WOODWITCH

SKYE MCKENNA

Illustrated by Tomislav Tomic

Praise for *Hedgewitch:*

'Magical in every sense of the word. So magical that I suspect Skye McKenna might actually be a fairy.' **Eoin Colfer**

'An enchanting contemporary classic. The writing is as magical as the story – a total treat.' **Piers Torday**

'There are only two sorts of fantasy story: the ones that feel fake and the ones that feel real. It's hard to explain the difference but you know the real ones when you read them and *Hedgewitch* is one of them.' **Philip Reeve**

'A richly inventive story.' **Gillian Cross**

'So full of magic and adventure – I wish I'd written it myself!' **Linda Chapman**

'Oozes magic from every page. The start of a cosy, compelling series for anyone who's ever wanted to be a witch.' **Aisha Bushby**

'The writing sparkles with magic while the plot bubbles with danger. There are friends to be made and an opinionated cat to win over. *Hedgewitch* sang to my inner witch and should NOT be missed.' **Julie Sykes**

'From the very first page, the story sweeps you into an utterly believable magical world, one filled with warmth, wonder, mystery and just the right amount of danger to thrill young readers.' **Aisling Fowler**

'Fantasy lovers should not miss *Hedgewitch*.' **Daily Telegraph**

'Vivid and thoroughly assured, *Hedgewitch* may well stand alongside the works of Murphy and Rowling in years to come.' **Literary Review**

'A twisty tale that brings together nature and folklore.' **i Weekend**

'Thoroughly magical and compelling...' **New Statesman**

'This transformative story about hope and standing by one's convictions is recommended for readers brave-of-heart...' **Readings Magazine**

'A magical story of adventure and friendship involving a cast of remarkable characters.' **The School Librarian**

'Packed full of mystery and imagination.' **BookTrust**

'Charming magical quest.' **LoveReading4Kids**

'This magical story feels like it will be an instant classic.' **The Week Junior**

'The start of an entrancing new series whose characters will quickly charm their way into the hearts of its readers, and encourage them to embrace the magic of the wild.' **librarygirlandbookboy.com**

'This feels like slipping on your pjs, and is a gentle read with just enough darkness to set your hairs on edge.' **misscleavelandsreading.com**

'For those with magic in their soul, *Hedgewitch* is a pure delight.' **lilyandthefae.wordpress.com**

'With echoes of Diana Wynne Jones and Alan Garner, *Hedgewitch* feels like a future classic.' **www.picturebooksnob.com**

'A spell-binding read full of evil magical folk and good witches.' **Toppsta Reviewer, aged 9**

'A great book full of magic, friends and fun.' **Toppsta Reviewer, aged 12**

'I really, really love this book. I couldn't stop reading.' **Toppsta Reviewer, aged 8**

Published in 2023 by Welbeck Flame
An imprint of Welbeck Children's Limited,
part of Welbeck Publishing Group.

Offices in: London - 20 Mortimer Street, London W1T 3JW &
Sydney - 205 Commonwealth Street, Surry Hills 2010

www.welbeckpublishing.com

A CIP catalogue record for this book is available from
the British Library.

ISBN: 978 1 80130 041 4

Printed and bound by CPI Group (UK)

10 9 8 7 6 5 4 3 2 1

For my father,

who taught me

how to find my way

through the woods.

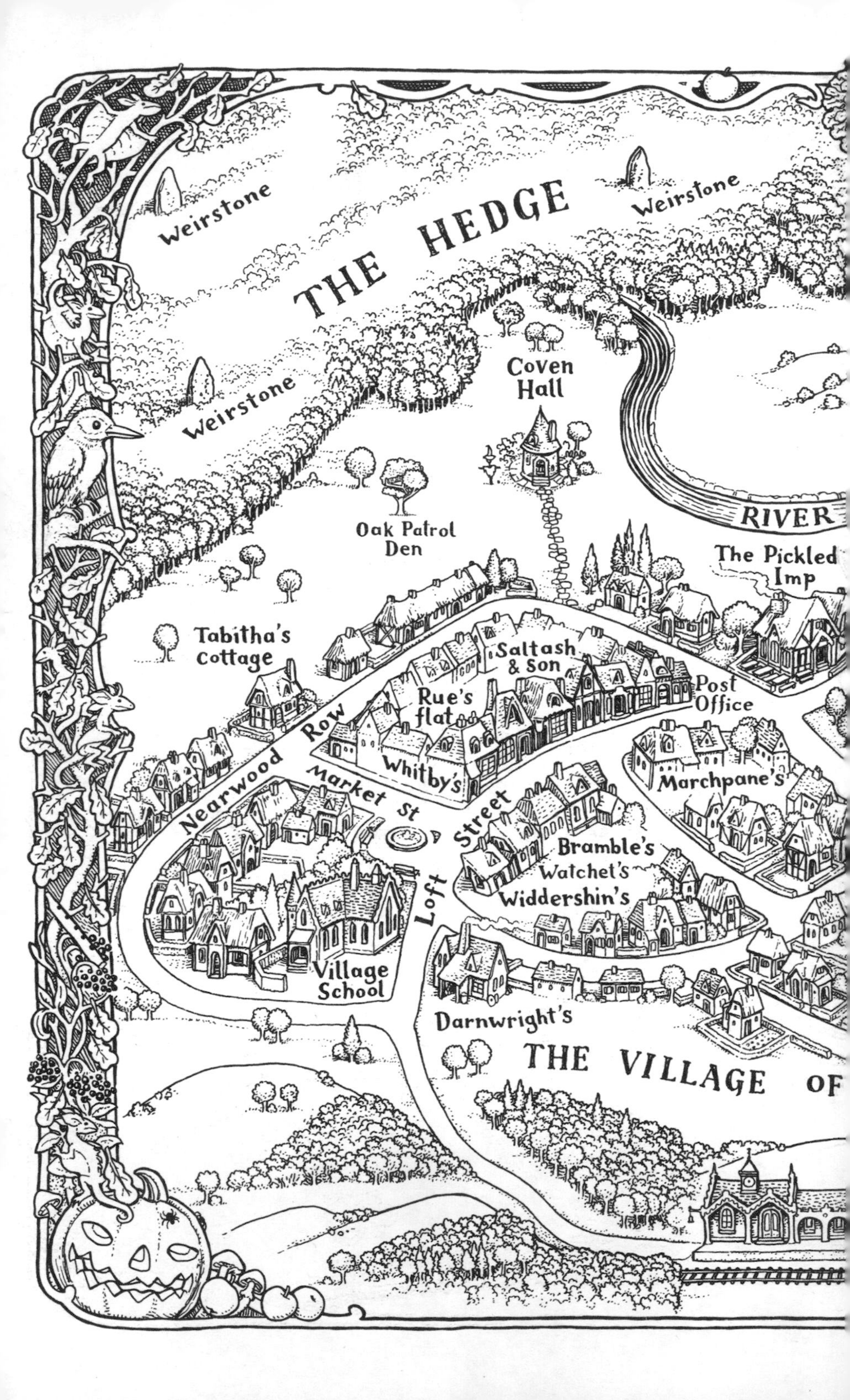

THE HEDGE
Weirstone
Weirstone
Weirstone
Coven Hall
RIVER
Oak Patrol Den
The Pickled Imp
Tabitha's cottage
Saltash & Son
Rue's flat
Post Office
Nearwood Row
Whitby's
Marchpane's
Market St
Loft Street
Bramble's
Watchet's
Widdershin's
Village School
Darnwright's
THE VILLAGE OF

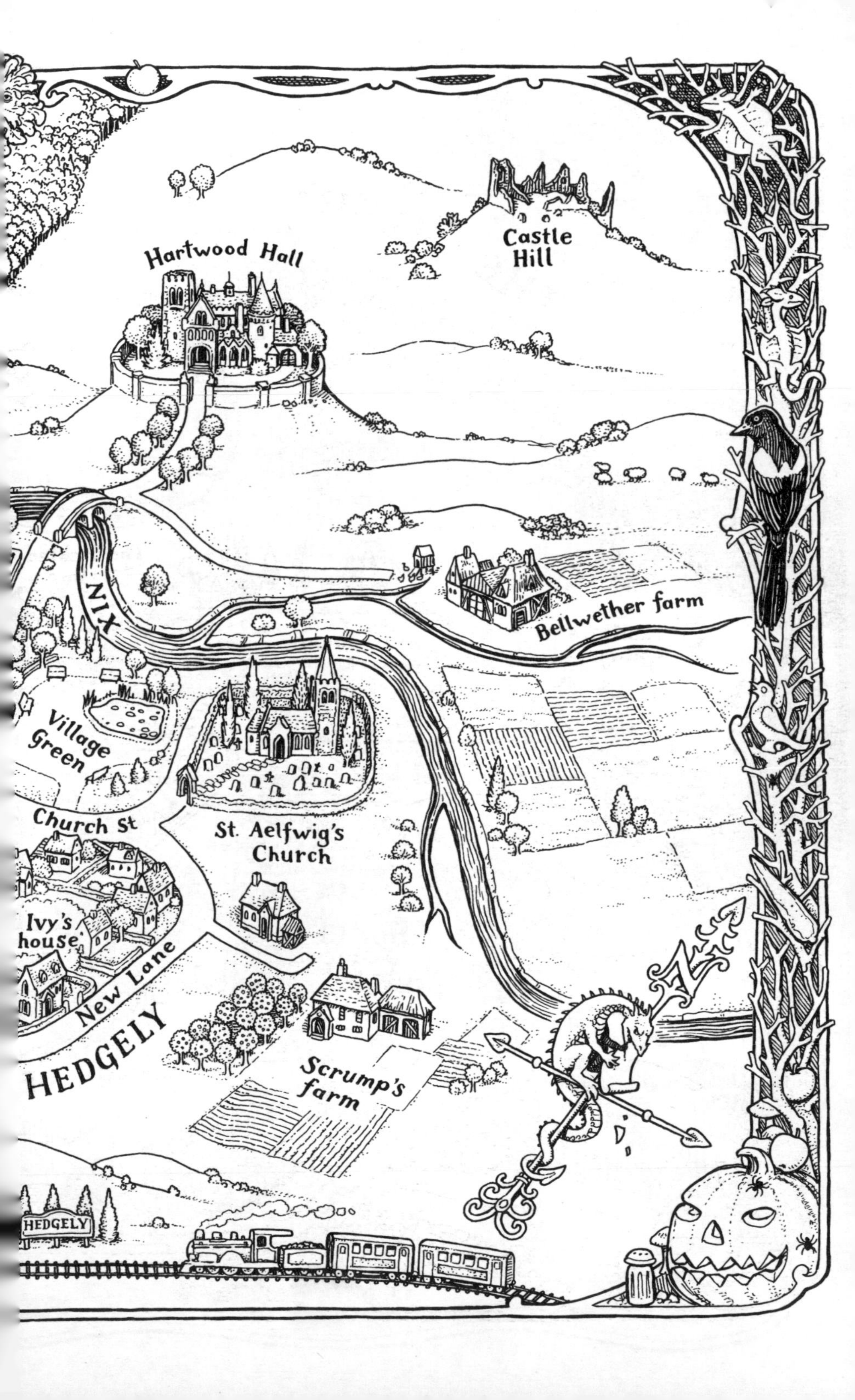
Hartwood Hall
Castle Hill
NIX
Bellwether farm
Village Green
Church St
St. Aelfwig's Church
Ivy's house
New Lane
HEDGELY
Scrump's farm
HEDGELY

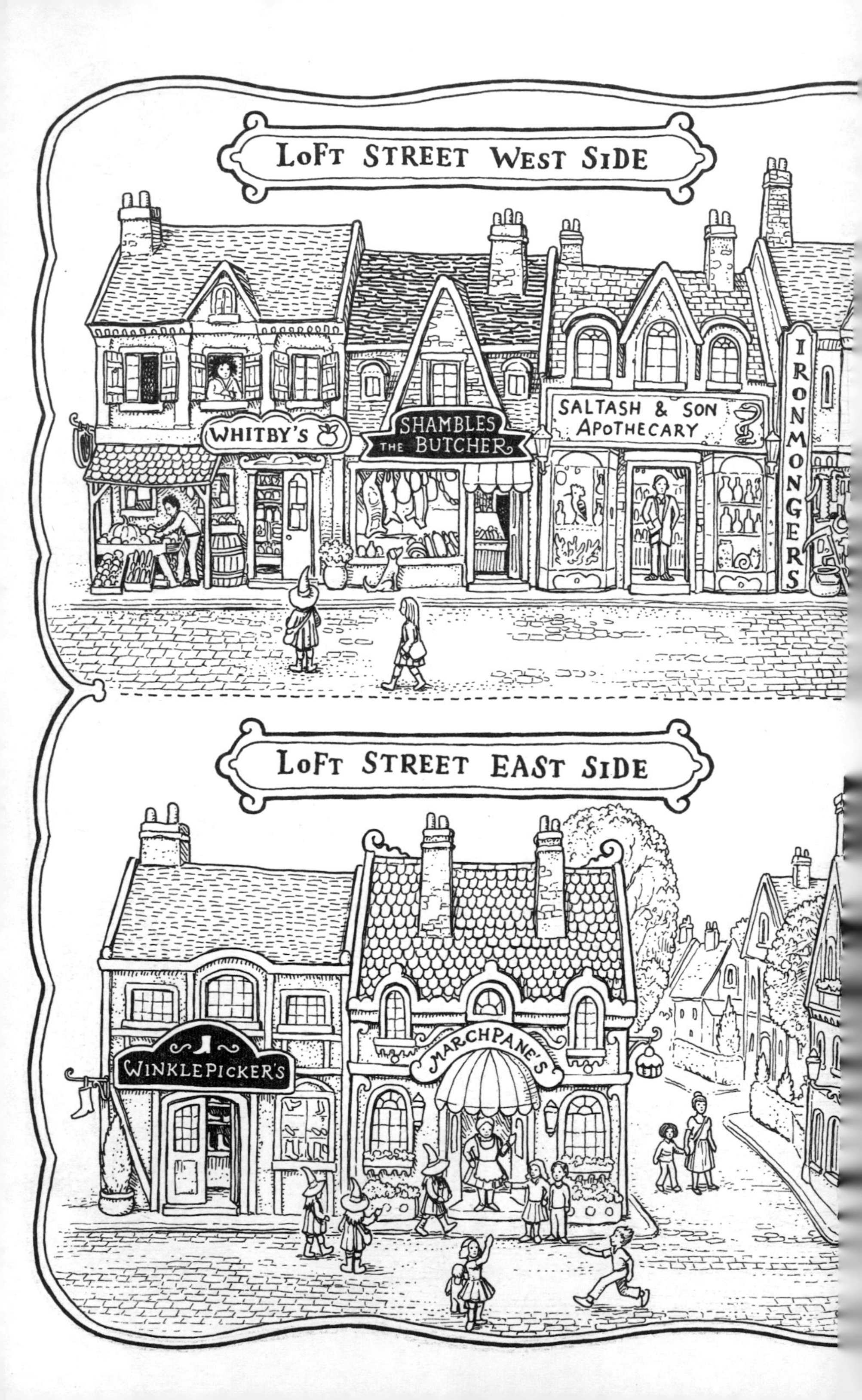
LOFT STREET WEST SIDE
WHITBY'S
SHAMBLES THE BUTCHER
SALTASH & SON APOTHECARY
IRONMONGERS
LOFT STREET EAST SIDE
WINKLEPICKER'S
MARCHPANE'S

TILLER & TELFOR
POST OFFICE
THE PICKLED IMP
W. E. BOBBINS
Bramble & Bloom
TEA ROOM
WATCHET'S
WIDDERSHIN'S BOOKSHOP

'Three are the Watchers within the wood
The trees have ears so you'd better be good.
One is wicked and one is wild
And one has big teeth to eat the slowest child!'

Hedgely schoolyard game

Chapter One

Fledgling Witch

Cassandra Morgan was brewing potions in the potting shed. Bent over a softly simmering cauldron, she measured out an ounce of powdered peppermint, a drachm of dried rosemary and thirteen drops of tincture of ginger. She'd been there for hours – so long, in fact, that Montague had given up chasing woodlice and was taking a nap amidst the cabbage seedlings. Now and then, the cat opened one golden eye to check on her progress and make helpful comments like, 'You've miscounted, that's fourteen peppercorns,' or, 'I'd grate the lemon peel finer, if I were you.'

Cassie was working in the potting shed because she had been forbidden by Mrs Briggs, the housekeeper, from using her camping cauldron indoors after accidentally setting fire to the moss-green rug in her bedroom. It was only slightly singed, but, as Mrs Briggs explained, there was a lot of wood in Hartwood Hall and a lot of antique furniture. Cassie had complained that she couldn't possibly work out of doors because she was trying to brew an enlivening elixir which required very steady temperature control – and it had been blowing a gale all week.

Brogan, the gardener, had taken pity on her and let her use his shed. So, there she was, amidst towers of terracotta pots and salmon-coloured geraniums, carefully feeding tinder grass to the fire beneath her small copper cauldron.

'It's supposed to be turning a shade of warm apricot,' said Cassie, checking her *Witch's Handbook* once more.

'It would, if only you would give it sufficient time and *keep stirring*,' said the grey cat. Montague was Cassie's familiar; he could do a little magic of his own, but mostly he was there to provide annoyingly practical advice at every opportunity.

'I haven't *got* time,' said Cassie, glancing at the clock on the potting shed wall. 'I need to get to coven after this.'

Cassie was determined to arrive with a bottle of perfectly brewed elixir and complete the tasks required to earn her white Potioner badge.

'You have ample time. You're only thirteen and the witch's craft takes years of hard work to master. Humans aren't like cats,' said Montague, grooming his whiskers. 'We are born with agility and grace whereas you must develop your skills through constant and persistent practice. There will be plenty more badges to earn and tests to pass after this one.'

But that was just the problem. As a matter of fact, Cassie had three problems.

The first was that she had started behind compared to the rest of the young witches in her coven. They had all grown up in the village of Hedgely, or in witching families elsewhere in the country, and had known about the world of Faerie and its dangers since they could walk. Cassie, on the other hand, had spent half her life in a boarding school in London. Her teachers had told her there was *no such thing as faeries* – but her teachers had been wrong, and when it came to the dangerous and deceptive faery folk she had a lot of catching up to do.

Cassie's second problem was that her mother, Rose Morgan, was still missing. It had been seven and a half years since Cassie had last seen her, but now she at least knew *where* her mother had gone. Cassie had seen a letter in which Rose explained that she planned to travel to Faerie, to find something precious she had lost, and that a friend had offered to help her do so. Cassie didn't know what her mother had been searching for, or who had helped her cross the border, but she was sure Rose had intended to return home.

Cassie's final, and most insurmountable problem, was her aunt. Miranda Morgan was Cassie's guardian, the Coven Mistress and the Hedgewitch; the warden who guarded the Hedge, the great tract of forest that formed the border between England and Faerie. She was the only person who could help Cassie follow her mother to Faerie, but Miranda had forbidden her from going – that is, until Cassie had earned her licence and was a fully qualified witch.

And so, Cassie needed to earn this badge, and all the others that stood between her and that final test. She had to prove that she had all the skills necessary to travel across the border, to survive Faerie and return safely home again.

'*Cassandra...*' said Montague softly.

She had to learn and learn fast if she wanted to prove herself to her aunt. There was no time for mucking about on broomsticks with the other girls or playing silly games like Blinkers. She had read the *Witch's Handbook* cover to cover, and she was determined that she would master every rune, every spell, every potion in it.

'CASSANDRA!' Montague hissed.

'What is it?' asked Cassie, drawn from her thoughts back to the potting shed and the geraniums and the orange flames that were licking up the sides of her cauldron.

'Oh no... no, no, NO!' she cried, blowing on the fire, but this only made the flames rise higher. The purplish-brown liquid inside was bubbling to a rolling boil, rising over the rim of the cauldron and pouring out, hissing as it reached the flames and letting off clouds of rosemary-scented steam.

'The watering can. Quickly!' said the cat.

Cassie grabbed the watering can and emptied its contents over the potting shed table, dousing the flames and flooding the workbench. The geraniums had been splashed with the diluted elixir and, one by one, they lifted their pink petals and began to sing. A wordless tune filled the potting shed as the plants formed a chorus, nodding their blooms to the strange melody.

Cassie sank down on her stool and sighed. In one careless moment she'd lost hours of meticulous work and the potion wasn't the only thing she'd ruined – her *Witch's Handbook* was soaked through, its pages dyed with clouds of aubergine.

'You'd better tidy this up before Brogan sees it,' said Montague, batting a paw at one of the singing geraniums which was rather off-key, 'or you'll be brewing potions outdoors all through the winter.'

By the time Cassie had mopped up the potting shed, raced upstairs to change into her pointed hat and witch's cloak and back down to the kitchen to hang her sopping handbook by the fire to dry, she was already running late.

'Here now, hold your kelpies!' called Mrs Briggs, turning from the bread she was kneading to pull a tray from the oven. 'I've baked hazelnut rolls; you can take them along to the coven hall for afternoon tea. Oh my, whatever happened to this?' She peeled away the cover of Cassie's handbook to inspect its sodden contents.

'I had a little accident in the potting shed.'

'Another?' said Mrs Briggs. 'Well, it will dry, but you can't go along without a handbook. Wait here a moment.'

'But I'm going to be late!' called Cassie, as the housekeeper disappeared through the scullery and up the back stairs.

Mrs Briggs returned a moment later with a small black book and passed it to Cassie. It was a *Witch's Handbook*, just like her own, with the swirling silver triskele on the front cover, only it was older, its pages dog-eared and yellowing.

'It was your mother's copy – found it last time I was in the attic and put it aside, just in case. All right, straighten that hat and don't forget the rolls!'

Cassie's broomstick, which was named Tantivy, thoroughly enjoyed the break-neck flight down the hill from Hartwood, over the river Nix, through the village of Hedgely and up to the coven hall. Buffeted by the wind, Cassie could barely control Tantivy's eagerness, but just now she was grateful for its speed as she and Montague skidded to a halt outside the hall. Normally, she would come to coven straight from school on a Friday afternoon, but today was the last day of the summer holidays and their first coven meeting since July.

The coven hall was a low, round building of yellow stone, situated on the outskirts of the village between the last row of houses and the looming shadow of the Hedge. It had a pointed slate roof, like a witch's hat, and was surrounded by a garden of flowering herbs. Just now there were poppies, pennyroyal and purple loosestrife, but Cassie did not have time to stop and admire them. She could already hear singing coming from inside the hall.

'The sky is clear as we fly on,
Beneath the dazzling stars.
We know their names and stories,
Their wisdom, it is ours.'

A dozen voices were raised together in the coven song; the meeting had already begun. Leaving her broom outside in the September sunshine, Cassie crept up the stone steps and slowly pushed the door ajar.

Chapter Two

The Whispering Woods

'The cauldron boils and bubbles,
A sweet and healing brew.
We gather herbs and flowers
To make our potions true.'

Twelve girls stood in a circle around the central hearth, along with a tall woman dressed head to toe in black – Cassandra's aunt, the Hedgewitch. Across the circle, a girl with dark, corkscrew curls and freckles spotted Cassie and grinned. Rue Whitby was Cassie's patrol leader, and one of her two best friends. She would not give Cassie away.

'The night is calm and peaceful,
The lamb bleats in his stall.
We guard the village and the home
From dangers great and small.'

The girls sang on. One voice rose confidently above the rest. It belonged to Ivy Harrington, the best witch in the coven, by her own estimation, and a thorn in Cassie's side since she'd arrived. Ivy stood tall and proud, her brass pins gleaming with polish and row upon row of badges on her ink-black cloak. She too had spotted Cassie and the smug smile she wore suggested she couldn't wait for the Hedgewitch to scold her niece for tardiness.

'For we are witches, one and all,
And we are not afraid
Of goblins, grigs and gwyllions,
Our wards and charms are laid.'

Creeping in as quietly as she could, with Montague slinking like a shadow at her side, Cassie joined the circle between Rue and Tabitha Blight, the third member of Oak Patrol and her other best friend. Tabitha gave Cassie a dimpled smile and made space for her, squeezing her hand as Cassie joined in with the final verses of the song.

'For we are witches, one and all,
A coven of the best.
Good friends who stand together
Through any threat or test.

For we are witches, one and all,
We know, protect and heal,
With noble hearts, loyal and kind,
And courage true as steel.'

The ring of young witches fell silent as the Hedgewitch addressed them. 'Today we return to our work after the long summer break, although some among us' – Miranda frowned at Cassie – 'appear to have forgotten the hour at which our meetings begin. I hope you have all spent the holidays practising your potions and wards and I look forward to seeing the progress you have made on your individual badge work, but now, a new season has begun. Autumn is the busiest time in the witch's calendar, with the great celebration of Hallowe'en ahead of us. Today we will be working on your Forager badges, collecting nuts and berries from the outskirts of the Hedge. Foraging not only provides us with ingredients for potion-making but is also an essential survival skill for any witch who finds herself lost in the wild. I remind you that witches never take more than we need and strive to leave no trace of our passing; there are faery folk within the woods who take offence at violence to their homes and are quick to punish the reckless forager. Now, if the patrol leaders would collect the baskets, we will gather outside.'

'You got off pretty light there, Cass,' said Rue, handing Cassie a wicker basket and hoisting her own over her shoulder. 'I thought she was going to roast you for sure! Late on the very first day back? "That's hardly befitting the Morgan reputation".'

Cassie sighed. 'I was trying to finish the enlivening elixir, only I botched it again. I'm never going to earn my Potioner badge at this rate.'

Fortunately, Montague had opted for a nap at the coven hall while they went foraging, so he couldn't tell Rue and Tabitha just how much of a disaster this attempt had been.

'Did you try adding the peppercorns one at a time, like I said?' asked Tabitha. 'I can help you next time if you'd like.'

Tabitha was easily the best potion-brewer in the coven and Cassie was sorely tempted. 'My aunt would *know* you'd helped me – I'm not sure how, but she would. It's all right, I'll get it eventually, I just have to keep trying and—' She stopped.

Blocking their path up to the woods was Ivy Harrington, flanked by Susan and Phyllis Drake.

'Here comes *Oaf* Patrol,' said Ivy. The Drake sisters sniggered. 'Sensible of the Hedgewitch, really, to put the three worst witches in the coven together. Saves us the bother of having to train you.'

Rue stepped forward. 'I know it's difficult for you, Ivy, but try to *think* for a moment and you might remember who it was that rescued you from the goblins at Midsummer. I'll give you a clue – it was the three witches standing before you wearing Argent Stars for their bravery!'

Ivy shrugged. 'You got lucky, that's all. Real witchcraft is more than reckless rule-breaking, and a *real* patrol like Thorn will beat you three hopeless daydreamers at any task.'

'We *are* a real patrol!' said Rue, fuming.

Tabitha grabbed her arm. 'Oh, drop it, Rue. She's just messing with you and we have work to do. Come on.'

They pushed past Ivy, Susan and Phyllis and made their way up the hill.

It was a glorious, sunny afternoon, but all around them were the first signs of autumn. Horse chestnuts littered the ground with glossy mahogany conkers and the wild crab-apples bore clusters of pink and yellow fruit. The grassy meadow that ran up to the Hedge had gone to seed and was starting to fade from purple to bleached gold. It rippled in undulating waves under the breeze.

The Hedge was the largest forest in England, and the oldest. A dense wildwood full of dark and tangled thickets, it had frightened and fascinated Cassie since she'd first arrived in the village. Within, she had encountered wisps and goblin nabbers, and the shape-shifting faery phooka. Yet Cassie knew she'd barely begun to uncover its secrets; that older and stranger things lived in its shadowy depths.

Rue and Tabitha spotted a line of hazels and hurried over to look for nuts, while Cassie wandered along the edge of the wood, gazing into the receding lines of trees. Although the sun was still warm on her back, a shiver ran down her spine. She always felt like this when she came near the Hedge – a curious mix of fear and longing, as though something within the woods was calling to her, beckoning her further in.

A rustling sound drew Cassie's attention to the branches above her. The leaves of the birches and wild cherries were just beginning to turn yellow and, as Cassie looked up into the golden foliage, she spotted a small horned head peering down at her. The head was attached to a serpentine body the length of a pencil case and covered in gleaming scales that faded from grass-green at its nose to sunset-red at the tip of its tail. As she watched, the wyrm spread its limbs, exposing patterned membranes, which it stretched out like wings. Cassie gasped as it fell from the tree and glided in a graceful circle, like a sycamore seed, until it reached the forest floor and scurried away under a pile of dead leaves.

'Daydreaming again, Cassandra?' asked Ivy, who was picking blackberries from the thorny brambles to add to her basket. It was already half-full of rose hips and haws, beech nuts, sloes and green acorns. 'It's only a leaf wyrm, they're everywhere at this time of year.'

'They're beautiful!' said Cassie, as another wyrm, this one pale lemon in colour, glided by.

Ivy sniffed. 'I suppose, but we're here to forage, not gawp at the wildlife. These,' she said, holding up a fistful of white berries, 'are snow-rowan berries, the rarest kind. I can't *wait* to show the Hedgewitch. What have you found?'

Cassie glanced at her empty basket.

Ivy laughed. 'I suppose it's to be expected, you're still only a fledgling witch, after all. You've an awful lot to learn before you make sapling witch, like me.' Ivy tapped the leaf-shaped pin on her collar.

Trying her best to ignore Ivy, Cassie scanned the leafy boughs and spiky shrubs before her, determined to find something just as impressive as the snow-rowan berries.

A breeze stirred the leaves and lifted Cassie's red hair, bringing with it the scent of dank leaf mould. Ahead of her, a beam of sunlight drew her attention to a solitary tree. It was a small, twisted thing, short and stunted beneath the taller oaks and ash trees, its spindly branches grey under yellowing leaves. She couldn't see any fruit or berries, but it might be worth a closer look. Brushing hair from her face, Cassie made her way around the tree, peering into the foliage until at last she glimpsed a cluster of tiny silver nuts, three of them growing off the same thin branch. She reached for them, but a hand snatched them away, snapping off the twig they were hanging from with a crack.

'I saw them first,' said Ivy.

'No, you didn't, you followed me!' Cassie protested.

'You don't even know what they are,' said Ivy. '*These* are silver seernuts – do you have any idea how rare they are? They're supposed to tell your fortune if you crack one open... ouch!'

'What is it?'

'Something pricked me—'

But Ivy's complaint was cut off by a rustling sound above her. Both girls looked up. The broken branch was still moving, waving back and forth as if writhing in pain. The branches around it had begun to move too, whispering and rattling together.

'It's just the wind,' said Ivy.

But Cassie could feel no breeze on her cheek now.

The disturbance passed from tree to tree, until the whole grove was full of the susurration of sighing leaves. Beneath the rustling they could hear something else – a murmuring of strange words, like a crowd of people whispering together in an unfamiliar language.

'Where is it coming from? I can't see anyone,' said Ivy. 'If this is Ash Patrol playing a trick on us I'll...'

Cassie was aware of just how far they had strayed from the rest of the coven. They had stepped into the Hedge and could no longer see the others – and they weren't human voices, of that she was sure. Suddenly, Cassie remembered the singing geraniums.

'I think...' She hesitated to say it. 'I think it's coming from the trees.'

The voices of the trees grew louder, the soft rustle of leaves punctuated by the creak of branches, the snap of thrashing twigs.

Ivy's eyes went wide. 'What is it? What are they saying?'

'I don't know,' said Cassie, but if she listened very hard, she thought she could make out just one word, repeated over and over again: 'daw-ter' they said. *Daughter.*

'Here, you can have them,' said Ivy, throwing the seernuts at Cassie's feet. 'I'm going back.'

As Ivy crashed away through the bushes towards the sunshine and the rest of the coven, the whispering voices ceased and Cassie crouched down to look at the nuts. One of them was cracked and a tiny golden spider crawled out of it and disappeared into the leaf-litter.

With one last glance at the now-silent treetops, Cassie went to find Rue and Tabitha.

Chapter Three

The Copper Beech

The witches of 1st Hedgely Coven returned to their hall with overflowing baskets of hips, haws, nuts and berries to process. The nuts would be candied for Hallowe'en treats and the berries made into hedgeberry jam, with help from Mrs Briggs, or into syrups and oxymels for winter chills. The last of the summer herbs – yarrow, goldenrod and hops – would be dried for later use in potions and wards.

After the meeting had officially ended, Cassie, Rue and Tabitha made their way towards the copper beech.

The beech tree grew on the grassy sward that led up to the Hedge, not far from the cottage where Tabitha lived with her grandmother. Rue had played beneath its shade with her brothers when she was younger, so when Oak Patrol decided they needed a den, she'd thought of it immediately. Of course, they had their patrol corner, but it was inside the hall they shared with Ash and Thorn Patrols, and anyone might overhear their conversations. No, what they needed was somewhere with a bit more privacy; where they could plan secret patrol business, or discuss important things, and the beech provided just that.

Properly, it should have been an oak tree, Cassie supposed, but she rather liked the copper beech with its spreading boughs of deep purple leaves and smooth grey bark into which generations of Hedgely's lovebirds had scored their initials. It was a mature specimen, some fifty feet tall, with its lowest branches well above their heads, making it nearly impossible to climb. But that was not a problem for the witches, as they arrived by broom. Once up amongst the canopy, they were all but invisible from below and they could see out across the village, over the river Nix to the hills beyond.

Oak Patrol had spent the summer holidays constructing a platform from bits of spare wood

Brogan had given them. Tabitha had brought an old carpet from her grandmother's and Rue had managed to secure some cushions her mum was throwing out, so they had the beginnings of a proper den. They even had a biscuit tin hidden in one of the upper branches in which they stored puck-mints, hobstoppers, liquorice bats and other such sweets, should sustenance be required. The girls had great ambitions for their den, including a roof of some sort so they could meet there even in the rain. But the days were still mild and nothing was lovelier than to lie back on the old rug, hands folded behind their heads, looking up at the boughs of the tree shifting in the wind and enjoying the mottled sunshine on their faces.

Tabitha and Rue were doing just that, Rue's toad familiar, Natter, squatted on her shoulder and Tabitha's Wyn, a soft white rabbit, stretched out beside her. They were still very much in summer-holiday mode, and it was only Cassie who sat up, perched next to Montague on a thick tree limb that hung over the platform and made for an improvised bench.

'I want to go for my Sapling test,' she said, looking up the details in her mother's handbook. She'd only just earned her Fledgling pin in the summer and was eager to progress to the next level of her training.

'You can't,' said Rue, rolling onto her front and looking up at Cassie. 'You need three skill badges first and you've only got one and a half.'

'I'll finish the Potioner badge this week,' said Cassie.

Montague sniffed. 'Provided you do not set fire to some other part of Hartwood Hall.'

'That still leaves one more,' said Tabitha.

'I suppose I could try for Highflyer,' said Cassie. She had failed the flying part of her fledgling test, but after a summer spent practising on Tantivy she was keen to prove that she wasn't entirely hopeless on the broom.

'I don't see why you're in such a fuss over this, Cass,' said Rue. 'You're starting to sound like Ivy. Witchcraft is meant to be *fun*, you know.'

Cassie frowned. 'You wouldn't find it so much fun if *your* mother was missing.'

'I think what Rue is trying to say is that you don't have to do everything on your own,' said Tabitha. 'We can help you, that's what patrols are for. Perhaps we ought to go for a badge together?'

Rue scrunched up her nose. 'We're already working on Forager with the rest of the coven. It'd be a lot of extra work.'

'But it would show everyone what Oak Patrol is capable of,' said Tabitha.

'I suppose so,' said Rue, pulling herself up.

'What about Star Gazer or Herb Grower?' Tabitha suggested, looking at the list in her handbook.

'Sounds dull,' said Rue. 'It ought to be something impressive, like Ward Weaver, or Curse Breaker!'

Tabitha frowned. 'I really think after the summer we've had we should stick to something a little safer – herbs and charms, some chanting...'

Rue yawned dramatically.

'How about this,' said Cassie, climbing down to join them and bringing her handbook with her. 'The Woodwitch badge – it's got some tracking tasks and healing too... a bit of everything in fact.' The badge description had caught Cassie's eye because there was a date next to it and a big tick, suggesting it was one of those her mother had completed when she was a young witch in Elm Patrol.

'Woodwitch?' asked Rue. 'Never heard of it.'

Cassie passed over her handbook and pointed.

Woodwitch Badge

Demonstrate the skills of wood-witchcraft by completing the following tasks:

1. Correctly identify thirteen native trees and know their magical properties
2. Make a poultice for treating imp-bites, cuts and scrapes
3. Lay a trail through the woods using faery runes
4. Make Followfoot powder and use it to track a coven mate
5. Spend one night camping in the woods

'Spend a night in the woods?' said Tabitha, reading over Rue's shoulder. 'Cassie, where did you get this handbook? It's an old edition. The Woodwitch badge isn't in ours.'

Cassie explained about her potions accident and her mother's book.

'At least it sounds better than Herb Grower,' said Rue. 'And it's an excuse to spend more time exploring the Hedge.'

'We can start with the easier tasks,' said Tabitha. 'Like identifying different trees – and I've made a poultice before, for magical first aid.' She began copying the list of tasks into her own handbook with the stub of a pencil.

'Well, should we go for it?' asked Cassie.

They both looked at Rue – she was the Oak Patrol leader and ought to have the final say.

Rue grinned. 'If it means more camping, I'm up for it.'

Wyn tugged on Tabitha's sleeve. 'Oh, I'd better go, my gran will be wanting her tea and I must start the potatoes and the laundry is piling up...' Tabitha hurried to pack everything back into her bag. 'Let's meet up again tomorrow and go over this list.'

Rue and Cassie watched Tabitha fly down from their den and away towards her grandmother's cottage. Tabitha's grandmother, old Mrs Blight, might be from a famous witching family, but as far as they were concerned, she was a terror in fur and tweed. She made Tabitha's life a misery, treating the girl like her personal maid, forcing her to do all the shopping, cooking and cleaning.

'She ought to keep the old cave-wyrm waiting sometimes,' said Rue, chewing on a beech twig. 'But that's Tabitha's problem all round – she's too nice.'

'It *is* nearly teatime,' croaked Rue's toad familiar, Natter. 'And it's fish and chips tonight, remember?'

'Dad promised to bring some back from Oswalton. If I'm not there Oliver will scoff all the chips. Catch you later, Cass!'

Chapter Four

The Cursed Teapot

Loft Street was closing up for the evening, the last few shoppers making their way home with baskets and packages or heading to The Pickled Imp for a drink. Walking home through the village with Montague, her broom tucked under one arm, Cassie had her nose buried in her handbook. Turning the corner, she passed Whitby's, Rue's family's shop, where you could buy anything from tinned beans to fresh chrysanthemums. The shop was shut but the lights were on in the flat above and she could hear laughter and excited chatter through the open window.

Across the street and leaning to the right at an alarming angle was Widdershin's bookshop. Cassie cast it a longing glance as she passed, thinking of the pocket money she'd been saving all summer. She nearly had enough for *Perfect Potions: A Primer*.

Then there was Saltash & Son's apothecary, where they bought the rarer ingredients for spells and potions, those they could not grow or forage themselves, and Marchpane's, the bakery and sweetshop which was still crowded, although it was nearly closing time. A group of Cassie's coven mates stood outside swapping boiled sweets from pink-striped paper bags. Alice Wong waved at Cassie, who was lost once more in the pages of her handbook.

'Cassandra!' hissed Montague, brushing against her legs to get her attention.

But Cassie was reading about faery runes for marking your path in the forest and did not see Alice, nor did she see the tall, dark figure standing in the street, not until she tripped over a lumpy carpet bag and fell right into her.

'A witch should always be aware of her surroundings,' said the Hedgewitch. 'She should not blunder about with her nose in a book, thoughtlessly tripping over people.'

'Sorry, Aunt Miranda,' said Cassie.

'Well, as you are here now, you can accompany me to Bramble's,' said the Hedgewitch. 'I received an imp from Selena Moor just before coven, requesting assistance, and yet I still managed to arrive at the coven hall *on time*.'

Cassie winced.

'And you can carry that,' said her aunt, pointing to the bulky carpet bag.

Following Miranda back up Loft Street, Cassie struggled under the weight of the Hedgewitch's carpet bag. She knew from experience that it contained not only a selection of powders, potions and preparations for any ill, magical or otherwise, but enough wardstones to sink a small boat. There was no easy way to manage it and she shifted the weight from one arm to the other, swapping it with her broom.

'Aunt Miranda, I've learned a lot over the summer,' Cassie began.

'I'm encouraged to hear it.'

'I'm so much better on the broom; I hardly ever fall off. My potions are... improving, and you said yourself my runes are almost legible. The next Crossing Night is only a month away – at Hallowe'en – and I feel I'm ready now, to go across the border, to find my mother.'

The Hedgewitch pressed a palm to her temples. 'Cassandra, we've been over this a dozen times: one does not simply stroll into Faerie – there are far worse things in those woods than wisps and goblins, and the Hedge itself is a labyrinth of twisting ways. Wiser witches than you have lost their mind in the depths of the forest.'

'But you know the Hedge, if you helped me find my way through—'

Miranda stopped and looked Cassie in the eye. 'I have a duty here, to this village and its people. That is one of the lessons you have yet to learn, one your mother never did: to value what you have as much as that which you have lost. Come now, we have work to do.'

The Bramble & Bloom tea room, affectionately known as Bramble's by the locals of Hedgely, was a small bow-windowed establishment a few doors down from Widdershin's. It had rather a lot of flowerpots positioned around the doorstep with blossoming clematis clambering up the sun-warmed stone, and was lit from within by a soft glow.

The Hedgewitch rapped on the door sharply. It was opened a moment later by a tiny woman wearing five or six cardigans in shades of violet. She had wispy purple hair held up in a nest of jewelled pins and bright-green eyes.

'My dears!' she cried. 'You have come at last! I have been so awfully worried, so truly, dreadfully afraid lest something worse should happen. I must call the Hedgewitch, I said to Emley this morning over breakfast – it just isn't my area of expertise but *she* will know what to do about it. Come in, come in, take a seat over there and I'll brew you each a pot. I've just put the kettles on.'

'Thank you, Selena, but that is not necessary, and I'm afraid we do not have the time,' the Hedgewitch said. 'Your imp mentioned a cursed item you have acquired?'

'But my dears, there is always time for tea!' said the woman, bustling around behind a counter where a pot-bellied stove supported a range of different kettles: fat copper kettles with curling spouts, tiny iron kettles decorated with dragonflies, shining steel kettles and a multi-tiered kettle made of green glass, like a tower of bubbles. Selena Moor caught Cassie looking at them.

'You are wondering why I should need so many different kinds, my dear?' she asked. 'Different teas require different water, at different temperatures.

Much like any of your potions, the brewing of fine teas is as much an art as a science.'

With a small sigh, the Hedgewitch acquiesced and took a seat at the table Mrs Moor had prepared for them, indicating for Cassie to join her. Cassie was relieved to have an excuse to put down the weighty carpet-bag and better observe her surroundings. It was the first time she'd ventured inside the tea room. Bramble's was usually crammed with villagers wanting a sit down, a cup of tea and a chat, but now, just past closing time, it was empty.

There were a dozen tables, each covered in a fine lace cloth with an unusual design of butterflies caught in cobwebs. Before them was a vase of purple asters and a small silver sugar bowl with clawed tongs. The walls were papered with a pattern of snakes and roses and there was a tiled fireplace, with two wingback armchairs positioned before it. Cassie thought it looked the perfect spot to read on a rainy day. From the rafters hung bunches of dried leaves and flowers, some Cassie recognised from coven and others that were strange and exotic. There was a bookcase at the back of the shop, but instead of housing books it was lined with hundreds of round tins with pictures on them – tea canisters, Cassie realised. It was a library of tea.

'Here we are then,' said Mrs Moor, bustling over with a tray full of teaware. It was only then that Cassie realised the woman had never asked them what they'd like, nor were there any menus on the tables. With practised efficiency, Selena Moor arranged the tea service before them: a pot each, cups and saucers, spoons shaped like flowering twigs and a small jug of cream.

'Lavender and lime-blossom for the Hedgewitch,' said Mrs Moor, indicating the purple teapot. 'And saffron sweetbriar for the young lady. This is your first time trying one of my teas, is it not? Add a little cream and honey, it'll go down a treat.'

Cassie glanced at her aunt, who had taken a sip of her tea. As she watched, the Hedgewitch visibly relaxed, her shoulders softening and even the sharp set of her brows somehow gentler.

She turned over her own cup and found a small furry ball curled up beneath it. It uncurled and stretched into the shape of a shrew. 'Do you mind?' it asked her.

'Oh, you've found Sorex. He likes to take his naps in the crockery sometimes. Here, I'll fetch you a fresh one,' said Selena, exchanging the disgruntled shrew for a new cup.

Cassie's tea came out of the pot yellow as pollen but softened to the colour of good beeswax as she added the cream and honey, pouring some into her saucer for Montague.

Mrs Moor pulled up a seat to join them, watching Cassie intently as she took her first sip.

It tasted of Turkish delight, of the roses that grew in her mother's garden at Hartwood, of Midsummer's eve, with a touch of wakefire woodsmoke. Yet there was a depth and sweetness to it, like toasted marshmallows. It reminded her of the spice-scented breezes that blew into her bedroom from across the Hedge on still summer nights. The warmth spread through her heart filled with lightness. All was well. She needn't worry about badges and tests, she would find her mother, everything would unfold just as it should.

'Now, Selena, this cursed item...' said the Hedgewitch, her voice softer than usual.

'Of course, of course. Just a moment, I'll fetch it.' The tiny woman leapt up and retrieved another tray with clean cups and an old china teapot decorated with a daisy chain motif. She filled it with hot water and brought it over, pouring them each a fresh cup.

'There now, try that and tell me what you think.'

Cassie and Miranda both took the offered cups and sipped. Cassie nearly spat hers out. It tasted like tears.

'It's salty!' she said, pulling a face.

'Selena, have you mixed up your salt and sugar jars?' asked the Hedgewitch, raising one eyebrow.

'Of course not. It's the pot! Whatever I put into it, chamomile or lapsang souchong, it comes out tasting like the briny sea!'

The Hedgewitch lifted the teapot carefully and inspected it, opening the lid to peer inside. 'When and where did you acquire it?'

'Last Tuesday, from Eris Watchet's shop.'

'I have often suspected Eris of dealing with goblin traders, but this appears to belong to our world – the design is ordinary enough, a daisy chain, and yet...' The Hedgewitch looked up at Cassie.

'Cassandra, what do you make of it?'

Cassie nearly choked on the mouthful of sweet tea she'd taken to wash down the salt. Her aunt was actually asking for her opinion? Her professional opinion, as a witch? There must be some powerful magic in Selena Moor's tea.

Gingerly, Cassie took the teapot and inspected it, just as the Hedgewitch had. It was still half-full of soaked tea leaves but, as she stared at them, they moved – not naturally with the swish of the water, but as though an invisible finger was pushing them around. Cassie got up and walked towards the window, making use of the last of the day's light to examine the pot. As she peered within, the leaves rearranged themselves into the shape of a face, a wicked, grinning face. With a sharp twist, the pot leapt from her hands. It shattered as it hit the stone floor, pieces of porcelain spinning in every direction and hot water splashing her cloak.

'Cassandra!' shouted her aunt, as both women rushed over. Cassie was unhurt, but the teapot was beyond repair, the daisy-chain pattern broken and the smell of salty tea in the air.

'Never mind, dear,' said Selena Moor, fetching a mop. 'It was of no use to me like that anyhow.'

But the Hedgewitch was frowning. 'Cassandra will, of course, cover the cost from her pocket money.'

Cassie sighed. *Perfect Potions* would have to wait.

Chapter Five

Sebastian Penhallow

As soon as they had left the tea room, Miranda began lecturing Cassie about handling other people's property – especially when that property was potentially cursed, although she didn't seem to think the teapot had posed any real threat.

'But what happened to the teapot to make it pour only salt water?' asked Cassie, hoping to distract her aunt mid-tirade.

Miranda frowned. 'Cursed items are created by faery folk, as pranks or punishments for humans who cross them. Faeries have the ability to bring out the worst in things, to twist their very nature – the way you might train a puppy to bite. Of course, they can enchant things too, enhancing their innate virtues. Such treasures are extremely rare, however.'

'Is Selena Moor a witch?' Cassie asked. She was thinking about the way the saffron sweetbriar tea had made her feel, although sadly the effects of Miranda's lavender tea seemed to have worn off.

'Of a sort, yes. She trained at Convall Abbey as a mender before coming here to open the tea room. She only does a little magic now, although her knowledge of herbs is second to none. You will, of course, write her a letter of apology, we can't have—'

'Hedgewitch! Hedgewitch!' came a cry from across the street. It was Mrs Mossley, the postmistress, coming at them as fast as her short legs could carry her. They stopped and waited for her to catch her breath. She fanned her round, red face with an envelope before catching herself and handing it over.

'A letter for you. I thought it looked urgent and you might like to have it before tomorrow's post – it's from *London*!'

'Thank you,' said the Hedgewitch, taking the envelope and inspecting the handwriting. 'It is from Elliot.'

'Ah, that charming brother of yours – will he be visiting soon, do you think?' asked Mrs Mossley, peering at the letter as Miranda began to open it.

Cassie's uncle Elliot worked at Wayland Yard with the wardens, the witches whose job it was to investigate faery-related criminal activity and to protect people from goblins and other faery threats. Elliot wasn't a witch himself of course – men never were, as far as Cassie could tell, but the work he did was very important nonetheless. Cassie hadn't seen or heard from him since July when she'd helped stop a warlock named Renata Rawlins.

'We shall see,' said Miranda. The postmistress hovered for a moment longer, staring at the letter hopefully until the Hedgewitch wished her good evening.

Miranda read the letter slowly as they walked up the hill towards Hartwood Hall. Cassie was rather annoyed at this, given that her aunt had only just scolded her for reading while walking. Finally, as they reached the stone gateposts topped with moon-gazing hares, Miranda folded the letter and tucked it away into her cloak.

'It's your cousin Sebastian, he is coming to stay with us for Hallowe'en.'

Cassie had never met her cousin, and so she did not know how to respond to the news of his imminent arrival. But the letter had seemed to trouble her aunt, and Cassie wondered if there was something else behind her cousin's visit, something Miranda refused to share.

Cassie's uncle arrived on Sunday, with his son in tow. Sebastian Penhallow had inherited his mother's surname, as was tradition in the old witching families. He was two years younger than Cassie and nearly a head shorter, but he had the same red hair that she shared with her mother and uncle and wore horn-rimmed glasses.

Sebastian stood in the great hall, hands shoved in his pockets and eyes fixed firmly on the polished floor. This might have indicated a certain shyness had he not been standing in the most wonderful room in the house, dominated as it was by the Hartwood tree. The tree rose through the floorboards, right up to the ceiling above, where stained-glass windows threw patches of multi-coloured light on its heart-shaped leaves. A spiral staircase wound about its trunk and its branches stretched out along the corridors of the first floor. When Cassie had first come to Hartwood, she'd stood in awe, enchanted by the way the leaves danced to the breeze of another world, the way the tree seemed to reach out and welcome her to the house and the magical new world she'd fallen into. But Sebastian was wholly disinterested and Cassie simply couldn't understand it. Perhaps he was used to such marvels, growing up as he had in a family of witches.

'Why, Cassie, you've grown an inch since I was last here!' said her uncle Elliot, beaming. 'And you look the picture of health, Miranda. No more troubles with goblins, I trust?'

'There are always troubles in Hedgely,' said Miranda. 'But we can discuss such things later, this must be Sebastian.'

Elliot prodded the boy forward to greet his aunt and for a moment Cassie felt sorry for him. Miranda, tall, thin and stern, was a rather forbidding woman whom Cassie had found a little frightening at first and, to be honest, still did. But Sebastian did not seem afraid; he took one look at the Hedgewitch and sniffed, turning back to his father.

'I can't believe you're leaving me *here*, with these people. Why can't I come to London with you? I won't get in your way, you can drop me off at the Science Museum on your way to work and—'

'Sebastian!' said Elliot, raising a hand to stop him. 'We've had this discussion already – you cannot stay in London, and it will do you good to spend some time away from Cornwall. These people are your family – your aunt Miranda is a very busy woman but she has kindly offered to take you in for the holidays so that you can experience a proper Hedgely Hallowe'en, and I expect a bit more gratitude!'

'But they're *witches*!'

Cassie was taken aback by this, and she saw Miranda tense up at the way he'd uttered the word, as if it were a bad thing, something to be ashamed of. Cassie had lived half of her life surrounded by people who thought neither witches nor faeries existed, but here in Hedgely there was no profession more respectable or sought after than witchcraft.

'Yes, and it's about time you understood what that means. Now, apologise to your aunt and cousin while I get your things from the car.'

He left Sebastian alone with them in the hall, but the boy neither apologised nor said anything to Cassie or her aunt, leaving the three of them in an uncomfortable silence.

'Cassandra, perhaps you could introduce Sebastian to the house,' said the Hedgewitch.

'I don't need *you* to show me around,' said Sebastian as Cassie led him up the staircase. 'I've been here before, when I was three, and besides, I never get lost. My father always has me read the maps when we're driving because I have a perfect sense of direction. We just got a new car, you know, it's a Vauxhall Wyvern.'

Cassie, who knew nothing about cars, thought it sounded rather like some species of wyrm.

'Mrs Briggs has put you in the yellow room,' she said, leading the way. 'It looks out over the drive, and you can just see the village in the distance. Here, this is you...' she pushed open a door with a brass lion on it. 'Most of the time there's a lavatory three doors down on the left, although sometimes it's three doors up on the right; it depends on the moon phase. Would you like to see the mirror room? I only discovered it last week.'

Hartwood Hall was not like ordinary houses, where doors usually lead to the same rooms each time and staircases always take you up or down, no questions asked. At Hartwood, you might go looking for the music room on the second floor and find yourself instead in the buttery, surrounded by casks and sacks of potatoes. The morning room, in which Cassie had liked to read on wet summer days, had recently vanished to be replaced by a room lined with floor-length mirrors and a blue glass chandelier. It took some practice, but the longer you lived in the house, the more you got used to it, or rather, the house got used to you, and sometimes even helped you by providing a convenient bathroom or a back door into the pantry when you wanted a midnight snack.

Cassie tried to explain all of this to her cousin as she led him down the long gallery, pointing out the north turret and her aunt's study – which was strictly off limits. She showed him the south turret, in which her own round bedroom could be found.

'What's that?' asked Sebastian, pointing to the fluffy grey shape curled up on the end of Cassie's bed.

'That's Montague,' said Cassie. 'He's my familiar.'

'I'm allergic to cats, they give me hives,' said her cousin.

'And I,' said Montague, stretching, 'am allergic to disrespectful boys, they give me the urge to sharpen my claws on their scrawny legs.'

'Come on, you must be hungry,' said Cassie, dragging her cousin away.

They found their way downstairs to the kitchen, with its great open fire and heavy oak table, hams and herbs and bright copper pots hanging from the rafters.

'I can't believe you don't have electric lighting,' Sebastian complained. 'Or a gas stove – how can you cook anything decent on that? It's like we're back in the Middle Ages!'

'Well, it takes a bit of practice,' said Mrs Briggs, ignoring his tone as she cut them both generous slices of marmalade cake oozing with orange jam. 'But once you get the hang of it, I do believe the woodsmoke rather improves the flavour.'

Sebastian rolled his eyes but took a large mouthful of the cake, all the same.

'Ah, it does my eyes good to see the two of you sitting there,' said Mrs Briggs. 'Just like Rose and Elliot all those years ago. The mischief those two got up to! Well, I've no doubt you'll be having your own adventures soon enough.'

Sebastian snorted and Cassie glared at him. She'd only spent half an hour in her cousin's company and already she couldn't wait to get away.

'Cassie, love, why don't you show Sebastian the gardens and the stable next?' suggested the housekeeper.

With a sigh, Cassie cleaned the last of her crumbs off the plate, not wanting to waste a morsel, drank down her bramble tea and headed for the kitchen door. 'Come on then,' she called to her cousin.

Sebastian was no more interested in the Hartwood grounds than in the house itself.

'You ought to fill in these paths with asphalt, then it wouldn't be so awfully muddy,' he complained as Cassie led him through the orchard where pears, plums and damsons were ripe for the picking and the early apples had begun to fall, scenting the cool air with their fermenting juices. Sebastian wore brand new gym shoes, which had been pristine white before they'd set out from the house but were now stained green and brown.

'It's a garden,' said Cassie. 'It's meant to be muddy.'

She showed him the vegetable patch, where Brogan's pumpkins, great orbs of green, white and orange, were beginning to swell up like balloons, and her mother's rose garden, which was still heady with scent, even though most of the other garden flowers had begun to die away. They walked past the walled garden, which was always kept locked, and along to the stable.

'Hullo, Peg,' said Cassie, greeting the silvery-grey horse with feathered hooves and offering her a sugar cube she'd saved from their tea.

Sebastian, however, wouldn't come close enough to stroke her dappled flanks. 'It doesn't look safe, and I'm sure it has fleas. Where do you keep the cars?'

'What cars?'

'You must have several at a great big house like this, and a chauffeur to drive them.'

Cassie frowned. 'But we don't need a car; we have our brooms and Brogan drives the cart when there's anything heavy to carry.'

Sebastian stared at her, wide-eyed. 'But what about me? How am I meant to get anywhere?'

Cassie shrugged. 'You'll have to walk, I suppose.'

Muttering, he followed her around the house to the drive. Elliot stood there, in front of a glossy black vehicle, deep in conversation with Miranda.

'Father, you can't be serious about leaving me here,' said Sebastian, rushing up to them. 'They don't even have central heating! I'll freeze to death – that's if I don't starve first.'

But Elliot only laughed. 'There's no danger of that with Mrs Briggs' cooking, I promise you, and the fresh air will do you good. I loved it here when I was your age. Why, I wouldn't be surprised if I come back to fetch you after Hallowe'en and you don't want to leave!'

Sebastian scowled, shoving his hands in his pockets. Cassie thought that was rather unlikely.

'Well, I'd best be off if I want to reach London by nightfall. Chin up, Sebastian, it's not as bad as all that.'

Miranda, Cassie and Sebastian watched the shiny new car pull out of the drive, crunching on the gravel and disappearing down the avenue of beech trees. Sebastian, his eyes red and glossy, ran back into the house. Cassie moved to follow him but her aunt stopped her.

'Elliot brought news from Wayland Yard – they've caught Renata Rawlins,' said the Hedgewitch. 'She made the ill-advised decision to return to London, went into hiding somewhere in Battersea, but they tracked her down.'

'What will happen to her?' asked Cassie. She'd quite liked Renata, until she'd discovered the witch was helping goblins steal children from all over Britain.

'The Witches' Assembly will meet to discuss her fate. I thought she might try to hide in the Hedge, or even cross the border, but the fact she returned to the city suggests she has accomplices, or that she hoped to turn other young witches to the Erl King's side. Elliot must see that, but he is ever the optimist, believes the best of everyone, until it is too late.' Miranda sighed. 'You showed Sebastian around the house?'

'Yes, but I don't think he enjoyed it much. Does he really have to stay with us over Hallowe'en?'

Miranda frowned. 'I want you to keep an eye on him, help him adjust to life here in Hedgely.'

'Oh,' said Cassie, feeling a shadow pass over her plans for the weeks ahead. She had badge work to finish and was determined not to fall any further behind at coven. 'But he's eleven years old, I'm sure he can look after himself.'

Miranda shook her head. 'He is not a witch and does not understand the dangers of the Hedge – you, however, have plenty of first-hand knowledge in that department. All I'm asking is that you keep him out of trouble. I trust that won't be too difficult?'

Cassie sighed. 'Yes, Aunt Miranda.'

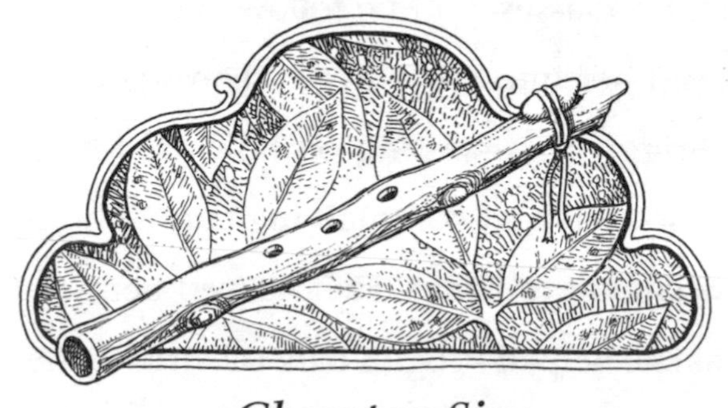

Chapter Six

Dances with Broomsticks

It was not difficult for Cassie to keep an eye on Sebastian during his first week in Hedgely, as he followed her everywhere. When she left her bedroom in the morning, there he was in the hallway, having already brushed his teeth and waiting to follow her down to breakfast.

On his first morning at Hartwood, Sebastian had inadvertently found himself in the Hedgewitch's private bathroom. Cassie had rescued him and, although he wouldn't admit it, she was pretty sure this appearance outside her bedroom door every morning was his way of ensuring he got to the breakfast table before his sausages went cold.

Sebastian followed her to school, where he was to join them for classes, and he followed her home again. He followed her into the village when she ran errands for Mrs Briggs, commenting on how old-fashioned all the shops looked and complaining about the lack of a Co-op, whatever that was. He followed her around the garden as she helped Brogan pick the first of the apples, a small, yellow-fleshed variety known as Imp Eyes, or dig up the potato beds, although he never offered to help with either of these tasks.

What he did like to do was talk. Sebastian could hold an entire conversation on his own, with very little input from Cassie, and indeed he seemed to consider any comment she made an unwelcome interruption. His favourite topics, aside from complaining about how backwards everything was in Hedgely, included cars, planes, space travel and how London was superior to anywhere else in the world. Cassie couldn't quite agree with him on this last point, as her memories of the city were dominated by Fowell House and the dreary suburb of Trite.

Hoping to steer the conversation in a more interesting direction, Cassie had asked Sebastian whether he liked to read and he had produced from his suitcase a stack of magazines titled *This is Your Future* which had a lot of pictures of flying cars in them. He spent the rest of the evening reading his favourite articles to her, and she soon regretted having asked.

By the time Friday came around again, Cassie was looking forward to coven even more than usual because she felt sure that Sebastian would not follow her there. Despite growing up in a witching family, her cousin had no interest in faery creatures, spells or potions, all of which he summed up as 'superstitious nonsense'.

But when Cassie and Montague arrived at coven hall after school, there was another new face amongst them. As the girls made the circle and sang their coven song, they couldn't help casting curious glances at the young woman at the back of the hall, perched on a stool, smiling and tapping her foot to the tune. She wore a bright-yellow cloak and a rather floppy witch's hat decorated with felt flowers. On her shoulder was perched a small blue and orange bird with a long beak – a kingfisher. Cassie raised her eyebrows at Rue, who only shrugged. Even the patrol leaders had no idea who she was, it seemed.

As they finished their opening song, all eyes turned to Miranda, who cleared her throat before beginning.

'Today we will review your summer badgework, but first, I have an introduction to make. Due to the events around Midsummer, and the ongoing investigation into the goblin kidnappings across the country, the Witches' Assembly have expressed some concern over your safety. Although I have assured them that *most* of my girls are too sensible to go wandering about the Hedge unsupervised' – here she frowned at Oak Patrol – 'they have nonetheless seen fit to provide you with further supervision in the form of an Assistant Coven Mistress.'

The young woman rose from her perch, beaming, and stepped over to join them, her familiar swooping after her in a flash of turquoise.

'Miss Early has come to us from the town of Knockshough in Ireland and her presence shall provide an opportunity for you to learn about some of the distinct traditions of Irish witchcraft. She will be with us until the end of the year, leading occasional meetings, and will be on hand should you require any additional assistance in your training.' Miranda's frown showed just what she thought of any girl who needed additional assistance.

'Hello there!' said Miss Early, trying to squeeze into the small gap in the circle Miranda had allowed. 'You can call me by my first name, which is Aoife. And I'm thrilled to be here with you. We're going to have such a wonderful time together and I can't wait to get to know each and every one of you.'

Cassie looked at the faces of the other girls, their expressions ranging from caution to confusion. Aoife Early, in her bright-yellow cloak and flowery hat, with a waterfall of loose brown hair and expressive hands could not have been more different to the Hedgewitch.

'In fact, I would like to start today's meeting with a very special activity that the girls back home in my coven just love! That is, if your Coven Mistress doesn't mind?'

Miranda opened her mouth to say something, but Ivy beat her to it. 'But we were going to present our summer badge work today!'

'Well, if there's time, you can show us what you've been working on after. Wouldn't it be nice to do something different, something fun to start off our first meeting together?'

'I'm not sure Ivy's heard of "fun",' Rue whispered in Cassie's ear.

'Marvellous! Now, if you'd all collect your broomsticks and meet me outside!'

The girls rushed to fetch their brooms, tripping over each other in the hurry. Cassie retrieved Tantivy from the Oak Patrol corner and followed Rue and Tabitha out into the garden.

'Do you think she'll have us doing broom races?' Rue asked, clutching Blaze, her own rather worn and beaten broom. 'Or stunts? I can show everyone that clockwise roll I've been working on.'

'Perhaps we'll be making broom polish, or practising flying with our familiars?' suggested Tabitha.

Cassie rather hoped not. Although her flying had improved over the summer, she still wasn't overly confident and she'd had just about enough of Montague's constructive criticism.

'Marvellous! Over here, girls, follow me!' called Miss Early, leading them through the coven garden and out into the grassy meadow.

The young woman was struggling with the weight of an old gramophone. Miranda followed as well, her arms crossed and her mouth drawn into a tight line.

'Very good, this will do splendidly,' said Aoife, setting the gramophone on a flat rock. 'I want you to form two lines, holding your brooms – that's right, you can face me for now.' Aoife had her arms outstretched as she guided them, her fingers fluttering.

'Now, I'm sure you're all wonderful flyers, and I can't wait to see what you can do, but for today, we shall keep our feet firmly on the ground.'

Rue sighed audibly.

'I want you to hold your broom in both hands and look at it – that's it.'

Cassie held her broom before her, feeling it twitch and stir between her hands. Tantivy had been her mother's broom once, and Cassie had only been flying it since her birthday in June, when her uncle Elliot had presented it to her. Her mother had, by all accounts, been an excellent flyer and it was to Cassie's great embarrassment that she was not.

'Just what is the point of staring at our brooms?' asked Ivy.

'I want you to get to know them better,' said Aoife.

'But it's only a stick – it's the witch who does the flying,' said Phyllis Drake.

'Ah, but as I'm sure you all know, a witch's broom is made of no ordinary wood. Who can tell me where it comes from?'

Nancy Kemp, the Ash Patrol second, spoke up. 'A witch's broom is made of whifflewood, from Faerie.'

'Exactly! And just as your familiars are not ordinary cats and mice and birds, but faery creatures with the power of speech and magical talents of their own, so too are faery trees special. I want you to really think of your brooms as independent beings, with a will and a spirit of their own. To think of flight as a partnership between a witch and her broom.'

It wasn't hard to think of Tantivy as an independent being, Cassie reflected – they frequently disagreed on things like which direction to fly in or whether Cassie should be perched on the broom or hanging underneath. Sometimes, she talked to her broom, but she couldn't see the point of staring at it. It wasn't as if you could make eye contact.

Aoife was fumbling with the gramophone. She set the needle and in a moment the field was flooded with the prancing melody of Vivaldi's 'Autumn'.

'Now I want you to feel the music! What is it telling you? What does it make you think of?'

The girls looked at each other, bewildered, as Aoife began to sway to the music. 'Embrace the music, embrace your brooms and when you are ready, dance!'

Rue coughed to hide a laugh. Ivy gave Aoife a wide-eyed stare of pure disbelief and the rest of the coven stood about clutching their brooms and looking warily from Aoife to the Hedgewitch while the strains of violins lifted above the meadow.

Only Tabitha seemed comfortable with Aoife's instructions. She stood, looking past them to a line of aspen trees that marked the path into the village, their branches lifting in a faint breeze from the Hedge, their bright leaves fluttering like brimstone butterflies. Smiling, she bowed to her broom and began to dance.

The rest of the coven turned to watch Tabitha as she waltzed about her broom.

Aoife clasped her hands together. 'Delightful! Simply delightful. This young witch has embraced the spirit of the thing. Now the rest of you, go on!'

Sighing, Cassie bowed to her broom as Tabitha had, and then walked around it in a circle, feeling utterly ridiculous. The other girls were laughing, but they too began to move, all except Ivy who stood to the side with her arms crossed, her broom hovering before her.

Tabitha was really quite good, a product of the dancing lessons she had at Clematis Academy, the fancy school she attended in the next valley. But it also helped that she wasn't bothered by the silliness of the thing, and rather seemed to be enjoying herself.

Rue had started getting into it too, although she was athletic rather than graceful, tossing her broom in the air and catching it, twirling it like a baton and then jumping over it.

Cassie was still turning in circles around Tantivy, unsure what else to do. She knew her aunt was watching her and so she ought to make an effort, but she had no experience to draw upon. Dancing was not something they taught at Fowell House, and the Hedgewitch did not own a wireless or indulge in music of any kind.

Tantivy had ideas of its own, however, and as she turned the broom began to rise vertically into the air, dragging her up with it. Soon her toes were barely touching the earth. She held on, grasping Tantivy with both hands as the broom took off, spinning her round and round and round.

'Stop!' she cried. 'Put me down!'

Rue grabbed one of her feet and pulled, but Cassie's shoelaces were untied and the boot came right off. The broom twirled Cassie around in the air, faster and faster. She was getting dizzy.

The other girls stopped their dancing to watch and at last Miss Early seemed to notice what was happening.

'Oh dear! That's very creative, but perhaps you should come back down now?' Aoife called to Cassie.

'I'm try... ing to!'

At last, Aoife lifted the needle from the record and the music stopped. Tantivy fell back to the ground, dropping Cassie in a heap. Some of the Thorn Patrol girls sniggered.

'Well, that was a wonderful start, but perhaps that's enough for today,' said the Assistant Coven Mistress. 'For those of you who are keen, I would like a few volunteers to learn some traditional Irish broom dances to perform at Hallowe'en.'

After coven, the three members of Oak Patrol walked back towards the village together.

'That wasn't witchcraft,' Rue scoffed. 'All that twirling nonsense. I mean, it was fun in a way, I suppose, but it's not going to help us catch goblins or protect the village, is it? If that's all she's going to teach us, we're better off with the old bat – I mean the Hedgewitch.'

‘I don’t know, I rather liked her,’ said Tabitha. ‘I spoke with her during tea break, she has all sorts of interesting ideas about modern witchcraft and new ways of doing things.’

‘What’s wrong with the old ways?’ asked Rue.

Cassie frowned. She had yet to decide what she thought of Aoife Early. Right now she was more concerned with having embarrassed herself in front of the coven and her aunt again, an occurrence that was all too common when her broom was involved. She thought she rather agreed with Rue though, they should be learning serious magic; that was what she needed to complete her training and find her mother.

Looking up to the Hedge, Cassie saw a small figure hurrying up the hill towards the trees, turning now and then to glance over her shoulder.

‘Hullo, isn’t that Ivy?’ said Cassie, pointing.

‘So it is!’ said Rue. ‘Where’s she off to?’

‘She’s gone into the Hedge, on her own. Should we fetch the Hedgewitch?’ asked Tabitha.

‘No, let’s follow her,’ said Cassie. ‘I want to know what she’s up to.’

Chapter Seven

Lost and Found

By the time Cassie, Rue and Tabitha reached the Hedge, Ivy had disappeared within its depths, swallowed by the twilight shadows. They found a narrow track where she had vanished.

Moving in single file, they followed the path into the woods. The trees were still and silent, the breeze having died off, and Cassie found it strangely quiet. When she'd first entered the Hedge in early May there'd been carpets of bluebells and a cacophony of birdsong. Now the cuckoos and nightingales had migrated somewhere warmer for the winter. Even the robins and blackbirds were too busy foraging to serenade them as they made their way deeper into the woods. Most of the trees still bore their summer greenery, but here and there were bursts of colour, field maples and rowan trees in clouds of yellow and red. Cassie spotted leaf wyrms and a nest of imps amidst their branches.

The signs of Ivy's progress were getting harder to identify as the path itself petered out. Paths in the Hedge tended to come and go, changing direction from one visit to the next, leading you in circles and sometimes vanishing entirely while you were following them, leaving you stranded in a leafy clearing or shady dell.

'It's getting dark,' said Montague, winding around Cassie's legs. 'Your absence will soon be noted if you do not return for supper. And, if I recall correctly, Mrs Briggs is preparing cheese and onion pie tonight.'

'We've well and truly lost the trail,' Rue admitted.

Cassie glanced back towards the village. They could still see the sky between the trees, but if they went much further they risked getting lost themselves.

'And it's growing cold. I ought to head home to light the fire for Gran,' said Tabitha.

'I just wish we knew what Ivy was up to,' said Cassie. It wasn't the first time they'd caught the Thorn Patrol witch wandering the Hedge on her own, searching for medicinal herbs and flowers. Ivy's mother was very ill, unable to wake from her enchanted sleep. Mrs Harrington had been cursed with the faery sickness, the *esane*, and her daughter was desperate to find a cure.

'What was that?' hissed Tabitha, turning round to peer into the shadows. 'Did you hear it? A voice...'

They stopped to listen and Cassie almost expected to hear the trees whispering again, but there was only a rustling in the leaves behind them followed by a low moan.

'Ivy?' called Cassie.

'It is not her,' said Montague, ears twitching and head lifted to sniff the air.

The girls exchanged worried glances. There were many faery creatures lurking within the Hedge, some merely mischievous but others truly dangerous to even the most experienced witches.

'I suppose we ought to look,' said Cassie.

Tabitha nodded. 'Someone might be hurt.'

There was another groan from the bushes.

'Oh, come on then,' said Rue. 'We've come this far, I'm not going back until we know what it is.'

Cassie clutched her broom all the same, ready to make a hasty retreat.

The three young witches stepped towards the sounds, pushing back the brambles that grew in their way, their fingers soon pricked and stained purple by the ripe berries. They were greeted by more moans and thrashing noises.

'Hullo!' called Rue. 'Who's there?'

Cassie brushed past an overgrown holly bush and stepped into a small clearing where a stout old man was crawling about on his hands and knees in front of a hazel tree. He wore no hat and his grey hair was standing up like thistledown. His hands and face bore fresh scratches.

'Where is it? Oh, where is it?' he muttered. 'I must find it, ohhhh...' he let out another moan.

'Farmer Scrump!' said Rue. But the man's eyes were glazed over and he clutched his chest with clawed hands, curling into a ball on the ground.

'Mr Scrump, can you hear us? We're here to help you,' said Tabitha, crouching down beside him. He was shaking all over. She removed her cloak and wrapped it around his shoulders.

'Sir, what's happened?' Cassie asked him. 'Are you hurt?'

'What's he doing all the way out here?' asked Rue.

'Cassie, my satchel,' said Tabitha. 'Find the hartshorn oil, the little yellow bottle, quickly!'

Tabitha was helping the man to roll over and sit up, supporting him whilst checking that none of his limbs were broken. The old farmer seemed dazed and confused; he was still babbling and didn't respond to their questions.

Cassie uncorked the hartshorn and waved it under his nose. He sniffed twice and sneezed all over her hands. She dug out her handkerchief and handed it to him to prevent a repeat occurrence.

The hartshorn appeared to be working – his eyes cleared and refocused on the three girls, the clearing and the state of his clothing.

'How did I...? Where are we?' he stammered, looking up at them. 'You're the Whitby girl, are you not? The one as I caught in my orchard last Sunday, stealing apples. But how did I end up here...?'

Rue ran a hand through her bushy hair, grinning sheepishly. 'That was *last* year, Mr Scrump.' She lowered her voice for the others. 'Do you think he's had a bump to the head?'

'Loss of memory or time, that's one of the nine signs of enchantment,' said Tabitha.

'When we found you, you kept saying "where is it?"' said Cassie. 'Have you lost something? Is that why you were in the Hedge?'

Old Mr Scrump looked at her, his expression blank as a sheet of paper. 'Was I now? Don't recall, don't remember wandering in here, neither. Was on my way home from The Pickled Imp. No recollection as to how I wound up here. Now, where's my stick...?'

'Here it is,' said Tabitha, handing him a walking cane that had fallen beneath the hazel.

'But your farm is east of the village and The Pickled Imp,' said Rue. 'This is the Hedge – you've come entirely the wrong way.'

'We'd better take him to the Hedgewitch,' said Tabitha, helping the old man up.

Cassie took his other arm, wrinkling her nose at the smoky scent of his wool jacket. As she touched him she saw the faintest shadow of something detach itself from the farmer and fade back into the woods.

'Did you see that?' she asked the others.

But Tabitha and Rue were looking back towards the path, leading Mr Scrump away from the darkening Hedge and towards the lights and safety of the village.

'There now, have a sip of that. You'll be right as rain in a moment,' said Mrs Briggs, pouring a cup of dandelion tea for Farmer Scrump and adding a spoonful of honey. The honey came from the Hartwood hives kept by Brogan and tasted faintly of roses and apple blossom.

They were seated in the kitchen, lit by the fire and a row of stubby beeswax candles. Cassie, Rue and Tabitha were perched on a bench that ran along one side of the great oak table, while Mr Scrump occupied the other, with the Hedgewitch watching him from her seat at the table's head. It was almost dinner time, and the smell of the pie Mrs Briggs had just pulled out of the oven was making Cassie's stomach growl in anticipation.

'Now, Mr Scrump, can you tell me everything you remember before the girls found you in the woods? Please do not leave out any detail, however insignificant it may seem,' said the Hedgewitch.

'Well, it was just as I was telling the girls. I finished up repairing that wall earlier than I'd hoped and so thought to reward myself with a drop of something down The Imp. I was there no more'n an hour, you ask Emley – he sent me on my way saying Mrs Scrump'd be on his case if I weren't home in time for tea. I stopped outside to light my pipe and have a moment, just to myself, see – it's that time of year when a man doesn't have much time to pause and reflect. There's the apples to be bringing in and I've got to watch out for fruit thieves too!' he said with a chuckle, winking at Rue. 'As I stood there, I noticed it had got dark all of a sudden, and I thought it must've been later than I thought so I headed off home, or at least I ought to have, but somehow I ended up in the Hedge.'

'When we found him, he was searching for something,' Cassie added, feeling this was somehow important and should not be overlooked. 'He kept saying "where is it?"'

'Well, I dropped my stick somewhere thereabouts, until this nice young lady found it for me,' said Mr Scrump, nodding at Tabitha.

'And you can't remember *why* you went into the Hedge?' asked Miranda. 'You didn't hear or see anything out of the ordinary?'

The old man shook his head. 'As I said, don't recall entering the woods to begin with. I'm a Hedgely lad, born and bred. I know better than to go wandering about in them there woods. Why, Mrs Scrump would have her head in a spin if she knew I'd been in there, she's awful frightened of the faery folk.'

'And well she should be,' said Miranda. 'You were lucky the girls found you before dark, although what they were doing wandering about the Hedge unsupervised, I, for one, would like to know.'

'Well, we should probably take Mr Scrump back to his farm,' said Tabitha quickly. She nudged Rue.

'Right! We'll make sure he gets home safe, leave it to us!'

The Hedgewitch raised an eyebrow. 'Brogan will take you both home in the cart with Farmer Scrump *after* I have had a word with the three of you.'

Mrs Briggs helped the old man out of the kitchen, bundling him under a knitted blanket for good measure, and Miranda turned to the girls.

'Now, which of you would care to tell me exactly what you were doing in the Hedge when you found Farmer Scrump?'

Cassie, Rue and Tabitha exchanged glances. They couldn't snitch on Ivy; the rest of the coven would consider it bad form, and besides, they didn't have any proof that Ivy had been there and she was sure to deny it.

Miranda sighed. 'Nonetheless it appears that Farmer Scrump was fortunate to have the three of you happen across him, and you did the right thing in bringing him to me. Whatever cast this enchantment upon him may still be abroad in the Hedge. Did you observe anything unusual in the woods?'

'I thought I saw something,' said Cassie. 'A shadow, it was very faint, and it went away when Mr Scrump came to.'

The Hedgewitch frowned. 'The Hedge is full of shadows, but there is something about this that I do not like. I want the three of you to stay well away from the woods, unless Miss Early or I are with you. If you notice anything else strange in the village, come to me at once.'

Cassie walked Rue and Tabitha through the entrance hall, beneath the spreading branches of the Hartwood tree.

'I wonder what really happened to Mr Scrump,' said Tabitha. 'Could he have been wisp-led, do you think?'

'He didn't see any strange lights,' said Cassie. 'And yet, he *was* looking for something...'

She was interrupted by a light rapping on the great oak doors and hurried to open them.

Standing on the doorstep was Aoife Early, clutching her broom and surrounded by a number of brightly coloured boxes and suitcases.

'I don't suppose you could help me with these?' she asked.

The girls stopped staring and rushed to relieve her, bringing everything into the hall.

As they were rearranging Aoife's luggage, Sebastian came down the stairs, his hands rammed in his pockets and a scowl on his face. He stopped at the foot of the Hartwood tree and wrinkled his nose at Aoife. 'Who's this?'

Aoife extended a hand, which the boy ignored, refusing to remove his own from his pockets. 'You can call me Aoife,' she said, beaming at him. 'Your aunt has very kindly invited me to stay here with you.'

Sebastian sniffed. 'Just what this place needs, more witches.' Without another word, he left in the direction of the kitchen.

'I'm sorry about that,' said Cassie. 'It's not you, he's like that about anything to do with magic.'

'Poor child,' said Aoife. 'I sense great sadness in his aura. A tragic story no doubt. Hmm, is that cheese and onion pie I can smell?'

Chapter Eight

Juniper Water

Life at Hartwood Hall was livelier than usual over the next week, as its two newest residents adapted to the quirks and routines of the house – and the house adjusted to its guests.

Sebastian still followed Cassie around, complaining about everything from the plumbing to the absence of a wireless. In the evenings he disappeared into his bedroom to write long letters to his father, which appeared each morning on the post-tray in the hall. Cassie had offered to catch an imp for him, explaining that it would be a much quicker way of getting a message to Elliot, but Sebastian had refused point-blank to have anything to do with faery creatures.

Aoife, on the other hand, followed her own strange routine. She was always at the breakfast table before Cassie and Sebastian arrived, although she did not touch the eggs, bacon and sausages that Mrs Briggs piled on their plates. Instead, she opted for a bowl of fresh fruit, drizzled in honey, and refused a cup of bramble tea in favour of her own strange concoction, which was as thick and green as pond slime.

'I like to be up before the birds,' Aoife explained. 'To feel the dew between my toes and greet the new day with open arms and great lungfuls of fresh air. You're welcome to join me for my morning callisthenics, Cassie. I think you'd find it quite invigorating.'

Cassie politely declined. One night, however, she awoke to find her window open and a cold draft blowing in. Crossing the floor to close the window, she saw the moon high in the sky over the Hedge, and a slender figure moving in the orchard below. Rubbing her eyes, she peered down and realised it was Aoife, dancing about in a circle beneath the apple trees, waving her arms in the air and singing.

'I don't think she sleeps,' Cassie said to Tabitha the next day, as they walked down Loft Street, kicking up the dry autumn leaves. 'And she's always burning smelly herbs in her rooms. She gave Sebastian a chunk of citrine to ward off "negative vibrations".'

'I'm afraid I don't see the problem,' said Tabitha. 'All witches use herbs and stones, don't they?'

'Yes, but not like *that*,' said Cassie, rolling her eyes. 'She offered to read my palm at dinner last night – you should have seen the look on Aunt Miranda's face, you know what she thinks about that sort of thing...'

But Tabitha was distracted, counting the pennies in her hand. 'Do you think I could stretch to bread rolls? They'd be so nice with the soup but I suppose a loaf would go further...'

Cassie and Tabitha were standing outside Marchpane's bakery, each with a basket full of groceries. They'd already been into Whitby's, where Rue was helping her mum stack shelves in the shop. Tabitha had spent twenty minutes choosing the perfect bunch of radishes, insisting that her grandmother would send her back if any were bruised or marked.

'Oh, but let's stop in at the post office first, Gran's out of stamps again,' said Tabitha. 'She writes to the *Hedgely Herald* every week, complaining about various things that bother her in the village. It's sort of a hobby of hers, although mostly I think she just likes to see her name in print.'

But as they approached the small shop with its red pillar box out front, they heard a commotion. Two women ran out of the post office, carrying baskets and dragging a young child, looking behind them as they hurried away.

Cassie and Tabitha rushed into the shop. Mrs Mossley was flapping about the place like a frightened hen. As they entered, she seized a large parcel from behind the counter and began ripping off the brown paper in which it was bound, tearing it to shreds which fell into an already sizable pile of torn wrapping.

'Where is it!?' she cried, her voice strangely high-pitched. She tore into the box and pulled out a pair of new ice skates, glanced at them and threw them over her shoulder, reaching for another parcel, this one small and round.

'Mrs Mossley!' cried Tabitha, rushing forward. 'Whatever's the matter?'

The woman's eyes were wide and unblinking. 'I need it! Where is it? I must find it!' she said in a shrill voice, tossing a tin of sardines to the ground and rifling through the unsorted mail for her next target.

'Please, Mrs Mossley,' called Tabitha, trying to reach her. 'What is it? What have you lost? Maybe we can help you find it... without all this mess.' She was wading through an ankle-deep pile of torn paper and string.

'Tabitha, something's wrong with her,' said Cassie, pulling her friend back. 'Don't get too close – look at her eyes.'

Tabitha stopped and together they watched the woman as she tore into another box, pulling out armfuls of hand-knitted socks. Mrs Mossley's eyes were glazed, her teeth bared and her hair, coming loose from its usual neat bun, stuck out in all directions. What's more, there was something wrong with her shadow. The afternoon sun threw it against the far wall of the shop and it seemed both larger and darker than it ought to be. There was a faint smell of smoke in the air, although there was no fire in the hearth.

'Go get the Hedgewitch,' said Cassie. 'She'll be in her study. I'll stay here and make sure Mrs Mossley doesn't hurt herself... or anyone else.'

Tabitha left her shopping basket with Cassie and ran.

The postmistress was throwing packages across the room. 'Too small!' she cried. 'Too big! Too soft!' At last she seized upon a shoebox-sized parcel and began to excitedly unwind the layers of paper and string enclosing it. When it revealed only a box of Sudson's Best Washing Powder she began to weep.

'What's the matter, Mrs Mossley?' Cassie asked, trying to distract the postmistress but keeping her distance. 'What are you looking for?'

The woman began tearing into some of the thicker envelopes. 'Treasure, it's treasure he wants. I must find it, I must take it to him!'

Soon she would run out of things to open, and then what? Cassie had already waved three potential customers away from the post office, telling them to come back later.

'Who?' asked Cassie. 'Who wants this treasure?'

Mrs Mossley lifted her head and stared through Cassie to the back wall of the post office. Her hands still clawing open letters she cried out, 'The king!'

Cassie turned to see a portrait hanging there, a middle-aged man, clean shaven and in dress uniform. 'King Robert?' she asked.

But at that moment the Hedgewitch rushed into the post office, followed by Malkin, her black cat familiar, and Tabitha, gasping for breath and clutching her side.

The Hedgewitch approached the post mistress, who was now using her teeth to tear open letters.

'How long has she been like this?' Miranda asked.

'Since we arrived, at least half an hour,' said Cassie.

'Stand back,' said her aunt, waving Cassie and Tabitha aside. She withdrew a small vial of clear liquid from her pocket and held it clasped in one hand as she opened the other, palm up, to form a cup. Pouring some of the liquid into her left hand she began chanting:

'By the bitter water of juniper, I release you.
By the cold light of the day, I release you.
By the sweet words of friends, I release you.
By the open hand of the witch, I release you.'

As she spoke, she flicked her wrist towards the postmistress, dousing her in the water; the air filled with a sharp green scent. Droplets fell on Mrs Mossley's hair, her face and her hands. She stopped ripping through her package and looked up, her eyes fixed on the Hedgewitch.

'From the bounds of this spell you are free,' the Hedgewitch finished, and as she said the final word Mrs Mossley slumped over the counter, like a puppet whose strings had been cut.

Cassie and Tabitha rushed forward, helping the woman to her feet and supporting her. The glazed look had gone from her eyes and she was shivering.

Tabitha found a wool blanket in the pile of opened packages and wrapped it around the postmistress's shoulders. 'There, it's all over now. You're safe, the Hedgewitch is here.'

'Who...? Where...?' Mrs Mossley stuttered. Coming to her senses, she took in the mess surrounding her. 'What on earth happened here? The parcels... who did this?'

'You did, Mrs Mossley,' said Cassie. 'You were looking for something – don't you remember?'

The postmistress shook her head, looking up at the Hedgewitch. She touched a hand to her face and hair, feeling the dampness of the juniper water.

'Someone or something has enchanted you, Mrs Mossley,' said Miranda. 'It is all right now, the spell is broken, and I will check the wards on your doors and windows. But first, I must ask – has anyone strange come into the post office? Have you had any unusual packages delivered?'

The woman shook her head. 'No, no, nothing unusual. I've been here all day, just the regular village folk coming and going. A little while ago I noticed it was getting dark terribly early, it does at this time of year, I suppose, and I went to open the shutters on the back window. That's the last thing I remember.'

Cassie glanced out the window; it was mid-afternoon and the sun was still high above them.

The postmistress was visibly shaken and Tabitha helped her to a seat.

'Very well, if that's all you can recall, you'd better close the post office for the rest of the day and lie down. I'll give you a restorative tonic but the best remedy is good food, sweet tea and sleep.'

'I'll help her upstairs, and make her something to eat,' said Tabitha.

Miranda nodded, 'Good. Cassandra, you'd better start tidying this up. I must speak to everyone who came to the post office today... there should be a book of accounts, yes, here it is. If anything untoward happens, send Malkin to fetch me.'

It took Cassie and Tabitha several hours to sort out the post office and get Mrs Mossley settled, so Cassie did not see her aunt again until tea-time. When she arrived at Hartwood, Mrs Briggs was cutting up seed cake and filling the big blue teapot with hot water. The Hedgewitch was at the table already, although Sebastian and Aoife were yet to come down.

Miranda was recounting the afternoon's events to the housekeeper.

'That poor woman,' said Mrs Briggs, buttering slabs of cake. 'Could be something she ate. Bad fruit, perhaps, or fish out of the Nix. Remember the time Rose and Elliot pulled that strange white fish out of the river? Cooked and ate it right then and there – they were sick as barghests for a week! Had awful dreams about being chased by pike. Should have brought it to me, I told them, you can't trust food as comes out of the Hedge!'

'Perhaps,' said Miranda, sipping her tea. 'Mrs Mossley has no memory of the incident, or how she came to be in such a state.'

'And she had a funny look about her,' Cassie added. 'In her eyes, as though she wasn't herself at all. And then there's Farmer Scrump. He lost his memory too for a while, and when we found him, he was *looking for something*, just like Mrs Mossley.'

'I suppose the two incidents could be connected, however, Mr Scrump was found in the Hedge – his state of mind is not uncommon among those disorientated by the woods. Mrs Mossley, on the other hand, swears she hasn't been near the Hedge. Either way, we'll need to get to the bottom of this before anyone else is affected. It's only luck that neither Mr Scrump nor the postmistress were hurt – luck and some resourceful young witches.'

Cassie was beaming at this rare compliment from her aunt when there came a tapping at the windowpane. There was a shadow behind the glass and, when Mrs Briggs got up, dusting the flour from her skirts, to open it, a black-and-white bird with a flash of bright blue on its wing swooped in to perch on the back of a chair.

'The Assembly send their salutations, Hedgewitch,' said the magpie, who was clearly a witch's familiar.

'Well met, Spica, to what do we owe this visit?' Miranda replied.

'Your presence is required for the trial of Renata Rawlins.'

Miranda's mouth was set in a firm line. 'The timing is unfortunate, I am needed here.'

'The warlock must be tried and you are the sole witness.'

'Not the sole witness,' said Miranda, glancing at Cassie. 'For how long will I be required?'

The magpie shifted from one taloned foot to the other. 'For nineteen days and nineteen nights. It is to be a blood-truth trial.'

Miranda shook her head. 'Impossible, I cannot be away from the Hedge for so long and so close to Hallowe'en.'

'It is not a request, but a summons. You are expected for the commencement of the trial on Sunday at noon.'

There was a moment's silence while the Hedgewitch regarded the magpie over her steaming tea and Cassie waited for her to answer.

'Very well, I will leave at dawn tomorrow.'

The magpie dipped his head in a little bow and flew back out of the window, his tail fanned and his claws catching on the sill as he left.

Mrs Briggs tutted. 'I wish they'd just use imps like everyone else.'

'Imps are not always trustworthy – you know that, Mabily,' said Miranda, rubbing her temples. 'And the Assembly are rather attached to both tradition and secrecy.'

'Well, imps are quicker and they don't damage the woodwork.'

Cassie rather liked the thought of having a bird for a familiar and being able to send secret messages to people. If she asked Montague to take a message to Rue he'd probably say he had more important things to do, like napping.

'Where is the Witches' Assembly?' asked Cassie.

'It is held at Caer Gwrachod, in Wales. Witches have met there for centuries to discuss important matters,' Miranda explained.

'Can I come?'

The Hedgewitch shook her head. 'Novice witches are not permitted to attend the Assembly; you must earn your licence first.'

'But I was there too, when Renata tried to kidnap Jane Wren. I was a witness.'

'Yes, and if you were older I would send you in my stead, but as things stand, it is not an option. I must go to Wales and you must promise not to do anything foolish while I am away.'

'What about Mrs Mossley, and Farmer Scrump?' asked Cassie.

'If there is any more trouble in the village, go to Miss Early.'

'But she's hopeless!'

'Cassandra! I will not have you talking about a qualified witch in that way. You will do as Miss Early tells you and show her the same respect you do me, what precious little that may be. I shall be back in time for Hallowe'en. I expect you to look after your cousin and stay out of trouble until then, if it is not too much to ask.'

Cassie sighed and reluctantly agreed. It would be strange not having the Hedgewitch around. Since Cassie had first come to Hedgely, her aunt had not left the village once. Although sometimes Miranda was so busy they rarely saw each other, Cassie always knew she was there, that the girls could go to her when anything truly frightening happened and she'd know how to solve it. Cassie had no such confidence in Aoife Early.

Chapter Nine

Shells, Bells and Summoning Spells

The leaves of the copper beech had turned from deep purple to rusty orange, falling in drifts and piles on the platform of the Oak Patrol den, leaving gaps in the canopy and beginning to reveal the girls' secret hideaway. Cassie swept away a pile of them with her broom, watching them flutter down to the ground as she told Rue and Tabitha about the magpie familiar's visit to Hartwood and Miranda's departure that very morning.

'And she's going to be away for nineteen days – until the week before Hallowe'en,' said Cassie.

'Sounds splendid if you ask me,' said Rue, flicking leaves off the den floor with her fingers. 'Almost three weeks without the Hedgewitch around – we can do whatever we like!'

'I suppose Miss Early will be running coven meetings,' said Tabitha. She was sitting cross-legged, with a small mortar and pestle in her hand, grinding up dried herbs to make Followfoot powder.

Rue laughed. 'As if Aoife will take her head out of the clouds for long enough to notice what we're up to.'

'But what about Farmer Scrump, and Mrs Mossley?' asked Cassie.

Tabitha looked up at her. 'I stopped by the post office this morning – Mrs Mossley is doing fine, says she's feeling quite herself again.'

'Yes, but I've been thinking about the way they were behaving. I'm sure there is something connecting them.'

'What, apart from them both being old and barmy?' asked Rue.

'While they were enchanted they were both desperate to find something. What if someone is using them to search for whatever it is? Someone who can't come and get it themselves? Mrs Mossley even tried to tell me what it was... some sort of treasure – she said it was for the king.'

Rue shook her head. 'Probably thought she was the Queen of Faerie or something.'

'Rue! That's got to be it. I thought she meant King Robert but what if she was talking about the Erl King?'

Tabitha looked up at her. 'The Erl King? What makes you think he's mixed up in this?'

'He was trying to get my key, remember? That's why he sent Glashtyn to trick me, and I almost gave it to him. Aunt Miranda said the key is one of the great and ancient treasures of Faerie.'

Rue frowned. 'But the Hedgewitch has the key now. Surely he's given up on trying to get it?'

'Yes, but she said *one* of the treasures – what if there are more? What if it's another faery treasure he's after and he's using the villagers to try and find it?'

'I suppose it's possible,' said Tabitha. 'Only, I don't see what we can do about it. We don't even know what they're looking for.'

'But we *do* know that neither Mrs Mossley nor Farmer Scrump have found it, and if whoever is using them is still looking, it could happen again. What if someone gets hurt next time?'

Rue frowned. 'And the Hedgewitch is away. If the Erl King wanted to cause trouble in the village, now would be the perfect time.'

A long, high-pitched whistle pierced their conversation and all three girls went to the edge of the platform to look down.

Standing on the grass beneath them, his hands stuffed in his pockets, was Sebastian.

'Hullo! I can hear you, you know, from down here. How do I get up? Is there a ladder or some sort of pulley system?'

'Oh, for stars' sake,' said Cassie. 'I suppose I'd better fetch him.'

'Can't we leave him down there?' asked Rue. 'This is supposed to be a *secret* den.'

'I promised Aunt Miranda I'd keep an eye on him, it's just this once.'

Cassie descended from the treetops on Tantivy, landing with only a slight wobble on the grass before her cousin.

'The only way up is by broom,' she explained. 'But Tantivy can probably manage the both of us, if you really want to.'

Sebastian raised one ginger eyebrow. 'Both of us, on that thing? I don't fancy falling to my death. Why can't you build a proper ladder? I could help...'

'Look, you can stay down here if you like, it makes no difference to me,' said Cassie.

'All right, we'll do it your way – I just hope you can control that thing.'

After a somewhat shaky ascent, Sebastian joined them on the platform of the den, planting himself firmly in the middle of the rug so as not to be too close to the edge.

'Huh, it's not *that* high up here after all. What are you three up to anyway? Brewing up slugs and lizards?'

'Actually, we're making Followfoot powder, it's for tracking people through the woods,' explained Tabitha, as he crouched down to examine her potion-making kit.

'What's this?' asked Sebastian, pulling a bottle of deep-red liquid out of Tabitha's satchel.

'Oh, that's Coltsfoot cordial, I made it last week. It's for winter coughs and colds. Would you like to try some? It tastes a bit like cherries.'

Sebastian dropped it back in the bag. 'No thanks! You'll probably poison me. Can't imagine why you waste your time with this stuff when you can just go to the pharmacy for some aspirin or penicillin.'

Rue and Tabitha looked at Cassie. She had tried to explain to them just how annoying her cousin was, but until now they'd not quite believed her.

'You should invest in a proper chemistry kit, you know, I can show you how to make sodium cyanide.'

Tabitha wrinkled her nose, 'Isn't *that* poisonous?'

'What are those?' he asked, pointing to a series of symbols that Rue had painted around the entrance and edges of their den.

'They're faery runes, to keep out *unwanted intruders*,' said Rue, dropping the hint like a load of bricks.

Sebastian sniffed. 'It's not like faeries are a serious threat these days.'

Cassie took a deep breath and tried to contain her rising irritation. 'That shows what you know. Only just this week, two people in Hedgely have been enchanted.' She told him about Farmer Scrump and Mrs Mossley.

Sebastian merely shrugged. 'Sounds like a couple of old folks having a turn if you ask me, nothing magical about it. Probably to do with the weather, a drop in barometric pressure, or something in the water—'

Cassie cut him off. 'But they were both looking for something, some sort of treasure.'

'Treasure, you say? I suppose there could be a Viking hoard or Anglo-Saxon burial mound around here somewhere – it's always possible in these backwards, out-of-the-way villages.'

Cassie saw Rue bristle at this remark. Oblivious, Sebastian continued. 'You'll want to conduct a proper survey, lay out a map and draw a grid on it. That way, you can search systematically. And of course you'll need a metal detector – I could probably build one with the right tools.'

'Or we could use a seeking spell,' suggested Tabitha. 'Like the one Cassie and Rue used to find the stolen children.'

Cassie shook her head. 'That was for finding people, and we don't have any more lanthorn flowers.'

'It's all superstitious nonsense anyway. This is the twentieth century, we're in the age of science and technology – I can't imagine why you'd waste your time with this stuff.' He scuffed one of Rue's runes with the toe of his gym shoe. 'Witches are just a load of ignorant women holding us back from real progress.'

All three girls stared at him, open-mouthed. Cassie, who'd had enough of this kind of talk after being subjected to three weeks of it, turned on him. 'How can you say that? Your mother is a witch and uncle Elliot works for Wayland Yard. They've spent their lives studying faery magic and trying to protect people from it. How can you say it's all nonsense?'

Sebastian scowled at her. 'You don't know anything about my family. You don't know what it's like to be banished to the middle of nowhere – to be shipped off by your parents and dumped in some hateful place—'

'Actually,' said Cassie. 'I do. I know exactly what it feels like. At least you know where your parents are, you know they'll be waiting for you when you finally go home.' She pointed towards the Hedge. 'My mother is on the other side of that wood, but she might as well be on the moon, frankly, because I have no way of reaching her. Witchcraft is the only hope I have of ever seeing her again. And this' – she spread out her arms in the direction of the village – 'is *our home*. Rue's, Tabitha's and mine, and the people who live here are neither ignorant nor backwards, they're warm and welcoming. The only hateful thing about this entire situation is that Aunt Miranda insists I have to put up with you!'

There was a brief, stunned silence.

'I never asked for this, for any of it,' said Sebastian, turning away from her.

'Come on,' said Tabitha, reaching for her broom. 'I'll give you a lift down on Aura.'

'Well,' said Rue, once she and Cassie were alone in the den. 'I suppose he deserved that, for being such a little beast.'

But as she watched her cousin clamber off Tabitha's broom and dash away from the beech tree, Cassie wasn't so sure.

'Girls, girls! Gather round, I have a simply glorious activity for you today!' called Aoife Early, her wooden bracelets clacking as she waved the young witches over from their patrol corners. It was their first coven meeting without the Hedgewitch, and everyone was curious to see what Aoife had planned for them. On the floor of the hall were spread an array of seashells, shards of broken china, fat glass beads, mismatched cutlery, and small silver bells. Each piece had a hole drilled through it and Aoife was beaming at them over a pile of branches and balls of string.

'Are we making wards?' asked Rue, somewhat doubtfully.

'Oh no, quite the opposite,' said Aoife. 'Now, can anyone tell me what faeries like?'

'What they *like*?' asked Heather Shuttle, frowning.

'Stealing children,' said Nancy Kemp.

'Cursing people,' said Anika Kalra.

'Leading travellers into bogs,' said Alice Wong. 'Oh! And turning milk sour.'

Aoife shook her head. 'No, I don't mean the harm they do us – I mean what they like for themselves, what pleases them.'

The girls all stared at her in confusion. When they learned about faery folk, it was to gain an understanding of how they might prevent them from coming near their homes and families, how to drive them away and undo the damage they caused.

'Think about it this way,' Aoife began again. 'You all know what materials deter faery people: iron and salt, clear running water, rowan, vervain and solwort. But what if you weren't trying to drive them off, what if you were trying to attract a faery?'

'Do you mean if we wanted to catch it? We made faery traps in the spring,' said Harriet Webb, the Ash Patrol leader and one of the most experienced witches in the coven.

Aoife smiled. 'Well, yes, you might need to call a faery to you for various reasons: to bind it, but also to gain information or assistance from it.'

'The Hedgewitch says you can't trust faeries,' said Ivy. 'They twist the truth and deceive you. They don't want to help us, so why should we ask?'

'Well, it's certainly true that the faery folk do not operate by our rules, laws and ideas of good behaviour, but that doesn't mean they can't ever help us. After all, they have magic beyond anything a witch can do, and sometimes the best way to prevent a faery creature causing harm is not to frighten it off, but to befriend it.'

Ivy laughed. 'That's ridiculous, we don't make friends with faeries, that's not what witchcraft is about.'

'Well, all I ask of you today is that you think about what might attract faery folk to a place, rather than driving them away.'

There was a long pause as the young witches considered this.

'Beauty,' said Tabitha, suddenly. 'Pretty, shiny things, like the sort you pay imps with for taking messages.'

'And food,' added Rue. 'They're always stealing the stuff, and you've got to put out milk and bread for brownies to keep them on your side.'

'Excellent, yes, and what else?'

Cassie thought about all the faery stories she'd read and remembered one about a fiddler who'd been stolen away to play at faery dances.

'Music,' she said. 'They like music.'

'Exactly!' said Aoife, beaming at Cassie. 'They love music, and songs and pleasing sounds. So today we are going to be making wind chimes from the objects you see here. It isn't as easy as it looks to make a pleasant-sounding chime, so I want you to experiment with different materials and see what works. We'll hang them up in the coven garden and see what sort of faery folk they attract.'

'But what if they attract something dangerous?' asked Heather Shuttle.

'With all the wards and protective herbs in the garden, you needn't worry about that. No, we're not likely to attract anything bigger than an urchen or a grig with these chimes, but even if we did, I'm sure you'd all be quite capable of handling it.'

Cassie and Rue exchanged worried glances, but Tabitha was already reaching for a pile of silver bells.

'This is complete and utter nonsense,' said Ivy, folding her arms across her chest. 'I'm not going to waste my time making silly wind chimes. When the Hedgewitch gets back, I'm going to tell her all about this!'

Ivy stomped off to the Thorn Patrol corner where she pulled out a copy of *The Witch's Own* magazine and sat down to read. Aoife sighed, but did nothing to stop her, instead helping Lucy Watercress untangle a ball of string.

'I hate to admit it,' said Rue. 'But Ivy has a point. I don't see what good making wind chimes will do. Why on earth would you want to attract bogles, imps and goblins?'

They were sitting on cushions in the Oak Patrol corner. It wasn't a corner in the strictest sense of the word as the hall itself was round, but a space along the wall set aside for their things. Cassie, Rue and Tabitha had decorated it over the summer with oak branches, green bunting and hand-drawn charts of magical herbs and fungi. There was a rack for their brooms and Mrs Briggs had made smaller cushions for Montague, Natter and Wyn. It wasn't as grand as the Thorn Patrol corner, which boasted a sofa and a wall-mounted potions rack, but it had begun to feel like their own space within the coven hall.

'I don't know, but I think there's something in it,' said Tabitha. 'I mean, if we worked *with* the faery folk instead of against them, maybe they wouldn't cause so much trouble all the time?'

'That's fool's talk and you know it,' said Rue. 'Faeries have been a threat to us for thousands of years; we're not going to change that with a few tinkly bells. Why, you might as well ask the Erl King over for a cup of tea and a slice of cake.'

Cassie had to agree with Rue for the most part. In the past year alone various faery folk had tried to trap, kidnap and drown her. The one time she had sought the assistance of a shape-shifting phooka it had deceived her, appearing as her mother and trying to make her give up the precious golden key. But Aoife's words had given her another idea, about how they could find out what was behind the strange behaviour of Farmer Scrump and Mrs Mossley, and what the villagers had been looking for while under enchantment.

'There was one thing Aoife said that made sense, though,' said Cassie. 'That bit about getting information from a faery. If the Erl King is behind what's happening to the villagers, surely his servants would know. If we could only talk to Burdock...'

'The goblin? He's as slippery as an eel,' said Rue.

'I know, but he's a filcher – a goblin thief. He knew the Erl King wanted the key; that's why he broke into my room to get it. If the goblins or the Erl King are behind this, he'll know, and he'll know what they're looking for.'

'But how do we find him and convince him to help us?' asked Tabitha.

'That's the difficult bit. Last time, he *had* to work with us because he owed me a favour and even goblins can't go back on their word. But I doubt he'd come running if we simply went into the Hedge and called for him. I'm pretty sure he's still cross about the Hedgewitch forcing him to help her find me, and we don't even know if he's around. But maybe, if Aoife is right, we could do something that would draw him to us.'

'I doubt he'll come running when he hears this,' said Rue, holding up her wind chime – an assortment of forks and broken pottery which clanked and clattered together. 'And there isn't anything about summoning faeries in the handbook. They hardly want young witches calling up banshees and bogles.'

'Let's ask Aoife, I bet she knows how to attract a goblin,' Tabitha suggested.

They got their chance when afternoon tea was served. It was getting cool enough for hot drinks now and they had sweet, spiced apple tea with Mrs Briggs' chestnut and chocolate loaf. Rue was licking crumbs from her fingers as they approached the Assistant Coven Mistress.

Aoife was tidying up near the Thorn Patrol corner, where Ivy was still sitting, reading her magazine and ignoring the rest of them.

'Of course, she can't just walk out,' whispered Rue. 'Wouldn't want to lose her badge for perfect attendance!'

Cassie nudged her to be quiet as they reached Aoife, who looked up at them, beaming. 'And how are you girls getting on with your chimes? Do you need some help?'

'Actually, we were wondering about goblins,' Cassie began. '*Hypothetically* speaking – if we wanted to attract goblins, not that we do of course, but what sort of things do they like?'

'Now there's an interesting question. Of all the faery peoples, our relationship with the goblins is among the most fraught. I am aware that the three of you had an encounter with some goblin nabbers in the summer, so I'm sure you know how dangerous they can be.'

'Oh, of course!' said Tabitha quickly. 'We don't really want to get mixed up with them again, we were just wondering.'

'Well, goblins are generally very wary of witches. There's little love lost between us and many goblins are wanted by the wardens for stealing, kidnapping and damage to human property. They're likely be suspicious of a witch trying to approach them, and see any invitation as a trap. However, *hypothetically* speaking, if you knew a goblin's name and put it into a summoning spell, you could probably get his or her attention. You'd also want to bring some sort of gift as a sign of goodwill.'

'But we don't know any summoning spells,' said Rue. Cassie elbowed her. Subtlety wasn't Rue's strong suit.

'I don't see why that should stop a patrol of clever young witches. Where do you think spells come from?'

'From witches' grimoires – their personal spell books,' said Cassie. She'd snuck into her aunt's study to find a spell in the Hedgewitch's grimoire once.

'Yes, but how do they get in those books in the first place?' asked Aoife

Cassie had never really questioned this. She'd thought of spells as ancient secrets passed down by generations of witches over the centuries, but she supposed they had to come from somewhere originally.

'Witches write them,' said Ivy, who had been eavesdropping and couldn't resist this opportunity to show Cassie up. 'Isn't that obvious?'

'Can we really do that, write our own spells?' asked Cassie, too excited by this idea to mind Ivy.

Aoife nodded. 'It isn't easy, mind you, but I encourage all my girls to give it a try.'

'You said we'd need a gift, too,' said Tabitha. 'What sort of gifts do goblins like?'

'I've heard they have a fondness for good, strong cheese.'

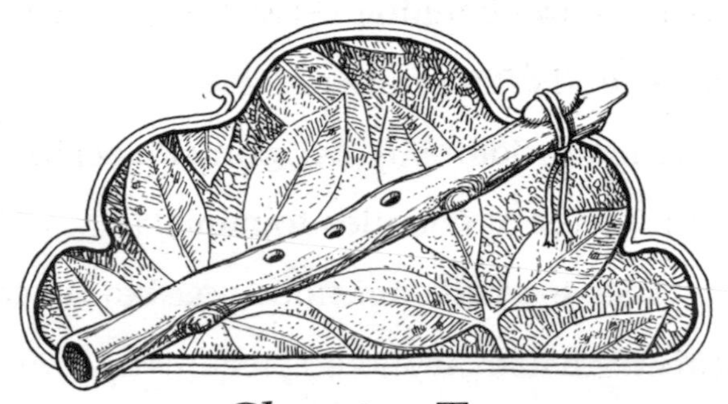

Chapter Ten

A Truckle of Blue Cheese

Oak Patrol met the following afternoon at the stump of an old elm tree growing just outside the Hedge. They'd changed into their hats and cloaks, even though it was a Saturday, because Tabitha insisted it was best to look like proper witches for what they were about to do and their uniforms might give them an air of authority.

'But he's only a goblin,' said Rue. 'And a rather small one at that.'

'It doesn't matter, if we want his help then we need to do the thing properly,' said Tabitha. 'Have you got the offering?'

Rue grinned and pulled a large, cloth-wrapped bundle from her rucksack. Opening it for their inspection she revealed a round of blue cheese, with a thick crust of mould on the outside. 'Mrs Bellwether's Best Hedgely Blue. It won a prize at the Midsummer Fair.'

'Phew! It doesn't half stink,' said Cassie.

'Smellier the better, he should pick this up from a mile away,' said Rue, placing it on the stump.

'Have you got the summoning spell, Cassie?' Tabitha asked.

Cassie flushed, she had been dreading this moment. It had taken her half the night to compose the summoning spell, as it was the first she had ever written. She'd looked up the words in her thesaurus and done her best to make it sound poetical, but even still, the thought of reading it aloud in front of her friends was mortifying.

'Yes, do you want to read it?' she asked, hopefully.

'No, you do it, I might get it wrong,' said Tabitha.

'All right,' Cassie cleared her throat. 'Here goes:

Goblin Burdock, wherever you are
Deep underground, near or far
We bring you gifts of luscious cheese
Hear my spell and come quick, please.'

There was a moment's silence before Rue burst out laughing.

'That was, well, very polite,' said Tabitha, biting her lip to keep from giggling.

'Luscious cheese?' howled Rue. She was buckled over with laughter, tears flowing from her eyes. 'Come quick, *please*?'

'It had to rhyme,' said Cassie, turning red. 'You try writing the spell next time if you're so–'

But Tabitha had grabbed her arm and Cassie looked up to see a pale figure crouched on the tree stump, sniffing their offering with his long pointy nose.

'Shhh!' said Cassie, while Rue tried to recover from her laughing fit. 'He's here.'

The goblin looked up, noticing them for the first time. 'Oh, it's *you*.' He glared at Cassie and began to climb back down off the stump.

'Wait! Don't go, we need your help!' she called.

The goblin sneered, flipping the tip of the dirty nightcap he wore back over his pointy ears. 'And why should I help *you*? You think his High and Horribleness rewarded me for the last time? You think they gave me a medal for leading two witchlings to the goblin market? For taking the Hedgewitch herself to the tower where his servant was working, where he nearly had the key in his grasp! Interfering, he said I was, fraternizing with the enemy. Me, Burdock, lover of humans?' The goblin spat on the grass and it withered to brown. 'I been thrown out, I have, no longer fit for the service. Filchers don't want me any more and it's all your fault!'

'I'm sorry, we had no idea,' said Cassie. It was difficult to feel sympathy for the goblin, but in truth, they had forced him to help last time. And then the Hedgewitch had threatened him when Cassie was in danger, so it was no wonder he hated humans really.

'But if you're not working for the Erl King any more, then what harm could it do?' she asked. 'All we want is information. People are getting hurt and we need to know why. We were sure a well-connected goblin, such as yourself, would know all about it.'

The goblin narrowed his eyes. 'What sort of infer-mation?'

'People in the village are being enchanted, they're being forced to look for something, some sort of treasure, against their wills. But when they snap out of it they can't remember what it is,' Cassie said. 'We thought, being in the business of precious things, you might know what they're looking for?'

'Well, as it happens I might know something about that,' said the goblin, inspecting his dirty nails. 'Word of these things gets 'round in the trade.'

'Oh, *do* tell us,' Tabitha begged.

'What you offering in exchange?'

'We brought you the cheese,' said Cassie. 'What else do you want?'

The goblin turned and a slow smile crept across his face. 'Well, nows I thinks about it, maybe there is something: a favour, such as you had from me before, to my regrets.'

When Cassie had first caught the goblin sneaking into her bedroom, looking to steal the key, she'd let him go free in exchange for a favour, which she and Rue had later claimed when they needed to find the goblin market.

'You can't,' said Tabitha. 'That's an open-ended bargain – he could ask you to do anything, to give yourself over to the Erl King even!'

'So little trust you witchlings have. What would his High and Horribleness want with *her*, now as she don't have the key no more? He's got plenty of children has the master, doesn't need another scrawny witch-child who likes to cause trouble.'

'Very well,' said Cassie. 'You have my word, a favour. Now tell us what the villagers are searching for.'

The goblin's eyes shone with victory and he clambered back up onto the tree stump, seating himself as if on a throne. 'Word is, the Lord of Rags and Tatters is looking for a thing, powerful thing, valuable thing.' He lowered his voice, leaning towards them so that they could smell his rotten breath. 'I hear it's a sort of weapon, a spear they say, old as the hills.'

'But why hasn't he sent the goblins after it, why use the villagers?' asked Cassie.

'Because none may touch it and live!' The goblin grinned, showing his pointy teeth.

'And he thinks this spear is hidden somewhere in Hedgely?' Tabitha asked.

'It was stolen by a human, a long, long time ago. Chances are you lot have still got it tucked away somewhere.'

Cassie, Rue and Tabitha exchanged worried glances. If the goblin was telling the truth, then it would not be long before another villager was enchanted and forced to look for the spear, and if they found it, they might not survive the discovery.

'The Erl King, how is he controlling them?' asked Cassie, turning back to the goblin. But the tree stump was empty; both Burdock and the truckle of cheese had vanished.

'I hate it when he does that,' said Rue.

'Well, I suppose he did answer our question,' said Tabitha. 'And at least now we know what the Erl King is after.'

Cassie frowned. 'Yes, but we don't know how he's enchanting the villagers, and if one of them manages to find the spear...'

'We'll just have to find it first,' said Tabitha.

'But if it was stolen hundreds of years ago, it could be buried or hidden or lost,' said Cassie. 'We don't even know where to begin looking.'

Rue grinned. 'I know someone who might.'

Watchet's Museum and Antique Shop, read the peeling letters on the sign above the blue door. The bowed window was filled with moth-eaten chairs and paraffin lamps, china dolls and silver egg cups, writing slopes and a nautilus shell. Everything was covered in a thin layer of dust and there was no light within. It was five o'clock and Tabitha had to rush home to prepare dinner for her grandmother, leaving Cassie and Rue to approach the antique dealer together.

'Maybe we should come back tomorrow,' said Cassie, reading the small card on the door which read: BY APPOINTMENT ONLY in tiny, neat print. 'I don't think it's open.'

Cassie had never been inside the antique shop before; it didn't seem the sort of place to welcome curious young witches.

Rue sniffed. 'Never is. Eris Watchet hates customers. You've just got to make a bit of noise, get her attention.' To illustrate her point, Rue rapped loudly on the door with one hand while yanking on the bell pull with the other, making a cacophony that had everyone on Loft Street stopping to stare at them.

A moment later, the door cracked open and a hand shot out, grabbing Rue by the collar and whisking her inside. Cassie rushed to follow, squeezing through before the door slammed shut behind them.

A lean brown face peered down at them from the gloom. 'What do you want with such a racket, eh?' The woman looked them over, taking in their pointed hats and cloaks. 'Witches, is it? What do you want? I haven't got all day.'

There was the sound of a match being struck and the hiss of flame meeting oil as a lamp flared to life, illuminating the rest of Eris Watchet. She towered over them, dressed in a neat three-piece suit, over which she wore an orange smoking jacket. Perched on her curly head was a round hat with a tassel hanging from it.

'We've come about a faery treasure,' said Rue.

'Ha! Treasure? Do you think I was born yesterday? Don't waste my time with such nonsense.'

'Please, we just want to ask you a few questions,' said Cassie. 'It's about a spear and, well, it could be dangerous.'

The shopkeeper sniffed. 'It wouldn't be much of a spear if it was safe, now, would it? Follow me, this way, and don't touch anything!'

The antique dealer made her way ahead of them and as she went she lit a second lamp, and then a third and slowly the dim shop sparkled to life. It was an Aladdin's cave, filled to the rafters with mahogany desks, gilt-framed paintings, Chinese vases, silverware, steamer trunks, brass candlesticks and leering wooden masks. There was so much clutter that the girls could barely move and when they looked up, they saw more chairs and tables fixed to the ceiling, their legs dangling down like swimmers'.

Cassie squeezed between a towering stack of old suitcases and a marble statue of a winged deer, wrinkling her nose at the peculiar smells that permeated the shop: the beeswax and linseed oil of polished wood, the animal scent of worn leather, a touch of incense even. The shop smelled *old,* as if the accumulated debris of the ages had preserved, in its scent, the memories of the people who had once owned these things. She peered into a speckled mirror. A stranger looked back at her, a fair-haired girl in a white nightgown. Cassie started and the reflection shifted to her own bewildered face.

'This way,' said Eris, leading them down a narrow aisle between ornate wardrobes. 'And mind you don't knock anything with those brooms.'

'How can it be a museum *and* an antique shop?' Cassie asked.

'It's a museum for people like you what's not planning on buying anything.'

Perched on the furniture were armillary spheres, crystal orbs, silver goblets and porcelain witches with bows on their brooms. As they squeezed between armoires and escritoires, a small, slender object resting on a table caught Cassie's eye. It was thin and white as bone, twisted and lumpy, with a row of holes down one side. It seemed to glow in the dim light of the shop. She stepped closer and before she knew what she was doing, Cassie was holding it in her hands. The flute was made of wood, smooth and surprisingly light. A cold shiver ran down her spine, her fingers tingled and she felt the overwhelming urge to raise it to her lips and see what sound it made.

Suddenly, a blur of grey and red feathers swooped into her vision, snatching the flute from her hands with sharp talons. '*Squawk!* No touching, no touching!'

Cassie stumbled backwards as the parrot wheeled around her head and flapped up to land on top of a lampshade, the flute clutched in one claw.

'No touching!' said the bird. '*Squawk!*'

'Whoa! Is that your familiar?' asked Rue.

'That's Barbarossa,' Eris replied. 'An ordinary African Grey, nothing magical about him. He is, however, a bit protective of my stock and not opposed to biting small fingers if they touch things they shouldn't.'

The shopkeeper paused before an ottoman and a pair of wicker chairs and proceeded to remove a pile of old magazines and feathered hats from them.

'Sit,' she commanded, waving them forward.

Cassie perched on one of the spindly chairs, unsure if it would take her weight, while Rue climbed onto the ottoman and Eris Watchet reclined in the other chair, pulling an ivory pipe from her pocket and stuffing it with snuffwart from a small silver box. Barbarossa flew down to land on the back of her chair.

'A spear, you say? Which century? I've a medieval glaive and some handsome pikes from the War of the Two Queens,' said Eris, gesturing at a row of rusty iron weapons along one wall.

'It might be older than that,' said Cassie. 'We believe it came from Faerie.'

'The faery folk don't make iron weapons, can't bear the stuff – only metals they'll touch are silver and gold but they're too soft to hold an edge. The goblins have learned to work copper and bronze, but if it's really old, it would be made of stone.'

'But how can you make a weapon out of stone?' Rue asked.

'Knapping, they call it – humans used to do it too, before they discovered smithing. Here, wait a moment.' Eris Watchet disappeared behind a desk and could be heard rifling through drawers and boxes. She returned with cupped hands and deposited several small, thin objects into Cassie's lap. Rue picked one up and held it to the light. It was a sliver of pale-green stone, roughly triangular and so fine at the edges that the light shone through it, like dark glass.

'Faery darts, from the tips of their arrows. Be careful, they used to dip them in poison.'

Rue dropped the dart back into the pile.

'You could hardly call it a spear, though,' said Eris. 'And I've never come across any bigger than that.'

'We were told it might have belonged to someone who lived here, in Hedgely, a long time ago,' said Cassie. 'Perhaps someone who stole it from Faerie?'

Eris frowned, blowing a ring of green smoke. 'Where'd you hear that, then? Who you been talking to?'

'Oh, just a friend,' said Cassie quickly.

'This friend wouldn't happen to have yellow eyes and pointy teeth, would he? Hmmm, now I think about it, there was another meddlesome child in here once... oh, decades ago, asking about a spear. A boy, with spectacles and hair like a startled dandelion.' She paused and gazed over their heads. 'Can't for the life of me remember his name.'

Cassie and Rue sat forward, eager to hear more.

'No, it's gone. Never was much good with names and faces. *Things*, though – I never forget interesting *things*! The "slaying spear", he called it, seemed to think he could find it too. Though whether he ever did...'

Suddenly, there was a great *BONG* as the grandfather clock behind Eris Watchet's chair began to sound the hour. Cassie and Rue started as all the other clocks in the shop hurried to chime in, delivering a cacophony of cuckoos, dings, dongs and dells.

'Six o'clock, six o'clock. *Squawk!*' cried Barbarossa.

Eris returned her pipe to her pocket and rose from her chair.

'That's enough questions, off with you, it's time for my tea.' She took the arrowheads back and herded the girls out into the street, slamming the door behind them.

Chapter Eleven

Rabbit Holes and Rowan Berries

It was a week since the Hedgewitch had left for Wales when the fog rolled in.

'Brogan said it came down from the Hedge overnight,' said Cassie.

'Thick as potato soup!' Rue complained, hoisting her broom over her shoulder. 'I very nearly crashed into a tree on the way up, and would have if Natter hadn't warned me.'

A croaky chuckle came from Rue's pocket. 'Toads aren't blind you know!'

‘I mean, we always get some mist around this time of year,’ said Rue. ‘But this is heavier than anything I can remember.’

Cassie had experienced London smogs, with their choking coal dust, but this was another thing altogether. It lay heavy in the valleys, and from the window of her turret bedroom she’d seen it pooling into misty lakes between the hills, obscuring the farmhouses and sheepfolds that lay within. It had been like waking up in a castle in the clouds, looking down into an airy otherworld.

As they walked downhill towards the village, they entered the fog like divers. Cassie held out a hand in front of her, it disappeared from sight almost immediately.

‘It’s blue!’

‘Faery fog,’ explained Montague. He was particularly difficult to make out, his blue-grey coat melding into the air. Only his amber eyes stood out like lamps. ‘Can you not taste it? This is no English weather. It has come down from the Hedge.’

As they descended the hill, the fog grew thicker and Cassie reached out for Rue’s hand so they wouldn’t be separated. The village was oddly quiet for a Saturday; even Loft Street was mostly empty, a few distant shadows all they could make out of other villagers who had ventured into the fog. The buildings themselves were tall, dark shapes, indistinguishable in the strange blue light, with small fuzzy squares of yellow for windows.

There was a screech of wheels on cobblestones and clatter of metal as a bicycle pulled up before them.

'Not a day to be out of doors,' said a tall, thin figure, whom they recognised by his voice as Police Constable Griffiths. 'I could have run you both down. Best head back inside until it lifts. Unnatural, this – never seen anything like it and I've been here twenty years!'

'I guess broom practice is out of the question then,' said Cassie, feeling slightly relieved. She didn't much fancy the idea of flying into an invisible wall or bush.

Rue sighed. 'I suppose we can go back to my place... Only, Oliver and Angus will both be in, so we'll be like sardines. Come on, I think it's this way.'

As they stumbled along, looking for signposts and trying to get a glimpse of the shops on either side to determine their approximate position, they heard a wailing cry. It was a man's voice and as they stopped to listen, it came again, this time in a low moan.

'Where's it coming from?' asked Cassie.

'Behind us, I think,' said Rue. 'It almost sounds like...'

'Is that the rowan tree? This must be the village green, only I can't see a thing.'

The ground changed to grass beneath their feet. 'Watch out for the duck pond!' warned Cassie.

'Oww! Too late.'

'What is it? Have you fallen in?'

'I don't think so, there's no water,' said Rue. 'Just a rabbit hole, I expect.'

Cassie tripped and found herself face first in the muddy grass.

'I don't remember there being so many rabbit holes on the green.'

'Ohhh, I must find it, I must...' said a man's voice from somewhere ahead of them.

'Dad!' cried Rue, rushing forward and disappearing into the mist.

Cassie dashed after her and soon saw the tall, dark shape of Mr Whitby.

'It isn't here! Why isn't it here?' he cried, raising something long and heavy and pushing it into the ground. It was a shovel. The pits they'd tripped in weren't rabbit holes; Rue's father was digging up the village green.

'What is it, Dad? What are you doing?' asked Rue, taking hold of her father's arm. He shrugged her off and went on digging.

'It has to be here.' There was a thud as the shovel hit a new patch of grass. 'I will find it, and then... and then...'

'What are you going on about? Leave it, Dad, come home with us,' said Rue, reaching for him again.

A dark smoky scent lingered in the air and tickled Cassie's nose. Ted Whitby cast a dark shadow before him on the grass. Cassie blinked. That wasn't right, there shouldn't be any shadows, not in this fog. She caught Rue's other arm and pulled her away.

'Don't get too close. He's been enchanted. It's just like before, with Farmer Scrump and Mrs Mossley.'

Rue stared at her, wide-eyed. 'We have to do something; he could break a leg, or worse!'

They both knew what would happen if Mr Whitby found what he was searching for.

'My aunt used juniper water, but we haven't got any... I don't suppose pond water will be much help.'

'Rowan berries!' said Rue. 'They're good against enchantment, and we just passed the tree.'

'Right, you gather some and I'll see if I can remember the charm Aunt Miranda used.'

Rue nodded and dashed off into the mist.

'It may not work, Cassandra. You should seek assistance,' said Montague.

'But the Hedgewitch is away, there's only Aoife... Could you?'

'I'll fetch the witch. Don't get too close, there's something off about that man, he doesn't smell right, even if he is enchanted.' Montague cast one last glance at the flailing figure of Rue's father and leapt into the fog.

'Cassie?' called Rue.

'This way!'

Thud, went Mr Whitby's shovel. 'It's here somewhere, it has to be!' he wailed.

'Here, I've got the berries,' said Rue. 'What should I do with them?'

'I don't know, get them on him somehow? I think I can remember the incantation.'

Together they approached Rue's father. Rue threw a handful of the bright-red berries at him; her aim was good but he merely brushed them off and went back to his digging.

'It's not working, Cass,' said Rue, her voice quavering.

'Try again, as I say the spell,' said Cassie. She cleared her throat and began in her best chanting voice: 'By the... oh, this bit is about juniper, I'd better change it:

By the bitter berries of rowan, I release you.
By the cold light of the day, I release you.
By the sweet words of friends, I release you.
By the open hand of the witch, I release you.
From the bounds of this spell you are free!'

Finally, Mr Whitby stopped what he was doing and stood, still as a scarecrow, on the grass. The spade fell from his hands and he turned to look at them.

'Rue? Is that you? Can't see a ruddy thing in this fog.'

Laughing, Rue ran forward to hug her father.

Although dazed and confused by his experience and the shock of finding himself on the green surrounded by clods of grass he had upturned, Ted Whitby soon returned to himself and the fog began to lift. Cassie found she could see her hand again when she held it out in front of her. Flying towards them over the green from the direction of the village, came Aoife Early, Montague close behind and her kingfisher familiar a flash of iridescent blue at her shoulder.

'Girls! Are you all right?' she asked, a worried frown crinkling her young face. 'What's happened here?'

They explained everything to Aoife on the way back to the Whitby's shop, where a very worried Mrs Whitby came out to retrieve her husband and fuss over him. Aoife asked the same sort of questions the Hedgewitch had asked Mr Scrump and Mrs Mossley, but Ted Whitby swore he couldn't remember a thing after he'd come down to make coffee that morning, and that he hadn't been to the Hedge or encountered anyone in the street.

Leaving Aoife to check the house wards and reassure Mrs Whitby, Rue took Cassie upstairs to her room.

'She hasn't a clue, you can tell,' said Rue. 'My dad could have really been hurt – what if he'd broken his foot with that shovel? Or what if he *had* found the spear? He could have died! That witch, with her faery-friendly nonsense, isn't going to do anything about this. She has us making wind chimes and dancing about like ninnies and meanwhile, someone or something is attacking people in the village, *our* village.'

Cassie frowned. 'We need to find the spear ourselves, before anyone gets hurt. If only Eris Watchet could remember that boy's name... the one who was looking for it all those years ago – perhaps he found it?'

'My mum might know, she remembers just about everyone who's lived in the village – and everything they said or did. Let's ask.'

The Whitby kitchen was a fraction of the size of the one at Hartwood, and Cassie marvelled that Rue, her parents and her three brothers could all fit around the tiny table. Drying clothes hung from a rack above the fire. Oliver's drawings and old school prizes decorated the walls. It was equally comfortable in its own way, Cassie decided, and the pepper-pot soup Mrs Whitby was busy stirring over the small gas cooker filled the air with a delicious, spicy smell that seemed to chase away the last of the fog.

'A boy with spectacles and hair like a startled dandelion?' asked Rue's mother. 'Well now, I suppose that could be young Toby Harper. He moved to Hedgely with his family shortly after your father and I were wed.'

'Does he live nearby?' asked Cassie. 'Can we go and speak to him?'

'Afraid not, dear, he went missing, fourteen years ago at Midwinter. He was a grown man by then. Mysterious business it was too. There's some as say he went into the Hedge – goodness knows *why*. There was a search, of course, the old Hedgewitch had everyone out looking, but they never found a single hair – and no one has seen him since.'

Cassie and Rue exchanged a meaningful look. It could be no coincidence that Toby had vanished on a Crossing Night, especially if he was mixed up with dangerous faery treasures.

'What about the rest of his family?' asked Rue.

'His parents moved away – it was too hard on them, I suppose, living so close to the Hedge after what happened. He was a quiet lad, young Toby, always scribbling away in those notebooks of his. Liked to read too, got a job helping Widdershin when he was a few years older than you two. You could ask Widdershin about him, if you're really interested. Of course, he was a good friend of Rose's too, but I imagine you know that already.'

'He was friends with my mother?' asked Cassie. Her mother had never talked about the people she'd left behind in Hedgely.

Mrs Whitby lifted the ladle to sample the simmering broth. 'She was terribly upset when he went missing. Blamed herself, poor dear, although I never understood why. That was right before she left the village, now I think about it.'

Chapter Twelve

The Boy who Drew Faeries

Widdershin's bookshop was the very last on the east side of Loft Street, a few doors down from Bramble's. Over the years its beams had begun to give under the weight of the shop's merchandise, until the upper floors were leaning out over the corner of the street. Its green door was so crooked that you had to tilt your head to one side to enter. However, the inside of the shop more than made up for this; every surface, from the teetering shelves, to the tables and floor, was piled high with books. It was somewhat dusty and difficult to navigate, but Cassie thought it was the best place in the world.

Cassie and Tabitha made their way between the shelves, stepping over fallen books and occasionally returning one to its place. Cassie had met Tabitha at her bus stop after school and told her everything they'd learned from Eris Watchet and Rue's mum, all about the faery darts and Toby Harper. As they entered the shop together, Cassie took a deep breath, enjoying the familiar scent of ageing paper and leather bindings.

The old hob was snoozing in a chair by the pot-bellied stove, a thin brown book clasped to his chest and two of his four pairs of spectacles perched on the bridge of his nose. As he snored, his feathery eyebrows went up and down and his long tufted ears flapped on his shoulders.

'Mr Widdershin?' said Tabitha, softly.

But Cassie had rather more experience with the bookseller and knew that once he'd drifted off no amount of polite cajoling would wake him. She reached for an open book on the overflowing desk and shut it with a loud clap and a puff of dust.

'Great blithering blind wyrms, what is it? Fire? Invasion? Are the military history books at each other's spines again?' asked Widdershin, his eyes still bleary with sleep. 'Oh, it's you, Cassandra. What do you want?'

'We wanted to ask you about a young man who used to work for you,' said Cassie. 'His name was Toby Harper.'

'Tobias? Yes, I remember him. Bright lad, used to help me around the shop – cataloguing, book-herding, that sort of thing. Very interested in the history of the Hedge and the village, he was. But history is a dangerous subject, I was forever telling him, especially when it comes to Faerie.' The hob flicked a scrap of paper off his lap. 'There's things buried in the past that some folk want to stay hidden. People think books are safe, tame things nowadays. Always encouraging their children to read, they are. But books can change you, change the way you see the world, and then there's no going back. Indeed, some have a will of their own.' His hand strayed to the ivory book chained to his desk. A glass eye set into its cover opened and blinked at him.

'Yes, but was he interested in anything in particular?' asked Cassie. 'Say, faery treasures or old weapons?'

Widdershin raised an eyebrow. 'It wouldn't surprise me if he was. Dangerously curious, that boy, ancient mysteries are all very well in books, where they belong, but when you humans start poking about with things you don't understand, well... you have a tendency to get yourselves in trouble, don't you?' The bookseller sighed. 'One of his notebooks is probably still lying about somewhere. He was forever scribbling in it. Had a red leather cover, I believe. Haven't seen the thing since he disappeared, but if you can find it, you're welcome to it. It's of little use to me!'

And with that the hob exchanged the pair of glasses he was wearing for another on a chain about his neck, hefted the fat ivory book open and began to read.

Cassie and Tabitha looked at each other in dismay. Widdershin's shop was about as organised as the aftermath of an avalanche. While some of the books were stacked properly on shelves, just as many were piled high in teetering towers, jumbled together in small hills or tucked behind various pieces of furniture. It was, under ordinary circumstances, one of the things Cassie loved about the bookshop; she never knew what she might find – a treatise on imp anatomy, a book of merrow lullabies, an astrological thesis of unfulfilled prophecies. She'd spent hours perusing the shelves and stacks, and yet she'd never seen a notebook that matched Widdershin's description.

'I suppose we'd better start in the history section, if that's what he was interested in,' said Cassie.

'There are sections?' asked Tabitha.

'Yes, sort of, only they're not all in one place. History begins there, behind that bust of a faun and finishes up somewhere over there, with the cookery books,' Cassie explained, pointing to opposite sides of the shop.

They spent the rest of the afternoon searching through rows and stacks of books, getting excited for a moment whenever they spotted a small reddish volume without a title on its spine. So far, these thrilling finds had turned out to be nothing but a collection of goblin love poetry, a book on the architecture of faery palaces and another containing assorted remedies for boils. While Tabitha found the latter of some interest, Cassie was beginning to fear they would never find Toby's notebook when, wandering down an aisle at the very back of the shop, where the shelves were lined with huge, heavy books of maps and engravings, she stepped on a floorboard and heard it creak.

Now, to anyone else, a single creaky floorboard in an old shop would not warrant much attention. Indeed, the floor, which was worn from the passage of many customers over the years, would be expected to give at places where the nails had pulled free. But Cassie had once made use of just such a floorboard in her boarding school dormitory, and she knew that particular type of creak meant that it could be removed entirely.

Craning her neck around the shelves, she waved at Tabitha, who was sorting through a crate of old annuals, and used the witch sign for 'come here' to summon her over.

While Widdershin had granted them permission to look for the book, Cassie wasn't sure he'd be happy with her ripping apart the shop itself, and she said as much to Tabitha. 'Could you distract him for me?'

Tabitha nodded and walked back to the shopkeeper's desk.

'Mr Widdershin, have you got anything on herbs for familiars? My Wyn has developed a sniffle and I was wondering if there was a potion I could brew for her?'

'Hmm, yes, I think there's a copy of *Wyrmwood's Formulary* back here somewhere.' The old bookseller led her down a crowded aisle. Cassie heard him cursing as he stubbed a toe and knocked over a stack of books. She would have to be quick.

Fortunately, Brogan had recently given Cassie a penknife, and she put it to good use prising up the board at the narrow end, where the nails were already loosened. She'd had experience doing this quietly, as she'd kept her own private library under just such a board and had sometimes wanted to access it during the night while her dorm-mates were sleeping. Getting her fingers underneath, she pulled it up and aside. It was very dusty and dark, but sure enough there was a space beneath. Cassie wished she'd brought a torch; she couldn't see a thing and would have to reach in and feel about, hoping that no book wyrms had made a nest in there.

At first she felt nothing but stone and dry dust, but then her fingers found something soft and rough. She fished it out. It was a book and, sure enough, once she dusted off the cover, there was red leather underneath.

Cassie did not get a chance to read Toby's notebook until later that evening, after Tabitha had rushed home to prepare a meal for her grandmother and Cassie had eaten her own supper with Mrs Briggs, Brogan, Sebastian and Aoife. All the while, the small red notebook called to her from her bedside table, where she'd left it. Singing to her of the secrets tucked within its pages.

Taking a cup of cocoa upstairs with her after supper, Cassie settled into her window seat while Montague curled in a ball on her bare feet. The past few nights had been truly chilly and his furry warmth was welcome.

The little red notebook began with a series of diary entries, written when Toby was still a boy and newly arrived in Hedgely. In them, he described his first day at the school – the same one Cassie attended now – and his initial impressions of the village itself. He'd known as little about faeries or witchcraft as Cassie had when she'd arrived, but had become immediately curious about the river hag, the imps that flitted about, the wisps he spotted in the fields at night and the stories of stranger, wilder things lurking in the Hedge. The entries included notes on the faery creatures he encountered and there were pictures: drawings of grigs and urchens and a bogle, and a rather good caricature of Widdershin himself. Toby had set out to learn as much about faery folk as he could and his entries were both detailed and, as far as Cassie could tell, as accurate as anything in the *Witch's Handbook*.

Cassie read on as the moon rose above the Hedge. Her mug was empty and the embers in the fireplace little more than glowing ashes when she came across the first reference to the spear:

I've been reading about the faery knights, men who travelled around the kingdoms fighting faery beasts, back before there were enough witches to handle that sort of thing. Most of them died young, it seems. The knights didn't know any magic, but some were said to have enchanted weapons. The most famous were Sir Pismire and Sir Snowbrow – but there was another who lived in Hedgely, Sir Egad. There's not much written about him, only a story about how he killed a great wyrm with a magic spear.

Over the next few entries, Toby grew more and more interested in the spear, visiting Eris Watchet and looking for any reference he could find in the books at Widdershin's. He discovered that Sir Egad had left no descendants, and that his manor house had burned down in a great fire. Toby came to believe that the spear was hidden in the village somewhere, and it soon became apparent why he was so keen to find it:

Sir Egad was real, I'm sure of it, and if his spear was too, then it must still be hidden somewhere in Hedgely. If it really is enchanted and I can find it, that will prove I'm just as resourceful as any of the girls, and the Hedgewitch will have to let me join the coven. Rose says that if I come by on

Saturday, when the old bat is out on her rounds, she'll sneak me into Hartwood. I just know I'll find an answer there!

'He wanted to be a witch!' said Cassie, reading between the lines.

'Who did?' asked Montague, opening a single eye.

'Toby Harper, the boy who was looking for the spear. He wanted to join the coven and the old Hedgewitch – it must have been great-grandmother Sylvia then – wouldn't let him.'

'Of course not,' said the cat, rolling onto his side. 'Whoever heard of a boy witch?'

'But he was desperate to learn about faeries and magic and the Hedge. It must have been awful being forbidden to join, and Mrs Whitby was right, he was friends with my mother!' Cassie checked the date of the previous entry and did some quick mental maths. 'She would have been only fourteen then, the same age as Toby. Maybe she was helping him search for the spear?'

Cassie turned the page, only to find that it was the last. The rest of the book had been ripped out, leaving a ragged stump of torn paper in the spine.

'It's missing, the rest of the pages are gone,' said Cassie, running her finger over the torn edges. Toby had gone to a lot of effort to hide the book under that floorboard – why had he also felt the need to tear out half the pages?

'Then I suppose we are at an impasse,' said Montague.

'Not quite,' said Cassie. 'There's one last entry on the back of this page.' She read it aloud.

'Rose showed me the Hedgewitch's grimoire yesterday. There's a picture in it, of the three faery treasures held by the Hedgewitches of old: a key, a cup and a spear. Rose says her grandmother still has the key, that she's seen it, but the other two were lost long ago. According to the grimoire, the last Hedgewitch to possess the spear was called Nimue.'

'I do not see how that helps your cause,' said Montague. 'This Nimue has likely been deceased for centuries.'

'Yes, but it isn't the first time I've heard that name.'

'When I met Ambrose, the man in the oak tree, that's the name he called me – *Nimue*,' said Cassie, sitting beside Rue and Tabitha on the banks of the river Nix after school the next day. They'd bought faery cakes from Marchpane's and ate them while Cassie summarised what she'd learned from Toby's notebook. 'I thought he was simply confused at the time, he'd been asleep for centuries after all, but according to this, Nimue was the second Hedgewitch, Morgana of Faerie's daughter – or her niece, it's a bit unclear.' Cassie handed them a book called *Legends of the Hedge* and pointed to a picture of a fair-haired woman in a blue dress.

'Can't say she looks much like you, Cass,' said Rue, licking crumbs from her fingers.

'Is there anything in here about the spear?' asked Tabitha, leaning over to read.

Cassie shook her head. 'No, but that's why I think we need to speak to Ambrose. If Nimue was the last Hedgewitch to have the spear, he might be able to tell us what happened to it – and why the Erl King wants it.'

'Do you think you could find him again?' asked Rue.

'The book wyrm led me to him last time, but I think I remember what that part of the Hedge looks like. I'd know if we were nearby.'

Tabitha frowned. 'But what if we can't find this tree? If we wander deep into the Hedge we're bound to get lost and if anything happens, well, the Hedgewitch isn't back for another week. What if we don't make it out before nightfall? And what am I supposed to tell Gran?'

'Tell her you're staying over at Hartwood,' said Cassie. 'And we can bring supplies with us. It'll be a chance to work on our Woodwitch badge too – you know we have to camp out for a night in the woods to complete it.'

'Shouldn't we talk to Aoife first?' said Tabitha. 'Tell her all about the spear and the Erl King; surely she'll know what to do?'

They both turned to Rue, who finished her cake in one bite and chewed thoughtfully.

'Face it, Tabitha, Aoife's no use. We're on our own in this, at least until the Hedgewitch gets back, and we can't afford to wait that long. What if the next person to be enchanted finds the thing? I say we follow Cassie's lead, head into the woods on Saturday and see what this Ambrose knows. We've been that far into the Hedge before and found our way back well enough, and besides, we can handle a few goblins and wisps. I think this is just what we need – Oak Patrol's first real expedition.'

Chapter Thirteen

An Expedition

The three members of Oak Patrol stood at the edge of the forest, looking into the depths of the Hedge. It was mid-morning and, despite the cool air which tickled their necks, the woods were a blaze of glowing umber. The ground was covered in an ankle-deep carpet of crinkly leaves. It was going to be impossible to walk with any stealth or silence through that, Cassie realised. Their progress would be heard by each and every creature in the Hedge. She turned to face her companions.

'I know I said we should bring some supplies, Tabitha, but do you really need all of these things? You won't be able to fly Aura with all that.'

Tabitha was struggling under the weight of an enormous rucksack, stuffed to the brim and hung with various amulets, potion bottles and small camping cauldrons. At her feet were two more bulging bags and a bundle of poles and canvas.

'You never know what we might need in there,' said Tabitha. 'And if we do have to spend the night, you'll be glad I've packed extra rations and a jar of witch salt.'

'Yes, but surely one type of cauldron would suffice?' said Rue, who was holding Tabitha's broom along with her own.

'I'd rather be safe than sorry,' said Tabitha.

'Well, we haven't got time to stand about arguing,' said Cassie, reaching for a bulky canvas sack. 'Here, let me take the tent poles at least.'

Rue shrugged. 'Go on, hand me one of those bags, you can't manage both.'

The burden of Tabitha's supplies thus shared between them, they took the first path they came across into the woods and followed its winding way between the tree trunks. They brushed through dry brown bracken, crunched through piles of field-maple leaves and squelched through muddy streams.

Redwings, rooting amongst the leaf litter, and squirrels, burying their hoards of acorns and hazelnuts, ignored the passing girls. Gone were the piping melodies of spring and summer birdsong, the Hedge in autumn was eerily quiet and filled with a golden-brown light. Some of the trees, already bare of leaves, were skeletal in their winter frames, revealing discarded nests which had been invisible in the summer green. Elder trees bore clusters of dark berries strung with spider silk, and the wild roses and hawthorn were bright with red hips and haws. They went as quietly as the rustling leaves and Tabitha's jangling cauldrons would allow them, but every noise they made seemed overloud, and when the wind passed through the canopy above them it brought a dry rustling, raining leaves down upon them in golden showers.

The going was pleasant enough in the sunshine, but after an hour or so the clouds rolled in, shutting out the light and blanketing the woods in a deep shade that made it feel more like late afternoon than midday. At one point they heard a loud bellowing sound which echoed off the trees. Cassie walked right into Tabitha, who fell over, unbalanced by her rucksack.

'What was that?' they asked in unison, looking wildly about for some terrible faery beast.

But Rue was laughing. 'It's just a fallow deer buck, they make that noise in the autumn, staking out their territory.' She helped Tabitha to her feet and stabilised her. 'Nothing to be afraid of.'

But Cassie still had goosebumps on her forearms.

There were mushrooms and toadstools everywhere, even more than they'd seen in the spring. Tabitha insisted on stopping now and then to collect particularly rare specimens, which she dropped into the fishing creel which hung at her waist. Cassie kept an eye out for any that formed circles on the ground; she was not keen to find herself trapped in a faery ring again.

To pass the time, Cassie began quizzing the others on their tree knowledge. They needed to be able to correctly identify and recite the magical properties of thirteen trees for their Woodwitch badge, but this would soon be challenging as the trees shed their leaves and fruit and the girls had to rely on the bark to recognise them.

'What do you think that one is?' asked Cassie, pointing to a muscular-looking tree up ahead of them, its leaves a vibrant yellow.

'Beech?' asked Tabitha.

'No, it's a hornbeam,' said Cassie, thumbing through the handbook. 'Also known as "ironwood" – it's a protective wood, good for wards, and the leaves can be used in wound-healing potions. What about that one?'

'Elm,' said Rue. 'Would you put that away? We've been walking for *ages* and I'm starving.'

They had only just passed the elm tree when they came across the first weirstone. It was in a small clearing, surrounded by a ring of bright-green grass and scattered with brown leaves.

Cassie was relieved to find the stone unbroken, its ring of carved faery runes complete. The weirstones had been created hundreds of years before, to guard the border and keep the more dangerous denizens of Faerie from crossing into Britain. However, the Erl King was determined to destroy them so his goblins could run freely between the worlds, and had tasked the warlock Renata Rawlins with doing so. Cassie touched the cool stone and thought about her aunt, far away in Wales, giving evidence at the trial. She would be furious if she knew what Cassie was up to, but they had no choice, they needed to find the spear before the Erl King did and one of the villagers was killed.

No faery creature could approach the weirstones, and so they decided it was the best place to stop for lunch and to reassess their plans for the next stage of the expedition.

Cassie had brought chicken sandwiches wrapped in wax paper and three slices of Mrs Briggs' lemon and poppyseed cake to share between them. The housekeeper often sent her off with a packed lunch, so she'd had no difficulty in obtaining these. However, Cassie felt a bit guilty about not informing Mrs Briggs of her plan. If they didn't find Ambrose and get back before nightfall, she would be sure to worry.

Tabitha set up a small ring of stones and erected a tripod with a cauldron over it to boil water and make tea. 'I thought we might want something hot to drink,' she explained. Rue was helping her light the tindergrass with a sparkstone, rather more keen on Tabitha's excess baggage now that food was involved.

Sitting around the little fire, from which a ribbon of blue smoke streaked up towards the grey sky, they shared out the sandwiches and cake and wrapped their hands around enamel mugs of hot peppermint tea.

'Perhaps we should turn back,' said Tabitha. 'We've been wandering about for hours and seen no sign of this tree of yours, Cassie. Plenty of oaks, but none of them with faces. If we take the same path back, and it doesn't change on us, we might even be able to find our way safely home for supper.'

'She has a point,' said Rue, her mouth full of cake. 'The further on we go, the less I like our chances of getting out again, but it does seem a waste after we've come so far.'

'We can't give up now,' said Cassie. 'Look, what if it's the path that's the problem? When I found Ambrose the first time, it was after I'd left the path and got completely lost in the Hedge.'

'Are you suggesting we should get lost deliberately?' Tabitha asked.

'I suppose it could work,' said Rue with a shrug. 'And Tab's brought enough food to keep us going for weeks.'

But Tabitha hesitated. 'Look, I know this is important to both of you, and I want to protect the village too, but don't you think we're just a bit out of our depth here? Even if we find this Ambrose and he can help us, however will we get home? The lanthorn flowers won't be blooming at this time of year.'

The last time Cassie had spoken with Ambrose, she'd plucked a glowing lanthorn flower from his branches to guide her home, but that was in spring. There were precious few flowers about now.

Cassie shook her head. 'I'm not saying we let ourselves get entirely lost. I've been reading about tracking signs for the Woodwitch badge. We can use them to leave ourselves a trail, to guide us back here to this clearing. Then we can find the path again, or at very worst, set up camp here by the weirstone.'

'Sounds like a plan to me,' said Rue, rising to her feet. 'Come on then, there's still a few hours of daylight left.'

Tabitha began to put away the tea things.

They set out again, this time eschewing the wide, dry path for a deer track that led into a thicker, darker part of the woods, where green holly reached out to catch their hair and they had to edge around thick tangles of dog rose.

The going was slower now, due both to these natural obstacles and the fact that Cassie, who was bringing up the rear, would stop every few minutes to leave some sign behind. This might consist of a small pile of stones on the ground, or sticks formed into Faru, the faery rune that looked a bit like an arrow, to indicate the direction they had come. Where the ground was obscured by deep drifts of leaves she sometimes scratched the rune into the bark of a tree stump with her pen knife, so that they would see it and know which way to turn.

The day wore on and they grew tired of walking. Tabitha in particular was struggling with the weight of her rucksack and kept requesting short breaks to catch her breath. They made one such stop at an enormous mossy log, the trunk of some long dead tree. It must have been a giant of the forest while it had lived; the width of its trunk stretched high above them, with jagged branches and roots jutting out of it.

Cassie looked up at the sky through the occasional break in the canopy and saw that it was getting darker, the setting sun tinting the grey clouds purple. Night would fall soon, and before that they'd have to pick up the trail Cassie had left and make their way back to the safety of the weirstone. It was frustrating that they hadn't found Ambrose, but the Hedge was vast; they could spend days walking through the woods without seeing the same tree twice.

Rue climbed up the great log and stood atop it, trying to see into the distance through the trees.

It was odd, Cassie thought. They must have come at least three miles from the weirstone by now – although distance was somewhat hard to judge in the Hedge – but they hadn't seen any faery creatures. Not a single imp or wisp. Even the ordinary animals had disappeared. Cassie had hoped they might come across the owl Nimblewing or one of the other familiars they'd rescued from the goblin market, who could help them with directions towards Ambrose's tree. Yet the forest was strangely quiet and seemingly empty, only the slight breeze stirring the dry leaves.

Tabitha was resting against the log, looking exhausted; she wouldn't be able to go on much further carrying that heavy pack. Cassie had just opened her mouth to suggest they head back when the log twitched. It was nothing more than a ripple beneath the cracked wooden surface, a few feet above where Tabitha was sitting. Cassie stepped back and looked more carefully at the fallen tree. There was something off about it, something about the way the branches curved up and back like great antlers, something about the claw-like roots that dug into the earth, and then if you looked at it just so, you could almost make out the shape of a broad, serpentine head. A deep hollow in the wood narrowed and widened again, letting out a gust of warm loamy air in Cassie's face. The log was *breathing*.

'Rue! Come down from there... now!' she hissed.

Chapter Fourteen

The Wood Wyrm

'What's the matter?' called Rue. 'Is Tab ready to move on? I can see pretty far from up here. If we keep along this path there's a grove of birch trees, didn't you say—' But she did not finish her sentence as the log she was standing on began to tilt upward at one end, rising away from the ground and sending her off balance. Rue caught hold of a protruding branch and crouched there as the log rose up before her, ripping away from the grass and brambles and leaving a scar of fresh earth. Beetles and centipedes scurried for cover.

The tree contorted and stretched, exposing an ancient, reptilian head with a crown of broken branches and a beard of dripping moss. A crack in the bark blinked open to reveal a great golden eye. The creature pulled one taloned foot and then another from the forest floor, rising up on all fours and sending a cascade of dry leaves to the ground.

'Wyrm!' Tabitha shouted. 'Run, Rue, run!'

But Rue couldn't get down, and they couldn't very well leave her behind.

Cassie mounted Tantivy, struggling to balance with Rue's broom tucked under her arm. She urged her broomstick up, kicking off the ground and pointing the handle towards the great wyrm, which had begun to shake its brown woody scales, dislodging clumps of lichen and small saplings that had rooted there. Rue was clinging on for dear life as the creature opened its dark mouth and let out an almighty roar. It was like the roar of the fallow buck, only a hundred times louder, and flocks of panicked birds rose into the air around it.

The wyrm's breath, a gust of decaying leaves and damp moss, hit Cassie side on and pushed her back into the treetops. She heard twigs snapping in her broom's brush, and would have fallen if not for the fact she was clutching Rue's broom in her left hand – it hovered at her side, allowing her to regain her balance.

Cassie kicked off against a tree trunk and flew back towards the beast. Rue's broom, Blaze, was pulling her on towards its rider.

'Here!' she shouted, hovering as close as she dared above the wyrm's scaly back. Rue looked up and Cassie threw Blaze down to her. Rue caught it, releasing her hold on the wyrm and rolled off, swooping out from under its shadow on her broom. Cassie caught up and together they sped away from the beast, which had now raised to its full height, its branching crown on par with the surrounding treetops. Down below they could see Tabitha, struggling through the undergrowth as she ran. But the wyrm had seen her too and dived after her, its great head snapping branches off the trees as it crashed after the small witch, who was burdened under her rucksack.

'Tabitha! Your broom! Fly!' called Cassie, wondering why she didn't jump on Aura and join them above the treetops.

'It's her rucksack, it's too heavy,' said Rue, leaving Cassie's side to fly back towards Tabitha.

The wyrm was closing in on them, its talons ripping up bushes and scarring tree trunks as it crashed after Tabitha. Turning to see the wyrm coming after her, Tabitha tripped on a tree root and was sent sprawling on the ground, cauldrons rolling away into the bushes as she tried to right herself. In a moment Rue was beside her, helping her shrug out of the rucksack and climb onto her broom, and the two of them were kicking into the air. The wyrm shot out its long scaly neck and opened its great maw as it reached for the two airborne witches. The jaws shut with a great crack, like a falling tree, catching the brush of Rue's broom as she shot away.

Rue and Tabitha joined Cassie above the canopy, hovering together well out of reach of the furious wyrm which, after one last effort to rise on its hind legs and reach them, came crashing down through the trees and thrashed away through the undergrowth.

'That was a great wyrm,' said Cassie, breathless. 'I didn't think there were any left in the Hedge. Did you see all the moss and lichen on its hide? It must be ancient.'

'Have to admit, I was a bit more concerned with its claws and teeth,' said Rue, panting as she caught her breath. 'You all right, Tab?'

'Yes, only, the wyrm... it swallowed our supplies.'

'Never mind that, we should probably be heading home anyway.'

The sun had now set and the first stars were twinkling to life in the deep blue sky. Below them was a sea of auburn, brown and gold, undulating in small waves and peaks where the largest trees broke through the canopy. Cassie had never seen the Hedge from above before, and only now did she fully understand just how vast it was. The trees stretched out in all directions as far as the eye could see, unbroken and unchanging. The western sky was still lighter than the east, and so they turned their backs to it and pointed the brooms towards Hedgely. But before they could set off, Rue's broom shuddered and dropped several feet in the air.

'Seems I lost more than a few twigs to that beast,' said Rue. 'I'm not sure Blaze will make it all the way back.'

Cassie looked down at Tantivy. Her own broom was uncharacteristically subdued and seemed to be shaking as it hovered above the treetops. She twisted to inspect the damage; it had lost nearly half its brush in their escape and was covered in deep scratches.

'Tantivy doesn't look too good either, Cassie,' said Tabitha. 'And Aura can't take more than two of us. I think we'll have to make our way back on foot.'

'Good thing you left a trail, Cass,' said Rue, as they landed back on the forest floor. But in fleeing the wyrm, they'd come far from their original route and the beast had left a tunnel of destruction through the wood, obliterating any of the small signs Cassie had left behind. They had no way of returning to the weirstone, and it was even darker there beneath the canopy.

'Well, you wanted us to get good and properly lost,' said Tabitha. 'I think you could say we've managed that.'

Oak Patrol set out in what they hoped was the right direction, carrying their damaged brooms over their shoulders and peering into the rapidly darkening woods. They were on high alert, listening out for any sign that the wood wyrm was returning. Moving single file along a narrow path, they soon found themselves going downhill.

'This can't be right,' said Cassie. 'We never went uphill on the way in.'

'Oh, who cares, as long as we're going away from that creature,' said Rue.

They were tired, hungry and increasingly irritable, which did not help matters at all.

The slope grew steeper, and they had to walk sideways, skidding down in showers of brown leaves and catching at spindly trees to stop themselves from slipping.

Great boulders rose up before them out of the twilight, covered in thick pelts of moss and looking to their tired eyes like hunch-backed giants and crouching wolves. As they went on there were more and more of these stones, until they found themselves in a rocky valley, following a channel between mossy cliffs that rose up around them.

'I don't like this,' said Cassie. 'It's like a maze down here – if we meet anything unpleasant, there's nowhere to run.'

But the only alternative was to turn back the way they'd come, so they carried on, deeper into the gully. It was greener there, and wetter, with the plush moss and sprays of delicate ferns clinging to the stone cliffs. They came at last to high rockface over which a spout of water fell, gushing out over the rocks and into a pool at the bottom. They paused on the sandy bank.

'Please, could we rest for just a moment?' asked Tabitha. 'My feet hurt.'

'It's your constant need to rest that got us into this mess,' snapped Rue. 'If you'd not brought that ridiculous rucksack, we'd never have stopped at the log, and we'd probably have made it home in time for dinner.' Rue was never at her best when she was hungry.

'If we had my rucksack, then we'd be able to stop and light a fire, make camp and some hot food rather than trudging on through this darkness into who-knows-what danger,' Tabitha snapped back.

'Oh, hush, you two, something might hear us,' said Cassie. They were making enough noise to alert half the forest to their presence. She didn't like this place, it was still and quiet but something about it made the hairs stand up on her arms. Cassie had the uncomfortable feeling they were being watched, that whatever presence lurked in the stones knew they were there. 'I suppose we can stop for a moment. How are we for supplies?'

Rue turned out her hat out on a rock. 'A dozen hazelnuts and some rosehips, although there's not much eating in those. It's hardly a feast.'

They had been foraging as they walked, but the pickings were slim and they'd seen nothing edible since they entered the stony valley. Rue shared out the nuts evenly, which made for little more than a mouthful each.

'Do you think we dare drink from the pool?' asked Tabitha.

It wasn't always safe to drink from streams and pools in the Hedge; the waters tended to have curious effects. Some, as Cassie had experienced, could return forgotten memories to you, but others could take your memories away, leaving you with no idea where you were or how you'd got there.

Cassie looked up at the waterfall. It was so dark now that the whiteness of the frothing water was all they could see against the mossy stone, except... Cassie climbed over the nearest pile of stones and squinted into the damp shadows. There were stairs cut into the rock, leading up and into the waterfall.

Curiosity is a marvellous thing for reviving the senses, and the three girls forgot their hunger and tiredness for a moment as they made their way up the steps. They found they could edge around and behind the spout of water without getting more than a little spray on their cloaks. There was a high, arched doorway cut into the rock and more steps leading up and through it.

'Are we sure about this?' asked Tabitha. 'Someone must have built all this – what if they're waiting at the other end?'

'As long as they have some decent grub to share, that's fine by me,' said Rue.

'Cassie...' said Tabitha.

'These stairs are old, really old. Look how thick the moss is. I think whoever made them has probably been gone for a very long time.'

The doorway and the narrow tunnel reminded Cassie of another ruin, one she had discovered within Castle

Hill, to the north of Hedgely. She reached out to scratch the stone wall and sure enough, her hand came away with a glistening coating, like the dried trail of a snail. Whoever had built this place had not been human.

They continued climbing up through the face of the cliff and strangely, although the path was dim, they could still see. Cassie stopped to look up at the stone above them and found a mat of vivid, glowing green.

'What is it?' asked Rue.

'It's a sort of phosphorescent moss,' said Cassie, who had read about it in *A Natural History of the Hedge*. 'It's called Goblin's Gold.'

'*Great*,' said Rue. 'Just what we need right now, a few friendly goblins!'

They followed the glowing trail of the moss up and out through the top of the cliff and found themselves in the open air once more. They were standing on the rough clifftop, and could see the gullies on either side as gashes of darkness in the rock. Above them, the clouds had broken up and a round full moon was peeping out at them from behind her misty veil.

They stood before a stone bridge that led from their cliff, across the chasm, to another, where they could just make out the shapes of trees and another stone archway. They had only two choices; to continue across the bridge or to go back down the steps the way they'd come.

'Might as well see where this goes,' said Rue. 'We've come this far.'

She led them across the narrow bridge. If they made a false step, there would be nothing to prevent them from falling down into the crevasse.

Cassie held her breath and tried to convince herself that it was just like climbing a tree. She exchanged a worried glance with Tabitha, who didn't seem to be enjoying it any more than she was, and somehow that helped.

Rue charged on, as happy as if she were walking down Loft Street, and was the first to reach the archway.

She took one look and rushed through it.

'Rue, wait!' Cassie called out. But she had disappeared into the shadowy dimness on the other side.

When Tabitha and Cassie joined her, they saw what it was that had so excited Rue.

They were on top of another cliff now, on a raised platform roughly circular in shape. On the ground a thick, luxurious green moss grew, soft as an Persian rug, and they were surrounded on all sides by slender white tree trunks looming like pillars out of the darkness. They reminded Cassie of birches, but they lacked the black eyes on their bark, and so she could not guess what they were.

But Rue was not looking at the trees. Before them lay a table, beautifully carved of stone, with stone benches on either side. There was an embroidered cloth on the table, soft velvet cushions on the benches and the whole scene was lit by dozens of candles in silver candelabras. However, they barely noticed these rich furnishings because the table was burdened by a hundred different plates and platters, each heaped high with some delicacy: fresh fruit, roast meats, soft bread rolls, desserts of spun sugar shaped like castles, gelled fruit in glass bowls, cakes and pastries and pies.

The girls stood there, stunned by the vision before them.

Chapter Fifteen

The Riddlewood

'Where did all of this come from?' 'Is it real?'

Rue stepped forward and picked up a bread roll, lifting it to her nose. 'Smells real. The question is, does it taste real?'

'Rue!' said Cassie and Tabitha in chorus.

Rue laughed, returning the roll to the table and dusting her hands on her cloak. 'Ha! Should have seen the look on your faces! Of course I'm not going to eat it, it's clearly enchanted and even I know better than to touch faery food, thank you very much.'

But she cast a longing glance over her shoulder as she rejoined them at the archway. 'I suppose we should head back to the waterfall and pick up our trail from there?'

'I don't think I could walk another step,' said Tabitha. 'And I really don't fancy going back across that bridge in the dark.'

They looked at each other in the dim light. Although they had entertained the possibility of camping out in the woods, and even made plans for it, now that they were faced with the reality of sleeping in the Hedge it seemed far more frightening.

'I suppose we could stay here for the night and look for a way home in the morning, when it's light?' said Rue.

'I'm not sure that's a good idea,' said Cassie. 'There's something strange about this place. Who put the food there and what happens if they return? I know it's dark and we're all tired, but shouldn't we keep going?'

Rue frowned, her gaze returning again to the heavily laden table. 'I'm not sure we'd be any safer down there, not with the wyrm prowling about. It won't reach us up here, the tunnel is too narrow.'

'And at least here we can see anything coming towards us over the bridge,' Tabitha added.

'Oh, all right, but we ought to take turns keeping watch,' said Cassie. 'I'll go first.'

It was a poor camp without Tabitha's tent and supplies. They shared the handful of rosehips Rue extracted from her pocket, nibbling the sour flesh and avoiding the seeds, and made their beds on the soft turf. The night was chilly and they had only their cloaks for blankets, but Rue and Tabitha were so exhausted that they were soon fast asleep, breathing deeply, their faces pressed to the pillowy moss.

Cassie sat with her back against one of the white trees and looked up at the ring of open sky above them. The clouds drifted by, occasionally revealing patches of deeper night sky. She made out the three bright stars of the Hunter's belt, and the saucepan shape of the Plough, following the line of the last two stars in the constellation up to Polaris, the North Star. If only their brooms weren't damaged; they could have used it to guide them home.

It was a battle to keep her own eyes open, but once the stars had progressed a good way she decided it must have been a few hours and woke Rue who sat up with a start, rubbing her eyes but agreeing to take the next watch. Cassie sank gratefully into the moss, pulling her cloak up to her chin. She was asleep before she knew it.

When Cassie woke, the air had chilled and there were beads of dew in her hair. Tabitha was still asleep, her small, dark form rising and falling with gentle breaths, but the flattened patch of moss where Rue had been sitting was empty. Dragging herself up, Cassie saw that the clouds had cleared entirely and the orb of the moon hung at the sky's zenith like a great lamp, telling Cassie it was near midnight. The clifftop was bathed in soft grey light, casting everything in black-and-white relief. Before her, the stone table was unchanged, the silver platters overflowing with glistening fruit, the bread still crisp from the oven, the pies untouched. It all looked so much more tempting than before.

Cassie's stomach ached and she forced herself to look away from the feast. It was then she saw Rue, her head of frizzy dark curls framed by the moonlight, and before her, a woman. The woman was fair as the dawn, her long silvery hair streaming out from beneath a crown of star-like jewels. She wore a gown of white silk which fell in a puddle of soft ripples about her feet. Her face was difficult to look at, like staring into a bright but artificial light and indeed, her whole body seemed to glow from within. She was like the faeries Cassie had imagined as a child, reading tales of their beauty, their enchanting sweetness, and she realised that part of her still longed for that. All the goblins and imps and bogles she'd seen had failed to live up to that vision and here, at last, was a creature so ethereal she seemed to be made of mist and starlight.

Rue was entranced, rooted to the ground as the woman approached, holding out her hand. There was something in it, and Cassie stepped closer to see what it was. The woman had not noticed her yet, her attention fixed on Rue. Cassie saw that that the thing she was holding was an apple, but no ordinary apple – it was red as poppies and glistened as if it were dipped in honey. It was too flawless, the dream of an apple; it could not possibly be real.

Cassie felt a cold breeze on the back of her neck and, turning, she saw that they were surrounded. More women, pale and beautiful as the first were standing around the table, their hands folded before them as if in prayer. Then Cassie noticed that the trees, the tall white trees that had encircled the table clearing, were gone. The women were moving in on them, closing ranks into a tighter circle. As they drew closer, Cassie could better see their faces; their eyes were gold and glistening, their lips red as the apple, red as blood.

Rue lifted her own hand, reaching to take the apple.

'Rue!' Cassie cried, suddenly gripped by fear. 'Don't touch it!'

But Rue had already taken the fruit, her eyes still on the faery woman. The other women hissed at Cassie, and she found she could not reach Rue; her feet were fixed to the spot on which she stood.

'Tabitha!' she called, and the small figure lying on the moss stirred, blinking away her sleep.

Rue was gazing at the apple in her hand, transfixed, she raised it to her lips.

Heavy footsteps echoed on the stone bridge. Twisting to look behind her, Cassie saw another figure approaching through the archway. He was tall, dark and broad, with something on his head, something like antlers.

The Erl King! He had laid a trap for them, and was coming to claim them.

However, as the new figure stepped into the moonlight she saw that she was mistaken – he did not wear the tattered black robes or stag skull mask that she dreaded, but a cloak of leaves that fell to his bare feet, and the simple garments he wore beneath were of bark. What had looked like antlers were twiggy branches that appeared to be growing out of his shaggy hair.

Time seemed to slow down as he approached them, and still Cassie could not move. The women in white hissed again and drew back.

The man in the cloak of leaves came towards Rue. He reached out one great, strong arm as if to strike her but instead, he slapped the fruit from her grasp and stood between Rue and the glowing woman.

'Be gone, you have no claim to this child,' said the man, in a voice rough and dry as oak-bark.

The woman's face twisted out of its beauty into pure fury, baring sharp teeth in a crimson mouth, her eyes flashing yellow. She stepped forward, raising slim white arms from the folds of her silken gown. Her hands were long and clawed. The man raised the staff he was carrying and Cassie saw that it was an axe with a head of sharpened stone.

The pale woman hissed once more, retreating back to the edge of the cliff. In an instant, she vanished. Cassie turned to see the other women were gone and the white trees were back in place, their leaves hanging limply, as if they had never stirred.

The shining candles on the table had blown out. The food had changed too. Where there had been sweet breads there were piles of dead and decaying leaves, the bowls of fruit were rotten and heaving with worms and beetles. What had been a roast boar was nothing but a dead pigeon and the fine tablecloths were rags of lacy cobwebs.

Tabitha was at Rue's side now, wrapping a cloak about her and holding a hand to her face, which had lost its usual warmth and life. Cassie found that she could move again, and rushed to join them.

'She's in shock,' said Tabitha.

'The child will be well, she touched the fruit but did not eat,' said the man. He towered over them, broad as a tree trunk, his skin as dark as old oak and his hair wild and tangled. From his brow sprouted twiggy branches and his eyes, above his great beard, were the colour of polished brass. He was clearly no human man, but he had saved Rue.

Cassie opened her mouth to speak, but he held up a broad hand.

'Come, it is not safe here.' He headed back through the archway and across the bridge, not waiting to see if they followed.

Cassie caught Tabitha's arm. 'I think he's a woodwose, I've read about them. They're supposed to be wild and dangerous; some say they're *mad*.'

'Well, we can't very well stay here, we need to get Rue away from these trees...' said Tabitha, eyeing the slim white trunks. 'And he *did* save her.'

Reluctantly, Cassie agreed and, supporting Rue between them, they followed the faery man.

It was not easy to keep up with the woodwose. He took great big strides and his cloak of leaves made it hard to see where he ended and the forest began. Despite his pace, he moved so silently and softly that he barely stirred a leaf and seemed to know exactly where to place his feet to avoid any loose stones or roots. Cassie and Tabitha stumbled along behind him, supporting Rue as best they could. They followed him down the narrow stone paths, turning left, right and left again. It would have been impossible for them to remember every turn but the woodwose never paused to consider his route. He stopped only when Rue stumbled on a loose stone and fell. Cassie and Tabitha helped her up. Rue's expression was vacant and her limbs limp.

'She's not well, can't we let her rest?' asked Tabitha.

'Not here,' said the woodwose. 'This is the Riddlewood. It is not a place to tarry by day, let alone by night, for many old and hungry things dwell in the shadows.'

Half-carrying Rue between them, they stumbled after him. Finally, after endless twists and turns they came out from among the mossy cliffs and began to climb upwards again. The ground was still stony and scattered with boulders, but the earth was drier here and, as they scrambled upwards, their arms and legs aching, they found themselves amongst pine trees and mountain ash. It was by far the wildest part of the Hedge they'd yet come to, with no paths or weirstones to signal that humans had ever been there.

Rue was struggling, she had not spoken since the encounter on the hill and had a faraway look in her eyes that worried Cassie. As Rue stumbled and fell once more, the woodwose took her from them and lifted her into his arms as if she weighed no more than a baby.

At last they came to a stone cliff, rising up before them and surrounded by a cascade of great boulders left there by some ancient river of ice. Twisted and stunted trees grew on the boulders, their branches contorted and draped in moss, their roots clasping the stone like gnarled fingers.

The woodwose walked up to the cliff, turned left and disappeared into the face of the rock.

Chapter Sixteen

Lailoken

Cassie and Tabitha ran up to the wall of stone where the woodwose had vanished, taking Rue with him. The rockface was rough and solid, yet he had walked through it as if it were made of nothing but mist.

'Come,' said a deep voice. A light appeared in a dark crack in the rock to their left and they went towards it, only to find a hidden doorway where one granite boulder overlapped another. It was no faery glamour, but a simple optical illusion that hid the entrance of the cave from anyone who came at it directly. Still, the doorway was narrow and Cassie marvelled that the woodwose was able to squeeze through.

Once inside, it took a moment for their eyes to adjust. The deep darkness of the cave was broken only by a small red light in a niche against one wall. At first, Cassie thought it was a low fire, but as she came closer she saw that it was a wyrm, about the size of a cat, with stubby horns and spots down its bright orange scales. Its eyes were closed but it appeared to be lit up from within by a soft light, as if it had swallowed a coal. The creature gave off a wave of heat which Cassie could feel as she approached.

'That is Pyrrha, she is a glow wyrm,' said the woodwose. 'She will not hurt you, but do not touch her or you will be burned. I do not like fire, it is the devourer of forests, but the child must be warmed.'

He placed Rue gently before the glow wyrm on a pile of soft furs. Tabitha fussed over her, chafing her hands and arms, and Rue seemed to wake a little from her torpor. The woodwose handed Tabitha a cup made of rough wood, brimful with some clear liquid.

'Birch sap infused with betony. Make her drink,' he insisted.

Cassie looked about her at the stone chamber, which she could just make out by Pyrrha's soft light. There was a natural ceiling some ten feet high, under which the woodwose could stand comfortably. What Cassie had mistaken for logs in the dimness, were revealed now to be pieces of finely made wooden furniture – chairs, benches, a table, several chests, even a bookshelf. A recess in the stone wall was filled with more furs and a quilt of woven swansdown; Cassie thought this must be the woodwose's bed. All around them were carvings of animals and birds, imps, wyrms and fish. Some were life-size, such as the sparrowhawk perched on the back of a chair, and others smaller, like the tiny leaf wyrm, carved of some blonde wood, which would fit in the palm of Cassie's hand. All were made with such detail and understanding of their subjects that they seemed to have thoughts, movement, life of their own.

Rue held the cup in her hands now, taking great gulps of the liquid, the warmth and life returning to her face. She sat up and looked about her.

'Whoa! Now this is what I call a den.'

Cassie and Tabitha laughed, delighted to see their friend returned to her former self.

'Here, eat,' said the woodwose, handing her a small, dark cake. 'It is made with nettle seed, it will give you strength.'

Rue eagerly devoured the food.

'Thank you,' said Tabitha. 'You've been so kind and we haven't even told you our names.' She made the necessary introductions.

'You may call me Lailoken. It is a name I was given by your kind, long ago, and although it is not my true name, it will serve you well enough.'

'Who were those women? Were they gentry?' asked Cassie, wondering if they had encountered the most lordly and powerful of the faery peoples. Although she knew she ought to fear them, she had long wished to see one, ever since she'd learned faeries were real.

'No, they were the wood wives,' said Lailoken. 'They appear as *wenfarth* trees by day, but by night they are as you saw them; beautiful, yes, but had you glimpsed them from behind you would have found them hollow as rotting logs.'

Rue choked on her drink and had to be thumped on the back by Tabitha.

'The wives have much glamour with which they lay traps for foolish humans,' the woodwose continued. 'If your friend had partaken of their food they would have drunk her life-spirit until all that was left was a dry husk, like these leaves.' He lifted the edge of a rug woven from dry grasses and appliqued with leaf skeletons.

'But they were *so* beautiful,' said Tabitha.

'And when has beauty made a thing less wicked? The most dangerous of our kind often seem dazzling to those who have not the witch-sight to see through glamours.'

'But we *are* witches!' said Rue.

'Then you ought to know better. You should not have slept upon that cliff.'

'I know, I mean, we should have known,' said Cassie. 'But we were so tired and, well, nowhere seemed safe and we thought we'd find our way home in the morning.'

'You would not have found your way out of the Riddlewood by moonlight or sunlight. It is an ancient place, strung with more tricks and traps than a spider's lair. You are fortunate that I was passing and that I found you before you encountered one of the nightwalkers, the willow-men or the tree hags, next to whom even the wood wives appear gentle as deer.'

The girls looked at each other as Lailoken spoke these strange names of creatures that sounded far more frightening than the hobs, imps and wisps of the *Witch's Handbook*.

'But now you must tell me, what are three young witchlings doing so deep in the woods?'

'I'm afraid we were lost,' said Tabitha, and she told him about the wyrm and how it had chased them and destroyed Cassie's signs.

The woodwose nodded as she spoke. 'You have met Galtres, then. She is the last of her kind and the oldest of the wood folk. She is one of the Watchers of the Ways.'

'The Watchers?' asked Rue. 'Do you mean like the song? *Three are the Watchers within the wood...*? But I thought that was just a children's game; we used to play it after school.'

'It is no game, although there are, indeed, three in number. The Watchers are the guardians and the guides of the old roads. There is more than one path to Faerie, more than one point of crossing, but the Riddlewood is the surest, if one can evade the wood wyrm and find their way through. Yet many have met their deaths or lost their minds trying.'

'But the goblins cross the border all the time, don't they?' asked Tabitha.

'Wily and numerous as they are, even goblins fall prey to the dangers of the old roads. Galtres is particularly partial to goblin-flesh.'

Tabitha shuddered.

'However, you have not yet told me what drew you to the Western Wood to begin with. What do you seek here that you would take such risks?'

'We were trying to find a friend of mine,' said Cassie. 'An old oak tree... or rather, a man in a tree. His name is Ambrose.'

'You seek the wizard?' The woodwose raised his bushy brows. 'And what business do you have with him?'

'We're looking for something,' said Cassie, wondering just how much she dared tell him. Lailoken had been nothing but helpful so far, but could they really trust him? He was faery folk after all. 'It's a danger to the people of our village, and we thought he might be able to help us find it before it does any harm. Do you know him? Can you take us to him?'

'He is known to me, yes, and if that is what you seek, I will lead you to him. But not until first light. You must rest here until dawn.'

He left them by the glow wyrm, returning shortly with a wooden platter on which were more of the nettle-seed cakes Rue had eaten, along with dried plums and wild cherries, hazelnuts candied in honey, golden roasted chestnuts, little green loaves that looked like balls of moss and tasted of herbs, tart slices of crab-apple and slivers of deer-milk cheese. To wash this down, they were each given a cup of the birch-sap drink, which tasted of springtime and snowmelt with a hint of woody sweetness. It was a simple meal, compared to the great feast they had left behind on the clifftop, but it was filling and they each felt refreshed after it and able to think clearly once more.

The woodwose sat a little away from them on a low stool, turning a lump of wood in one hand. In the other he held a stone knife with a knapped edge, like the darts Eris Watchet had shown them. As the girls ate, a long feather emerged from the wood, and then a wing, and slowly it began to reveal the head and body of a bird, as if it had been trapped in the wood, waiting to emerge.

After their meal, Tabitha insisted that Rue rest, and although she tried to stay awake to watch over her charge, it wasn't long before they were both sleeping peacefully. But Cassie wasn't ready to turn in just yet.

The soft light of the glow wyrm was reflected in Lailoken's eyes and illuminated the branches that grew from his dark curls. It was a face that might have been frightening, had they met under different circumstances, but Cassie decided all of a sudden that she *could* trust him. There was nothing false or secretive in that face.

'If someone wanted to cross the border to Faerie, how would they get past Galtres and through the Riddlewood?' she asked.

'They would need a willing guide, another of the Watchers,' said the woodwose, hollowing out the beak of the bird and sending curled shavings of wood into a pile on his lap.

'You're one of them, aren't you? One of the Watchers.' Cassie asked, trying not to let her eagerness show. 'Could you show me the way to Faerie?'

'Humans, even witches, have no business in the sunless lands. Whatever you think to gain by crossing, you stand to lose a great deal more. None who go that way return.'

'But my mother is there, she travelled to Faerie seven and a half years ago, on May Eve – were you the one who helped her cross?'

'It was not I,' said Lailoken. 'But there is another who may aid the rash and desperate. Hyldamor, whom some call the Elder Mother. She is a wood hag, but far older and more wicked than the rest. She is called "mother" because she offers aid to those who have lost their way, and her gifts and powers are great.' He frowned and turned his knife to carve the bird's long tail. 'Hers is the easier path, but as with most things in this world, those who take the easy way pay the steeper price. Speak no more of this – be grateful for the sun on your face and the warmth of hearth and home, for these things are more easily lost than you imagine.'

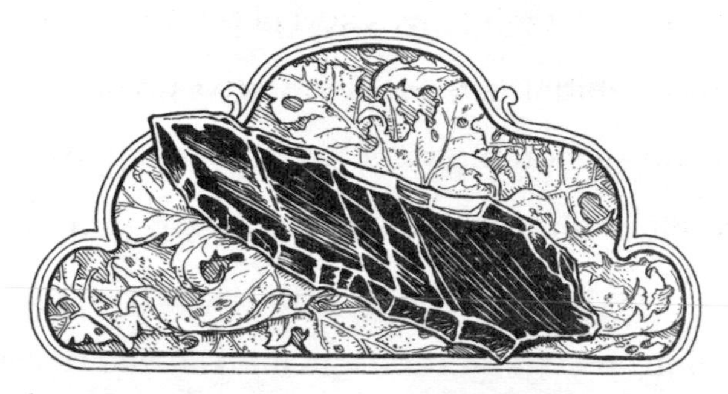

Chapter Seventeen

The Gossip of the Forest

Cassie woke several hours after dawn, when the sun entered the stone chamber through a natural chink in the ceiling. Rue still slumbered beside her on a pile of furs by the soft light of the glow wyrm. Lailoken's swansdown quilt lay over them and it was warm and light as a cloud.

Sitting up, Cassie saw that neither Tabitha nor Lailoken were in the cave, and with some anxiety she found all three of their brooms gone too. She followed the beam of light back to the entrance and emerged into the day, shielding her eyes at the sudden brightness. The morning light had filled the small rocky glade before the cave with shining gold, broken here and there by the rowan trees, their leaves and berries pillar-box red.

'Cassie!' Tabitha called to her. She was standing beside the woodwose clutching her broom, which gleamed in the sunlight. Lailoken held Rue and Cassie's brooms, one in each of his big hands. Cassie ran over to join them. She almost didn't recognise Tantivy. Lailoken had restored all three brooms to their former glory while the girls slept, replacing lost twigs in their brushes and weaving in new ones, sanding out chips and scratches in the handles and polishing them with oil and beeswax until they shone.

Cassie took Tantivy from the woodwose; it hummed in her hand and she could not resist joining Tabitha on a quick swoop around the glade. Their boots grazed the tops of the pine trees, startling wood pigeons. It was good to fly again, for the sheer joy of it, and to feel Tantivy strong and lively once more.

She landed before the woodwose with only a little wobble, and thanked him.

'A very fine piece of whifflewood, that,' said Lailoken. 'If a little exuberant. I should like to meet the tree it came from.'

'Have you ever seen a whifflewood tree?' asked Cassie.

'Indeed I have, they grow on the Wafting Mountains

of Faerie. Some believe it is their roots that hold the very stones aloft.'

Cassie felt a tug of the same desperate longing she had whenever she thought about crossing the border into Faerie.

They set off after a meal of soft green bread with rosehip jelly and deer's milk sweetened with honey. Rue was equally impressed with the restored condition of her broom, which had seen the greatest change of all. Blaze had been a bit worse for wear even before the wood wyrm, but now it had a completely new brush of birch and fir. Rue wanted to fly all the way home, but Lailoken insisted they follow him on foot if they still wanted to meet with Ambrose.

Without the woodwose to guide them, the three young witches would have been lost again within minutes. There were no paths to follow through the Riddlewood and the deep shadows of the boulders and cliffs high above them often obscured the guiding light of the sun.

Lailoken led them downhill, from the rocky promontory that hid his cave and through the labyrinth of mossy cliffs and ferny gullies into which they had wandered the night before. He would not let them pause to rest there, and they were discouraged from speaking or making unnecessary noise. But the woodwose passed them a leather flask filled with cool spring water and nettle-seed cakes to nibble on as they walked.

At last, they came out from amongst the cliffs and began to climb uphill through a stand of beech trees, their calves aching and their breath heavy with the effort. Lailoken began to show them the signs by which he navigated the woods. Compasses did not work within the Hedge but there were, he explained, other natural markers that might help them find their way when they could not see the sun or stars.

'You must learn to listen to gossip of the forest – the trees speak in their own language, to those with ears to hear it, but even humans might read what is written by bark and branch.'

He made them stop to observe the mossy boulders, which had their thickest pelts on the northern side where the sun did not dry them out. Pausing before the tallest beech, the woodwose showed them its long anchor roots, pointing south-west and protecting the tree from strong winds. He made them look up to find where the canopy of leaves was most dense on each tree, reaching for the high southern sun, and search for rusty lichens which, like the mosses, grew always in the northern shade of the trunk. Cassie found herself looking at the trees in a whole new light; each was a compass, a waymarker that could lead them home.

When they finally came across a weirstone, Cassie, Rue and Tabitha rushed towards it in relief, but Lailoken held back.

Of course, thought Cassie, *faery folk won't come near them.* What meant safety for the witches would have the opposite effect on the woodwose.

'I do not often come this way,' he explained. 'The stones, they bind the forest like an iron chain. All that is truly wild and free keeps to the west of here, but we must go on a little further to reach the wizard.'

They crossed a stream and passed through a grove of young birch trees, and Cassie began to recognise the way – it was here she'd met the book wyrm. Soon they were among oaks, old, twisted and wizened, sprouting tufts of twiggy whiskers. Their girths were great columns and many had crowns broken with age.

'They say the oak grows for three hundred years, lives for three hundred years and dies for three hundred years,' said Lailoken. 'But in the Hedge, they may live twice as long. These trees are the true elders of the woods; they remember the wars between our peoples, they remember the first Hedgewitches and a few of them remember the time before.'

The woodwose led them to the greatest and oldest of the oaks, and they crunched through knee-deep leaf litter, looking up at the almost bare branches.

When Cassie saw the wrinkled face in the trunk, its eyes shut tight and its mouth closed, she ran forward with a shout of delight.

'Ambrose!'

Slowly, the eyes opened, looking out at her with the same warm humour she remembered.

'Well, if it isn't the little witch who woke me up yesterday. You're back again, I see.'

'Yes, only it wasn't yesterday! It was months and months ago.'

'Hmmm? Is it autumn already? I thought I felt a chill. Rather unpleasant, having to give up one's coat of leaves just as the frost sets in, but then, trees all begin to sleep in the autumn; their thoughts go underground, deep, down into the roots where it is warm and dark. That is where they keep their secret council, you know. But who is this I see? Lailoken, old friend, is that you?'

The woodwose stepped forward. 'Yes, wizard, it is I. If I had known you had awoken, I should have come to greet you sooner.'

'Ambrose, we need your help,' said Cassie. 'We think the Erl King is looking for a faery treasure – a spear. We've been trying to find out more about it and came across a name you mentioned once: "Nimue". She was the last Hedgewitch to possess it.'

'First the key and now the spear, you say. What mischief is that boy up to, I wonder?' Ambrose frowned, the burls of wood above his eyes bunching together. 'Yes, I know well this so-called treasure, although it has brought nothing but ill fortune to those who have sought it. It is usually called the Slaying Spear, but its true name is Rhongomiant. It was made of nightglass from the mountains of Faerie and brought to these lands by the Wanderers. The spear brings death to all it touches, whether a blade of grass or the strongest man or beast – none may resist. It is a tempting power, but one that ultimately destroys the possessor, as it did the last faery knight.'

'Sir Egad,' said Rue. 'What happened to him?'

'The poor fool wished to prove himself a hero. He ventured deeper and deeper into the woods, killing mortal and faery beasts alike, but it was never enough. The spear had given him a hunger for death, until nothing would satisfy him, nothing but a great wyrm. There were two of them within the Western Wood in those days, and a terror they were, for nothing could kill them, not even cold steel. Their names were Melchet and—'

'Galtres!' said Cassie.

'Indeed, however it was Melchet whom Sir Egad tracked to his lair, and there they fought, for although he possessed the spear, it is no easy thing to kill a great wyrm. They say you can still see their battleground, for there no green things will grow and only the skeletons of trees reach toward the sky. Sir Egad slew Melchet, but was killed himself as the wyrm fell upon him.'

'What happened to the spear?' asked Tabitha.

'The people of your village reclaimed the knight's body. He was something of a hero to them in death and the spear passed into the hands of the first Hedgewitches – Morgana and after her, Nimue. It is the very reason I sought her out; I wished to possess the spear, for I felt it might be the answer to the great task I had taken upon myself, but she kept it from me and hid it well and after a time I was diverted by other matters. All for the better, for I would have likely succumbed to its deathly power, as did Sir Egad and others before him.'

'Then it might still be hidden, after all these years,' said Cassie.

'That is all I can tell you, young witchlings. Of all the treasures, it has the darkest heart, if you fix your will upon it then it will drive you to destruction. Leave the spear where it lies, if you want my advice.'

Cassie frowned. That was all very well if the spear remained hidden, but the Erl King would continue to use the villagers to seek it, and what if one of them, by chance, came across it?

Lailoken glanced at the sky, where dark clouds were gathering. 'I must return these three to the fields beyond, while the sun is still high.'

Ambrose closed his eyes once more, ready to return to his slumber. 'It is good to see you, young witchlings, but heed Lailoken's warnings – he knows the wood better than any. And do not seek the spear, for its power is no gift to the one who wields it, and it always claims its keeper in the end.'

The woodwose led them east, and as they walked the trees thinned and grew younger. Cassie looked at them differently now, wondering what they whispered beneath the soil, from root to root.

At last, they arrived at the edge of the woods, and before them lay the grassy slope that ran down to the village. The houses stood warm in the afternoon sunlight, like a row of baked loaves, steam curling from their chimneys.

'This is as far as I venture,' said Lailoken, coming to a halt amidst the shadows of the trees. 'Here, this is for you.' He held something out to Cassie and she took it, turning it over in her hands. It was the small wooden bird she had seen him carving in the cave. Its wings were folded and its beak was open in song. Every feather on its breast was carved in tiny strokes and it had a hole in the tip of its raised tail into which you could blow, making the whole thing into a whistle.

'It is a nightingale,' he explained. 'If you should find yourself once more in great need, blow on this and help will come, whether from me or some other quarter.'

‘Thank you,’ said Cassie, thinking of all the woodwose had done for them. ‘It’s beautiful.’

They said their goodbyes to Lailoken and together they left the Hedge behind and made for the village. They had been gone a day and a night, and were eager for a proper meal and their own beds.

Chapter Eighteen

Faery Dust

It was late afternoon by the time Cassie returned, tired and bedraggled, to Hartwood Hall. The gardens were cast in purple and orange by the fading light. Cassie breathed in a lungful of crisp autumn air, picking up the scent of windfallen apples and the dry leaves raked into piles on the drive. Blue-grey smoke rose from the vegetable garden, where Brogan was tending a bonfire, and wreathed the turrets of Hartwood Hall. Overhead, a skein of geese were announcing their arrival from the north. Cassie was relieved to be home and was already looking forward to one of Mrs Briggs' pies, followed shortly by a hot bath.

But as she flew towards the great oak door she saw two figures standing on the steps – a tall, thin man in a black helmet and next to him her cousin, his gaze fixed upon his shoes.

What was Police Constable Griffiths doing at their house? She had only been gone one night – had Sebastian called the police? Cassie urged Tantivy on to reach them.

'Good evening, Miss Morgan,' said PC Griffiths. 'I was just about to knock when I saw you coming up the drive.' He looked her up and down and Cassie realised how she must appear, caked in mud and leaves, her hair standing out like a fox's brush.

The policeman cleared his throat. 'I am aware that the Hedgewitch is away on business, and I take it you are in charge here in her absence?'

Cassie wasn't quite sure that her aunt would see it that way. She wondered where Aoife had got to. 'Aunt Miranda's not back until Thursday. Has something happened?'

'Well, it's young Sebastian here. Now, I know boys of his age can be somewhat... excitable, you might say, and get themselves into trouble, but we can't be having this sort of behaviour in the village, miss, it simply won't do. I'm quite sure the Hedgewitch would say the same, were she here.'

Cassie looked from the police constable to her cousin, who was still examining his shoelaces, a frown on his pale face.

'What has he done?' asked Cassie.

'Been caught taking things from the Whitby's shop. Nothing valuable, mind, just a magazine and a roll of sweeties, but still, we have to nip this sort of thing in the bud, I'm sure you understand.' The policeman adjusted his collar. 'Now, Mrs Whitby says she won't be pressing charges, but I need your assurance the lad will be taken in hand and this won't happen again. Next time there will be *consequences*.'

Cassie realised her mouth was hanging open. She shut it and nodded. 'I understand. Thank you for bringing him home. I'm sure it won't happen again and I'll go to Mrs Whitby tomorrow and apologise.'

PC Griffiths smiled at her. 'There now, that's all I need to hear. I'll leave him in your care, Miss Morgan.'

Cassie and Sebastian watched him retrieve his bicycle and cycle off down the road.

'You stole sweets from Rue's shop?' she said, turning on her cousin. 'Why on earth would you do that? You get loads of pocket money from Uncle Elliot and even if you've run out, you can always ask Mrs Briggs for some change.'

Sebastian scowled, looking up at her for the first time. 'It's not about the money. You wouldn't understand.'

'No, I don't understand. I leave you alone for five minutes and you turn to amateur burglary!'

'And what should I do instead? Sit around all day on my own?' asked Sebastian. 'While you run off and have all the fun with those girls from coven? I know you were out all last night – you went looking for the treasure, didn't you? I told you I could help and you left me behind, *again*!'

Cassie sighed. 'We couldn't have brought you, Sebastian. It was far too dangerous and you're not a witch.'

'I KNOW THAT!' he shouted, hands balled into tight fists.

Cassie saw that once again she'd struck a nerve. She could still remember what it was like to feel left out of things from her days at Fowell House and Miranda *had* tasked her with keeping an eye on her cousin. Perhaps if she'd spent more time with Sebastian, she could have prevented this.

'Look, if you swear not to do anything like this again I won't tell Aunt Miranda, and you can come with us next time we go into the Hedge, all right?'

Sebastian looked unconvinced. 'You'll really take me into the woods? Promise?'

'Witch's Honour,' said Cassie.

'Now then,' said Mrs Briggs, appearing in the doorway, her arms crossed. 'That was Constable Griffiths I saw just now, heading down the drive, was it not? I don't suppose you'd like to explain just what he was doing on our doorstep, young man?'

Sebastian shoved his hands in his pockets and scowled.

'And you, Cassandra, don't think a couple of pillows can fool me, I wasn't born yesterday. Your bed's not been slept in, you've missed three meals and there's glowing moss in your hair. You two have a lot of explaining to do. To think what the Hedgewitch would say if she were here!'

Cassie went over to the Whitby's shop the following day after school to apologise, but Mrs Whitby waved her out the door with Rue and they walked down to the village green to meet Tabitha. Cassie still could not understand what had possessed Sebastian to steal from the shop and he refused to talk about it any further.

'Don't worry about it, my mum says boys are prone to irrational behaviour,' Rue said with a shrug. 'And she should know, she's got three of them.'

'I can't help feeling like it's my fault, though,' said Cassie. 'I should have been keeping a closer eye on him. He's a nuisance but I never thought he'd do something like this...'

Tabitha frowned. 'Is he still writing to his father every day?'

Cassie nodded. 'Uncle Elliot doesn't always reply, though, I think he must be terribly busy. We only get a letter from London once a week.'

'Well, look at it this way, perhaps Sebastian didn't want the sweets – as you say, he gets plenty of pocket money. I suspect what he really wanted was to get in trouble.'

Rue gaped at her. 'But that's crazy!'

'Yes, just crazy enough that your uncle might hear about it and come to get him,' said Tabitha.

As far as Cassie was aware, word of her cousin's behaviour had not yet made it to Elliot, but if Tabitha was right about Sebastian's motivations, she worried what he might do next to try and get his father's attention.

Cassie sighed. 'I just hope Aunt Miranda doesn't find out about it. I'm supposed to be watching out for him. I'll have to think of something to explain our night in the Hedge too – Mrs Briggs will tell her if I don't do it first.'

'Perhaps we ought to tell the Hedgewitch the truth?' said Tabitha. 'About the spear and the wyrm and everything Ambrose told us. I hate to say it, but hasn't all of this gone a bit beyond us?'

'I still think we could find the spear ourselves,' said Rue. 'We know for sure this Nimue had it, and that she hid it somewhere. Just think, if we found it and saved the village, everyone would have to admit that Oak are the best and bravest patrol in the coven!'

'But what about your father?' said Tabitha. 'What if someone else is enchanted before we find it? They could *die*, Rue.'

Cassie hesitated. She knew Tabitha was probably right, and it was the Hedgewitch's responsibility to protect the village, after all. If her aunt knew about the spear, she'd be sure to forbid the girls from looking for it, saying it was far too dangerous. But, in her heart, Cassie wanted to agree with Rue – they were *so* close now, she couldn't let it go just yet. And what's more, her mother was mixed up in all of this somehow. Rose Morgan had been friends with Toby Harper, and when he'd disappeared fourteen years ago she'd blamed herself and run away from Hedgely. Her mother, the Erl King, Toby Harper and the spear – it was all connected somehow, but she couldn't quite see it.

As punishment for staying out all night, Mrs Briggs gave Cassie additional chores around Hartwood. The housekeeper insisted they have the house looking spick and span before the Hedgewitch returned. Cassie spent her afternoons sweeping, mopping and scrubbing for all her worth.

On Tuesday, Mrs Briggs led Cassie into the feasting hall. It was the largest room in the house and had a musicians' gallery, a hanging chandelier and a tapestry depicting a hunting scene: a train of nobles on horseback following a white stag. Along one wall was a huge fireplace with a mantlepiece from which carved faces and creatures emerged as if trying to break free. Cassie thought one of them rather resembled the woodwose. It was not a room they used much, being large and draughty and far too formal for everyday meals; instead it was reserved for when the Hedgewitch had visitors, or for important festivities.

'All right, duck, you try that on while I fetch you my second-best duster,' said Mrs Briggs, handing Cassie an apron printed with purple pansies. She returned with a brightly coloured feather duster. 'Boobrie feathers, only thing that works on faery dust. Just be sure to shake it out in this bucket. You don't want to get any in your eyes. And don't go tipping the stuff outside either, does odd things to the vegetables and Brogan won't be pleased.'

Cassie applied her duster to the mantlepiece with a little too much energy and sent a cloud of sparkling powder into the air, making them both sneeze and cough.

'Oh, my green garters! You can't go at it like that, this isn't ordinary dust, you know. Hold your duster like so, and use a gentle flicking motion.' The housekeeper demonstrated, scooping the powder into a copper bucket.

Cassie brushed dust from her sleeves and hair. It was very fine and glistened in many colours, reminding her of the powder she'd encountered at the ruins beneath Castle Hill and in the Riddlewood.

'Where does it all come from?' she asked.

'Well, most of it comes from the Hartwood tree,' Mrs Briggs explained. 'The tree was here even before the house was built. Its roots run deep beneath the cellars and its branches hold up the roof. As you know, it likes to change things now and then, create a new room, shift a corridor, block up a window, and whenever it does it leaves dust behind. That's faery architecture for you – pretty enough to look at, I'll grant you, but more than it's worth to clean.'

'The dust is left behind by faery magic?' asked Cassie.

'Quite. Wherever there's been a glamour or a great number of the folk gathered in one place you'll find it. Even imps and the like leave a trail of the stuff with their constant coming and going. It's something to do with the way magic interferes with this world – a sort of side effect, if you like. There's a book about it in the library, if I recall, and the Hedgewitch could probably explain it better. All I know is that it gets into every nook and cranny – it's the very bane of my existence!'

Cassie froze, her feather duster held in mid-air. Had she heard right? 'The library? Do you mean there is a library, *here*, at Hartwood?'

'Well, there was. It went missing when the brownie left.'

'How does a library go missing?'

'I'll tell you if you'll dust the moulding down there – my back will punish me tomorrow if I go bending down all day. That's it, nice gentle motions. Well now, there used to be a brownie in the house, Gwili was his name. Good at his work he was too, never had any trouble with bogles or creepy crawlies when we had a brownie, and now, look at this! Every autumn, as soon as it starts to rain, in they come!' Mrs Briggs scooped up a small yellow spider in the palm of her hand and tossed it out an open window.

Cassie had accompanied the Hedgewitch on her rounds and met the brownies of other houses in the village. The house-sprites protected their households and knew everything that went on under their roofs. Yet it had never occurred to her to wonder why they didn't have one at Hartwood.

'The house used to behave itself better too, when we had a brownie to mind it,' Mrs Briggs continued. 'None of this moving bathrooms about or locking you out of cupboards when it's in a huff because the guttering is blocked. But shortly after your great-grandmother,

Sylvia Morgan, died and Miranda became Hedgewitch, they had a row, her and the brownie.'

This didn't surprise Cassie at all.

'Can't even recall what it was over, something went missing I believe, and she blamed Gwili, but he swore he had nothing to do with it and it all went downhill from there until he packed up and left. Moved in with a nice family over Oswalton way, I hear. We've been without one ever since, more's the pity.'

'Couldn't we get another brownie?' Cassie asked.

'What, do you think they grow on trees? No, your aunt upset poor Gwili so much that he spread the word. We're on the brownie blacklist, I'm afraid, and will just have to make do without!'

'But what about the library?' Cassie asked, trying to bring Mrs Briggs back to this crucial detail.

'Well, it was your aunt's favourite place in the whole house. There's books in there on everything a witch could need: potion formularies, histories, travel accounts of Faerie. I'd find her asleep in there some nights, head on a pile of books. When the brownie left, he wanted to punish her, so he hid the library. It's still here in the house somewhere – your aunt spent months looking, but she couldn't find it. Had to move her things to the study in the end, but she still misses that library. Now, *there's* a room that could do with a good clean, I'll warrant – must be a foot of dust in there by now.'

Chapter Nineteen

The Trial of Renata Rawlins

When Cassie came downstairs for breakfast on Thursday morning it was to find her aunt sitting in her usual place at the head of the table, a bowl of porridge before her, alongside a cup of nettle tea and a copy of the past week's *Hedgely Herald*. She looked up when Cassie entered.

'I see that Ted Whitby has been the latest victim of these strange enchantments, but that you and Rue handled the situation admirably well.'

Cassie flushed at the unexpected praise. 'He's all right now, Aoife gave him a restorative potion.' She slid onto a bench and exchanged a look with Mrs Briggs, who was frying eggs. The housekeeper had obviously not told Miranda about Cassie's night in the Hedge, or her aunt would have begun by lecturing her. Cassie knew Mrs Briggs expected her to be the one to do the telling, but as soon as she did the half-smile on her aunt's face would vanish, to be replaced by the usual weary disappointment and she couldn't quite bring herself to do it, not yet.

'I am surprised by your unusual patience, Cassandra. I assume you wish to know about the outcome of the trial?' asked her aunt.

'Yes, of course,' said Cassie, reaching for the bread and butter and avoiding Mrs Brigg's gaze as she poured the tea. She *did* want to know about the trial and the Witches' Assembly and what had happened to Renata. The fact that it would delay her telling her aunt everything for a few more minutes was just an added benefit.

'Renata pleaded guilty – she could hardly do otherwise after what we witnessed. Prattled on about changes on the way and witches becoming powerful again – as if witchcraft has ever been about power. Our magic was always intended to protect others, to heal and to understand. It is the oath we all swear to, and those who break it must face the consequences.' Miranda took a sip of her tea. 'However, I fear the Erl King's network is far wider than we had imagined.'

'Does that mean there are more warlocks?' asked Cassie.

'Renata has given us the names of two – one operating in Cornwall, and another in Scotland. It took three witches and a rather strong infusion of lunaria to extract the information from her. Although, if there can be one good thing to have come out of this trial it is that the Assembly is taking the threat more seriously now.'

'I still don't understand why anyone would choose to work for the Erl King.'

Miranda paused. 'Before England went to war with Faerie, before the Treaty of Rosehill, our worlds were not so very distant. There were far more faery folk in this land, and the ancient witches travelled to Faerie, returning with a deeper understanding of magic. Some among our number see that time as a sort of golden age, they long to return to it and are willing to destroy all we have gained – safety, security, peace – to turn back time. The Erl King promises them access to all the wonder and

Hedge. We're working on the Woodwitch badge you see, as a patrol, and it's one of the requirements—'

'After I expressly forbade you from entering the Hedge without supervision? Really, Cassandra, I would have thought after your experiences at Midsummer you might have learned. And the Woodwitch badge was removed from the handbook years ago, for precisely this reason. Where on earth did you learn of it?'

'From my mother's handbook, but I—'

'You should have cleared it with me first. But of course, you knew there was no way I would have authorised such a reckless endeavour. You wish to prove yourself a responsible and capable witch but the minute I leave, you pull foolish stunts like this! *Really*, Cassandra, you must learn your limits. You are still a fledgling witch – you are *not* ready to face the dangers of the Hedge on your own.'

Cassie opened her mouth to argue but shut it again just as quickly. Her hands were balled into fists on her lap. She had intended to tell Miranda everything, about the spear and Nimue and the Erl King, but she dreaded to think how her aunt would respond. And besides, if they could find the spear themselves, that would prove to the Miranda that she was more than just a fledgling, that she was ready to go through the Hedge and find her mother.

'Hedgewitch,' said a lilting voice from the doorway. Aoife stood there in a long orange dress, her hands full of bunches of wheat. 'I know you've only just returned, but there's someone here for you. I've let him in to the entrance hall. I hope that's all right?'

Police Constable Griffiths stood in the hall, his helmet in his hands, looking flushed and uncomfortable and glancing now and then at the portraits of past Hedgewitches that covered the walls.

'Ah, Hedgewitch, so sorry to disturb you, and so early in the morning, but there's been another theft you see, well, a break-in actually.' He adjusted his collar. 'At Eris Watchet's shop. Something valuable's gone missing this time.'

Miranda drew herself up to her full height, which was several inches taller than the policeman's. 'And? Isn't that your business to sort out? Last I recalled, my responsibilities in this village do not extend to catching human thieves – unless you believe this to be goblin work?'

'It's not that, ma'am, it's only that your nephew...' He paused and swallowed. 'Well, he's been caught nicking things before and I told Miss Morgan here, that if it happened again...'

Miranda turned to Cassie. 'Is this true, Cassandra? Where is Sebastian?'

Cassie raced upstairs to fetch Sebastian from his bedroom. He came down to face the policeman in his pyjamas and didn't seem at all embarrassed about it.

'It wasn't me,' he said, calm as you like. 'I've never been near that mouldy old shop. What use would I have for some rotten antique?'

'Come now, boy, this will all go easier for you if you tell the truth. Where were you last night?'

'I was stuck here, of course. Bored out of my wits if you must know.'

'Can anyone in the house corroborate this story?' He looked at Cassie and she tried to think. When had she last seen her cousin? He'd been at breakfast yesterday – she could remember him having a particularly large helping of Mrs Briggs' pancakes, but she hadn't seen him at lunch. Dinner had been pumpkin and pork pie and, now she thought of it, Sebastian had left rather early after only one helping, claiming he was feeling unwell. Aoife had offered him one of her herbal tonics but he'd only pulled a face and gone up to his room.

'He was at dinner with us, at about six o'clock,' said Cassie, hoping that would satisfy PC Griffiths.

'And after that? Did anyone in the household see him?'

'I went to bed!' said Sebastian, his voice breaking. 'Why don't you believe me? You're all against me here, you have been since I arrived!'

'That's enough of that,' said Miranda. 'The boy says he didn't do it. You have absolutely no evidence Sebastian was involved, and until you do I ask you to kindly take your accusations elsewhere.' There was a steely edge to the Hedgewitch's voice.

PC Griffiths tried to protest, but ended up stuttering out an apology and leaving with his hat between his hands.

As soon as the door had shut behind him, Miranda turned to her niece and nephew. 'And just what was the good constable referring to when he mentioned a previous incident?'

Cassie and her cousin exchanged a meaningful look. It appeared that a further confession was due.

With only five sleeps until Hallowe'en, 1st Hedgely Coven were fully occupied with preparations for the Crossing Night. There was to be a procession through the village, followed by a feast at Hartwood Hall, and there was still so much to do.

Ash Patrol had commandeered the large cauldron on the central hearth, over which they were melting beeswax in a double boiler. Harriet Webb was dipping long cotton wicks into the molten gold liquid and hanging them from the broom rack. When they had begun to cool and solidify, Alice Wong took them down to carve protective runes in the soft candles and roll them in dried herbs. These would be handed out to people in the village to be lit on Hallowe'en, keeping them safe from harm.

Eliza Pepper and Anika Kalra of Thorn Patrol were making toffee apples with fruit from Farmer Scrump's orchard, boiling sugar in smaller cauldrons and dipping the glossy balls in crushed nuts they'd foraged from the Hedge. With the Hedgewitch nominally in charge again, Ivy deigned to participate once more. Of course, her apples were the shiniest and most evenly coated.

Heather Shuttle, Lucy Watercress and the Drake sisters were practising a traditional Irish broom dance under Aoife's instruction, while Nancy Kemp accompanied them on the tin whistle. Twirling about the coven hall, they leapt over their brooms, swinging them in the air so that the others had to duck.

'That's it, girls, feel the music,' called Miss Early, wafting about the room. 'Let the spirit of Hallowe'en guide you!'

The hall was full of dripping wax and sugar, flying feet and brooms.

'It's only a matter of time before the spirit of Hallowe'en ends up with a waxed apple or a toffee-coated foot,' said Montague from the safety of the Oak Patrol corner.

Cassie, Rue and Tabitha were surrounded by turnips and mangelwurzels, which they were doing their best to carve with their pen knives, hollowing out the insides to make jack-o'-lanterns. It was hard work, however, as the solid vegetables resisted their efforts and they were soon in need of Tabitha's poultices and plasters for nicked fingers and thumbs.

'I was under the impression they were supposed to wear frightening grimaces to scare away faery folk?' said

Montague, inspecting Cassie's attempt. 'That one looks as if it's drooling in its sleep.'

Her lantern did have a rather lop-sided and lazy expression. She put it aside and reached for another turnip.

'I don't see why we couldn't use pumpkins,' said Cassie. 'Brogan's grown an absolute mountain of them and Mrs Briggs is running out of things to put them in. So far this week we've had pumpkin scones, pumpkin soup, pumpkin roly-poly, stuffed pumpkins, pumpkin pudding...'

'The Hedgewitch says turnips are traditional; she doesn't approve of imported vegetables,' said Tabitha. 'Here, what do you think of this one?'

She held up her own – it had a rabbit's whiskered face, modelled on her familiar's, and a red bow tied around the stem at the top.

'*Terrifying*,' said Rue.

'So, what did the Hedgewitch say when you told her about the spear?' asked Tabitha.

Cassie flushed. 'I didn't, not exactly. I told her we stayed overnight in the Hedge because we're working on our Woodwitch badges. She was furious – I didn't dare tell her the rest. Rue's right anyway, we can find it ourselves, and when we do she'll see just how resourceful we are as a patrol.'

'We already earned the Argent Star – they'll have to invent a new badge to give us for heroism and bravery!' said Rue, eyes gleaming.

'That's all very well, but what if we don't find it? What if the Erl King's servant enchants someone else from the village?'

'Shh!' hissed Cassie.

Phyllis and Susan Drake were approaching from the Thorn Patrol corner, munching on shards of leftover toffee. 'You'd better keep an eye on that cousin of yours, Cassandra,' said Phyllis.

'Our mum says we ought to lock our doors, with a thief on the loose,' said Susan.

'What are they on about?' asked Tabitha.

'Haven't you heard about the break-in at Watchet's?' said Susan. 'The whole village is talking about it.'

'PC Griffiths says it was Sebastian Penhallow,' said Phyllis. 'Just goes to show there's a bad apple in every family.'

'And sometimes there's two,' said Rue, glaring at the sisters until they stalked off.

'That can't be true,' said Tabitha, once Phyllis and Susan had gone. 'You don't think he did it, surely?'

Cassie sighed, putting aside her knife. 'He says he didn't, and I want to believe him, but...'

'He *was* caught nicking sweets from our shop,' said Rue.

'Well, sweets are one thing, but I can't believe he'd do something like this,' said Tabitha. 'Did Griffiths say what was taken?'

'He only said it was a valuable antique,' Cassie replied. 'He was more interested in finding out where Sebastian was that night and the thing is, I can't say for certain. He left dinner early... He could have snuck out and I doubt any of us would have noticed.'

Rue attacked her jack-o'-lantern with vigour. 'And you said it yourself, Tabitha, he *wants* to get in trouble.'

The Hedgewitch strode into the centre of the hall, clapping her hands to get their attention.

'I'm pleased to see that standards have not slipped in my absence and that you are well prepared for Hallowe'en. However, in just two short months, another of the Crossing Nights will be upon us – Midwinter. Although it may seem early to begin thinking about snow and mistletoe, we must soon begin rehearsals for the Midwinter play if we're to be ready in time for the solstice.'

'Yes!' said Rue, grinning. 'We did *Saint Aelfwig and the Nuggle* last year, it was brilliant. I got to play an imp.'

Aoife stepped forward, beaming. 'The Hedgewitch has kindly asked me to direct this year. She tells me there were some small mishaps at last year's play, and that additional practice might be needed to iron out any costume and set issues.'

'Heather was playing a tree, the Faery Thorn,' Rue whispered. 'And Phyllis and Susan were meant to cut her down, but Susan swung too far and knocked Mrs Blight's hat off and then Phyllis trod on Heather's toes and they all went down in a heap, bringing the backdrop with them and setting fire to Heather's branches. It was fantastic!'

'This year, we will perform *The Wyrm, the Witch and the Faery Knight*. I'm sure many of you know the story. I've been watching you closely and have selected girls for each part.'

The coven broke into excited chatter and discussion at this – clearly some of them knew the story and already had ideas about which roles they'd like. Cassie, Rue and Tabitha exchanged glances. Was it a coincidence? Or did Aoife know something about Galtres and Sir Egad?

Aoife had to raise her voice to be heard over the hubbub. 'It will be a grand opportunity for creative expression! I look forward to seeing what each of you bring to your roles. The cast will be as follows...'

The room fell silent as every girl in the coven listened in to hear which part she would be given. Aoife unfolded a square of paper and read aloud, 'Narrators: Eliza Pepper and Harriet Webb, with Nancy Kemp providing musical accompaniment.'

This was no great surprise, Eliza and Harriet were the leaders of Thorn and Ash patrols, and the oldest girls in the coven, and Nancy was wonderful on the tin whistle.

'The wyrm will be performed by a team made up of Susan and Phyllis Drake and Anika Kalra.'

The three Thorn Patrol girls looked quite pleased with this and immediately formed a huddle to discuss who would be the head, body and tail.

'Tabitha Blight will play the Faery Queen, with Rue Whitby as the Knight.'

'Huzzah!' said Rue, rather too loudly.

'The lead role, of the Hedgewitch Morgana, will be played by Ivy Harrington,' announced Aoife.

There were gasps of surprise at this. Ivy had been openly critical of Aoife's activities and barely participated since the Hedgewitch had left, and yet she'd been rewarded with the best role in the whole play and was looking smug as ever.

'That should have been you,' Tabitha whispered to Cassie. 'Isn't Morgana your ancestor?'

'The villagers will be Alice Wong, Lucy Watercress and Cassandra Morgan,' Aoife continued. 'Heather, you will be the sheep taken by the wyrm.'

'Well, at least you won't be the sheep,' said Rue. 'Poor Heather.'

Cassie nodded and tried to smile, it could be worse. She probably wouldn't have too many lines to learn as villager number three, and she was still new to the coven, so she could hardly expect a starring role. Besides which, Midwinter was two months away, and they had more important things to worry about.

Aoife was handing out scripts and Cassie flipped through the pages to see if she had any lines to memorise.

'*Oh no! Not my sheep*,' read Ivy, standing over them. 'You've only got the one line, Cassandra, shouldn't be too difficult for you.'

'Oh, shove off, Ivy,' said Rue.

'Actually, I'll be needing both of you to rehearse with. Morgana has two scenes with the knight and a rather long bit with the Queen of Faerie at the end here, see? I don't want either of you forgetting your lines and letting me down – we'd better meet up after school on Monday and read through these together.'

Rue sighed, but reluctantly agreed, if only to make Ivy go away and leave them alone.

'Now I *really* wish you were playing Morgana!' said Rue.

Chapter Twenty

An Uncommon Thief

The following Monday, Cassie met Rue and Tabitha at Bramble's after school. Selena Moor had pulled out all the stops to decorate the tea room for the season. There were jack-o'-lanterns on every table, grinning with flickering light; stacks of pumpkins around the fireplace and doorway, black bat-bunting draped across the mantlepiece and windows, and muslin ghosts wafting between the bunches of herbs that hung from the ceiling. The ghosts fluttered and flapped in a rather eerie way whenever someone walked by.

The tea room was packed, and Cassie and Rue were relieved to see that Tabitha had managed to secure them a table by the window. They joined her, dumping their school things and sinking into their seats.

'I got away early, since we're supposed to be meeting Ivy,' said Tabitha. 'Where is she, by the way?'

'Said she had to run some errands first,' said Rue. 'Typical Ivy – she's the one that insisted on extra rehearsals in the first place.'

'Here you are my lovelies, sorry to keep you waiting but we're quite overwhelmed today, as you can see!' Selena Moor arrived with a heavily laden tray and began to distribute the tea things before them. 'Town's buzzing with rumours and speculation after the break-in – there's some as thinks the goblins were behind it and others...'

'Who think my cousin did it,' said Cassie softly.

'Well now, we should never be too quick to jump to conclusions, that's my motto,' said Selena, placing a tray of sticky gingerbread between them to share. 'Let's see, there's elderflower and eyebright for Tabitha, dandelion and dock for young Rue and a raspberry and red clover for you, Cassandra, oh and a tray of Marchpane's best parkin.'

'But you've given us four teapots?' said Cassie.

'Of course, the rosemary and red sage is for young Miss Harrington, when she arrives.'

The girls looked at each other. None of them had told Selena that Ivy was to join them. 'Now, if that's everything, I've just heard the bell go. I may be a witch, but I can't make tables out of thin air!'

Selena bustled off, leaving them to try their teas. Cassie's was sweet and tart, bursting with berries, and soon cleared her head, making her feel more alert and decisive.

Rue took three sugar cubes from the small cauldron on the table and dropped them into her cup.

Tabitha tugged on Cassie's sleeve. 'Look, there's Eris Watchet!'

They turned to see a tall, thin woman in a tweed suit duck through the door and approach the counter where Selena Moor was trying to boil six different kettles at the same time. Selena saw her and the two fell into a hushed conversation.

'I bet they're talking about the break-in,' said Rue.

'Oh, I wish we could hear what they're saying,' said Tabitha.

Cassie stood and picked up the sugar-cauldron. 'I'm going to get us some more.'

'But there's still loads...' said Rue.

Cassie shot her a look.

'... oh, I see. Well, get me another slice of parkin, while you're at it?'

Fortunately, the tea room was so busy that Cassie could weave between the tables without drawing too much attention to herself and come to stand beside a large vase of cosmos flowers and poppyseed heads that just about hid her from view. She had to listen very hard to tune out the general commotion, but she could just about make out the voices of Selena and Eris Watchet.

'That's the last time I purchase teaware from your shop, by the way,' said Selena. 'You should have seen the look on Miss Bobbin's face when I served her salty Darjeeling!'

'Huh, probably did her a world of good. That woman is positively insipid. And besides, I gave you a discount. You know my policy – no returns.'

'Well, there's not much left to return anyhow, another customer dropped it.' Selena explained. 'I do worry about where you get some of your stock though, Eris, and whose hands it might fall into.'

'Nothing wrong with my stock, or my suppliers, it's *thieves* I'm concerned about. Whoever got into my shop last week did so without breaking a pane of glass, or waking Barbarossa – and he sleeps with one eye open. No, if you ask me, there was witchcraft involved.'

'So you don't think it was the boy then? PC Griffiths seemed quite convinced...' said Selena.

'Ha. PC Griffiths couldn't find a stolen flute if it up and played him a reel!' said Eris. 'No, the boy would have taken some shiny gewgaw – a knight's helmet, or something else impressive to show his friends. I doubt he knew anything about the flute, even if he is the Hedgewitch's nephew. No, if you ask me, it's an uncommon thief who would leave all the jewellery and silver and take that flute...'

There was a pause. Eris lowered her voice even further. Cassie had to push her face into the flowers to hear.

'It was sold to me by Sir Henry after his wife... well, you know what happened to Tamsin. Brought in a box of her things, he did, that flute among them. Didn't think much of it at the time, but he seemed especially keen to get rid of it.'

Cassie heard the tinkle of water as Selena poured Eris another cup. 'Well, no doubt the poor man was grief-stricken, didn't want any of her possessions around to remind him. This flute now – what was it made out of? Ivory? Silver?'

'Elder wood,' said Eris.

'Elder wood? Are you sure? It's awfully unlucky to carve elder wood; I don't know a witch that will touch the stuff. An uncommon thief, indeed – who'd want such a thing!'

Cassie tiptoed back to their table and replaced the sugar. She quickly told Rue and Tabitha everything she'd heard.

'And another thing, I've seen the flute – when Rue and I went to ask Eris about the spear. I picked it up, gave me a strange feeling to touch it.'

'Do you think it's enchanted?' asked Rue. 'Or cursed?'

'I'm not sure exactly, but Eris said that it was made of elder wood.'

'But none of this helps us with who took it,' said Rue. 'Although she's probably right about Sebastian – what could he want with it?'

'No, it can't have been Sebastian. Eris said the thief came and went without a trace, she thinks witchcraft was involved.'

By the time Ivy deigned to join them, they'd all finished their tea and cake and had just about exhausted the topic of who might have broken into Eris Watchet's shop to steal the flute and why they might want it. Cassie was sure that it must be the same person who had been enchanting the villagers to find the spear. Rue agreed that they had another warlock on their hands, but Tabitha wasn't quite so sure, although she was convinced that Sebastian had nothing to do with it.

Ivy came into the tea room looking flushed. Clutching her school satchel, she made her way over to their table.

'Well, come on then, I haven't got all day and we can't very well practise in here,' she said, casting glances around the room.

'You're the one who's late,' said Rue.

'And Selena Moor made you a pot of tea, it's still warm enough to drink,' said Tabitha.

Ivy frowned. 'I haven't got time, come on, we can rehearse on the village green. But we don't need you, Cassandra, you're not in any of the important scenes.'

'Either Cassie comes or we don't,' said Rue.

'Very well, I suppose she can make herself useful and prompt us. Come on then!'

As they made their way down Loft Street towards the green, Cassie noticed that Ivy wasn't her usual prim and proper self. There were small leaves and twigs caught in her short black hair and she walked with a slight limp, favouring her left leg, which had several thin red scratches on it.

'Right, are you both ready? I've already memorised my lines, but I expect neither of you have,' said Ivy, placing her satchel carefully on the grass.

'What happened to you?' asked Rue.

Ivy dusted down her skirt. 'Nothing. Let's get on with it, shall we?'

'You haven't been into the Hedge again, have you?' asked Tabitha. 'Hallowe'en is only a few days away—'

'I can look after myself, thank you very much. Now, if you're both done fussing, let's start with the scene where I... I mean where Morgana brings the knight back from the brink of death with her potion.'

'But I've got loads of lines before that,' said Rue. 'And my battle with the wyrm – that's the best bit!'

'Well, we haven't got the wyrm, so we might as well start with *my* first line. You lie down over there, like you're dead.'

Rue looked at the rather muddy patch of grass Ivy was pointing to and frowned.

'Oh, let's just get this over with,' said Tabitha. 'I have to get home in time to make dinner.'

'My fair knight!' began Ivy in a high-pitched voice, 'What mortal wound have you sustained?'

Cassie was reading ahead in her copy of the script when, out of the corner of her eye, she spotted something sticking out of Ivy's satchel. At first, she thought it was a twig that had somehow got lodged there, and so, she began to pull it out.

'Arrrrgh!' groaned Rue, from where she lay on the ground.

Tabitha laughed.

'You're supposed to be a dying knight, not a pirate, try that again,' directed Ivy. 'I will not be upstaged by your nonsense. This is a very serious play.'

The twig was straight and light and made Cassie's fingers tingle as she touched it.

'Assist me, oh kindly witch, for I am not long for this world!' cried Rue, her voice overwrought with suppressed laughter.

'Fear not! For I bring you a tonic. You shall not die this day,' said Ivy, bending over Rue and miming feeding her a potion.

Cassie lifted the twig out of Ivy's satchel and rose to her feet. There was no mistaking it, it was the very same she'd seen in Eris Watchet's shop – the flute made of elder wood.

'What are you doing?' screeched Ivy. She rushed at Cassie and snatched the flute from her hands. 'That's mine! How dare you go through my things.'

'It was you!' said Cassie. 'You broke into the antique shop, you stole the flute – and you're letting Sebastian take the blame!'

'Shhh! Keep your voice down!' hissed Ivy.

'Why should she?' asked Rue, coming to Cassie's side. 'Why shouldn't we go straight to PC Griffiths and tell him all about this? Or the Hedgewitch, for that matter.'

'How could you, Ivy?' asked Tabitha. 'Whatever possessed you?'

Ivy grabbed her satchel and stuffed the flute back inside to hide it. When she turned to face them, there were tears in her eyes despite her furious glare. 'You don't understand, none of you do. This is my last chance, they're sending her away!'

'Sending who away?' asked Tabitha.

But Cassie already knew. 'Your mother,' she said.

Ivy nodded. 'They're taking her to Convall Abbey.'

'The witches' hospital,' said Rue. 'But that's in Devon.'

'She's not getting any better. The Hedgewitch says it's the only place they might be able to help her.'

'But surely that's for the best,' said Tabitha. 'And you can still go and visit her—'

'You don't know a thing, Tabitha Blight. Once she's gone there'll be nothing I can do to help her, this is my last chance.'

'But the flute?' asked Cassie. 'Why did you steal it?'

'The flute belonged to my mother – I only took it back.'

'Tamsin... Sir Henry – they're your parents? It was your father who sold the flute to Eris Watchet?'

'He sold all her old witchcraft things. But the flute can bring her back, the part of her that was taken across the border. It can summon a person all the way from Faerie. *She* told me.'

Cassie felt a cold wave of realisation wash over her. Ivy's mother had been sick for years, lying in an enchanted sleep. Cassie had seen Mrs Harrington herself when she went with Miranda on her rounds and the Hedgewitch had informed her that part of the woman's spirit had been taken by the faery that cursed her. Ivy was going to try to bring her back. Yet it was not this that had sent a chill down Cassie's spine. No, what had occurred to her in that moment was that the flute could help her too – that it might be able to call back her own mother.

'She said I have to blow it three times on Hallowe'en,' said Ivy.

'Who is this "she" you keep going on about?' asked Rue.

But Cassie was one step ahead of her. Lailoken had told her about the third Watcher, the one who helped the rash and desperate. 'The Elder Mother – you've been looking for her, that's why you've been sneaking off into the Hedge these past weeks.'

'She called to me, in my dreams – she said she could help me, if only I brought her the flute. She said that she could bring my mother back.'

'But she's a crazy old tree hag!' said Rue. 'You can't be serious, you should know better than anyone not to trust the faery folk – it was one of them that cursed your mum in the first place!'

Ivy clutched the flute to her chest. 'You can hardly lecture me, any of you! You'd do exactly the same thing in my place – Cassie already has!'

Cassie bit her lip. Ivy was right, she'd stop at nothing to find her mother, to have a chance to bring her back from Faerie. Even now, she was tempted by the very presence of that flute. 'We can't tell on her. After everything I did in the summer, trying to get my mother back – the phooka.'

'But Cass, we have to do something!' said Rue. 'She'll get herself killed, and if she opens a way into Faerie, well, she could let anything through!'

'The Elder Mother is dangerous,' said Tabitha. 'Lailoken said she always claims a price for her help.'

'Then I'll pay it, whatever it is. I don't care.'

Cassie reached out a hand towards Ivy. 'Let us help you. We can return the flute to Eris, no one needs to know who took it—'

'Ha! You just want it for yourself, now you know what it can do. Well, you can't have it. It's mine and I'm going to use it.'

'We can't let you,' said Cassie. 'Not if it puts everyone in Hedgely in danger.'

'Just try to stop me!' said Ivy, and with a furious glare, she dashed away up the road, clutching her satchel and the wooden flute tight.

Chapter Twenty-One

All Hallows' Eve

'Well, I still think we should tell the Hedgewitch,' said Tabitha. 'I know it's not good form to snitch, but Ivy could get hurt...'

Cassie shook her head. 'Don't you see? It's worse than that. The police are already involved and if we tell my aunt, Ivy won't just lose some badges and get a lecture, they could haul her before the Witches' Assembly – as a warlock.' Cassie had visions of Ivy joining Renata Rawlins at Hexham prison. She might be the most annoying witch in the coven, but even Cassie didn't think she deserved that. She, of all people, could understand exactly how desperate Ivy was.

‘We’ll just have to stop her ourselves. Tonight we keep watch – if she tries to sneak away, we follow.’

They were huddled together at the edge of Hedgely’s market square while the rest of coven milled about. The Hedgewitch was inspecting them, one patrol at a time, and any girl whose cloak was askew or whose pins were not brightly polished was made to sort herself out. Miranda would not, she explained, lead a coven of shabby and untidy young witches through the village on one of the most important nights of the year.

Aoife was handing out baskets full of amulets, toffee apples and the beeswax candles rolled with herbs and spices that Ash Patrol had made. Each girl also had a jack-o’-lantern on a stick to light their way, and Cassie was pleased to see some of her better efforts amongst them. As the sun set over the misty Hedge, the night turned cold and the girls were grateful that Mrs Briggs had been put in charge of provisions, handing out pumpkin scones and piping hot mulled apple juice to warm their hands. Some of the villagers had begun to gather to watch the start of the procession.

‘Where is Ivy?’ asked Cassie. ‘She ought to be here by now. You don’t think she’d sneak off before we even started?’

Rue sniffed. 'And miss out on earning her event badge? Not likely.'

'There she is!' said Tabitha. 'Talking to Susan and Phyllis.'

Cassie sipped her juice. 'Keep your eyes on her, we can't let her out of our sight.'

This was easier said than done, as the night fell around them and a grey mist rolled up from the river Nix. It was an ordinary mist, Cassie noted, not a faery fog, but it made faces indistinct and created a hazy glow around each lantern.

'Gather around, girls, let's make sure you're all here!' called Aoife in her sing-song voice. 'Nine... eleven... where's Heather? Oh, there she is, thirteen, grand! Now, if you're all ready, we'll be having our first chant, *A Lantern Bright* – ready? And a one, and a two, and a three...' Aoife waved her hands like a conductor. Together, the coven lifted their lanterns and their voices and began to sing their first Hallowe'en chant:

'When dew falls on each blade of grass,
And night comes calling early.
When dusk chases the farmer home,
And the winds cry hurly-burly.

When summer lays its head to rest
And winter rises from its bed,
You'd better lock your doors and set
A lantern bright beneath the lead.'

Cassie craned her head to look for Ivy, finding her at the front of the group before the assembled villagers. Of course – Ivy would never miss a chance to show off her fine singing voice.

'*When wild cries break the nightly peace*
And strange things sneak and slither,
We witches walk the lonely roads
And chase them hither-thither.'

Cassie tugged Rue and Tabitha by the elbows until they were just behind Ivy.

As the coven finished the Hallowe'en chant to a round of applause, Lucy, Heather, Phyllis and Susan broke away from the group. Each carried her broom and, at the start of a piping jig from Nancy Kemp, they began the Irish broom dance Aoife had taught them.

'Would you three stop breathing down my neck?' hissed Ivy, turning to Cassie, Rue and Tabitha.

‘Give us the flute and we won’t have to,’ Cassie whispered back, casting a glance in the Hedgewitch’s direction. Her aunt was frowning at them.

The broom dance went fairly well, all four girls remembering the steps and keeping to time. The only problem was that none of them had thought to practise while wearing their hats, and so they lost them, one by one, to the arcing sweeps of each other’s brooms. The villagers cheered, however, and seemed to consider this part of the fun.

Finally, it was time to begin the procession proper and the thirteen young witches, in their hats and cloaks, lanterns borne aloft, left the market square and walked down Loft Street. It was an old tradition, the Hedgewitch had informed them, for the witches of Hedgely to beat the bounds of the village on Hallowe’en night, ensuring that all was well and driving off any lurking faery folk. They would visit each home, one by one, bringing them candles and amulets to ward off any threat.

The coven formed a crocodile, walking in pairs between the shops, passing Whitby’s and Saltash & Son’s, Watchet’s and Widdershin’s, Marchpane’s and Bramble’s – all of whose windows were illuminated by jack-o’-lanterns.

Cassie, who was near the front of the procession with Tabitha, kept craning her neck around to catch a glimpse of Ivy, who was at the very back with Anika.

As they walked, Aoife led them in a rather rowdy Hallowe'en chant about a bogle named Clap-Cans, that involved a lot of foot-stomping and hand-clapping, which Cassie felt sure was bound to send any faery with a love of music running away with its fingers in its ears.

They stopped first at Mrs Mossley's house, behind the post office, and Heather Shuttle stepped forward to rap on the door. There was a jingle of keys, the barking of a small dog and the door swung open. The postmistress, clutching her Yorkshire terrier, smiled at them and uttered the formal question, 'And who comes calling on All Hallows' Eve, be you wight or sprite?'

Wight was an old word for a living human being, the Hedgewitch had informed them.

Lucy Watercress, who was Heather's partner in the line stepped forward to give the response, 'We are witches, come to wish you well and safe on this night.' She held out her basket and Mrs Mossley selected a candle and an amulet to hang on her door and dropped a few coins in as payment. All the money they collected would go to the hospital at Convall Abbey and the home for retired witches in Knaresborough.

They thanked her and sung another verse of the chant as Lucy and Heather ran to the back of the line, letting the next two girls step forward with their basket and lanterns.

In this way, the coven made their rounds of the village, stopping at every house and home, and singing as they went. It would have been rather fun, if Cassie, Rue and Tabitha hadn't been desperately watching Ivy the whole time in case she slipped away and made for the Hedge.

'Come on, we're next,' said Tabitha, tugging on Cassie's elbow. They had, it seemed, drawn the short straw, for when Cassie knocked on the dark wood door of a rather imposing old house, it was answered by none other than Silas Saltash.

Cassie blanched. The apothecary, from whom they occasionally bought the rarer herbs and spell ingredients they could not grow or harvest in the wild, hated children and young witches especially.

He glowered at them. 'And who comes calling on All Hallows' Eve, be you wight or sprite?'

Saltash stared down his long nose at Cassie and at first she forgot the words she was meant to say, but then she realised the old man was wearing his dressing gown and slippers and this made him a good deal less intimidating.

'We are witches,' she managed to stutter out, 'come to wish you well and safe on this night.'

Saltash pulled his lips back in a half-sneer, leaning forward to inspect the contents of Tabitha's basket. At last, he selected a long, slim candle and dropped tuppence, shutting the door in their faces.

Rue winked at them as they made their way to the back of the line, from where Cassie could more easily keep an eye on Ivy.

By the time they'd visited everyone in the village, and their baskets were empty, it was nearly midnight and bitterly cold. The mist curled around their boots, nipping their stockinged knees and they were all happy to follow the Hedgewitch uphill to Hartwood, chatting and walking together in small huddles against the chill.

Oak Patrol walked behind Ivy and Phyllis Drake, who were counting the donations they'd received to figure out if they'd made the most that night.

'Maybe she *won't* try anything,' said Tabitha. 'I know Ivy may be a bit reckless sometimes, but she's no fool.'

But Cassie wasn't so sure. She wouldn't feel safe until the sun rose in a few hours and the long night was over.

Hartwood Hall was a blaze of light. There were jack-o'-lanterns in every window, grinning and grimacing at the girls as they made their way up the drive. Inside, they were met by Mrs Briggs, who herded them into the feasting hall, the grand room Cassie had helped to dust and decorate. A great Hallowe'en supper had been laid out for them, illuminated by dozens of candles. There were sugar imps and toffee apples, pumpkin pies and mash o' nine sorts, honey-glazed ham, soul cakes and a fruit loaf called a barmbrack, which Aoife had baked herself. Inside, she explained, were small charms which would tell your fate for the rest of the year.

The other Hedgely witches, Selena Moor and old Mrs Blight, were already helping themselves to the food, and Brogan was perched on a stool in one corner, tucking into a large mushroom turnover.

Lanterns and baskets, cloaks and hats were scattered about the room as the girls descended upon the feast, hungry after their night's exertions. But Cassie, Rue and Tabitha had barely reached the table when Mrs Briggs found them. 'Come along and help me with this punch bowl,' she said, rounding them up. 'We'll be needing more glasses too, and I could do with six more hands!'

Sebastian was in the kitchen, eating a solitary supper.

'What are you doing in here?' Cassie asked. 'Come and join us in the hall, there's an absolute mountain of food and—'

'And a dozen witches who all think I'm a thief,' said Sebastian.

Cassie winced and exchanged a meaningful look with Rue and Tabitha. They all knew who the real thief was, but they couldn't clear Sebastian's name without betraying Ivy – at least, not yet.

'We know you didn't do it,' said Tabitha. 'And we're sorry. Can we bring you anything?'

'I'm fine, don't let me spoil the fun.'

When they returned from the kitchen, bearing even more platters and plates of food, Cassie looked around the room for Ivy. She'd been standing by the fireplace before they'd left, reciting her lines for the Midwinter play before an audience composed entirely of her own patrol.

'She's gone!' hissed Cassie, and Tabitha had to rescue the plate of hazelnut biscuits Cassie was carrying before they ended up on the floor.

Rue made a quick round of the room, stopping to talk with Eliza Pepper, Ivy's patrol leader, and returning with a frown on her face.

'Ivy said she had to go home early, but I bet she's off to the Hedge.'

Miranda was showing Aoife the carvings on the old mantlepiece and this was, no doubt, why Ivy had chosen this moment to slip away. If they hurried, they might still catch her before she reached the woods.

Grabbing their cloaks and brooms, they slipped out through the entrance hall, making for the drive. The night was dark and moonless, and the mist still clung beneath the trees, but as they reached the beeches, they could see a figure flying ahead of them, her pointed black hat vanishing into the fog.

'Ivy!' Cassie called, but the girl sped away from them.

Mounting their brooms, they raced after her, and by the time they'd reached the stone bridge they had nearly caught up. But to their surprise, Ivy did not follow the river Nix up to the Hedge, but turned left, speeding down a dark lane that ran between some cottages and the village green, towards St Aelfwig's.

'What's she doing now?' asked Tabitha.

'She knows we're following, perhaps she's trying to lose us.'

By the time they came out of the dark lane, into the churchyard itself, Ivy was nowhere to be seen.

Chapter Twenty-Two

Followfoot Powder

Cassie, Rue and Tabitha found themselves standing just inside the lychgate, surrounded by looming stone monuments and the tall spires of yew trees. Ahead, the church rose out of the mist, reaching its square Norman tower into the starless sky. The clock on the tower showed that it was two in the morning, but no bells rang and the stained-glass windows were all dark.

'Let's go back,' said Tabitha, hesitant to take another step between the tombstones. 'We've lost her.'

'She's got to be here somewhere,' said Rue. 'She must be hiding.'

magic of Faerie and that temptation proves too great. But in turning their backs on us, they turn away from humanity, and from the responsibility we have to protect those we love.'

'What will happen to Renata now?'

'She'll be locked away in His Majesty's prison at Hexham – they have a special wing for witches and their familiars, although it has not been used in a very long time. No, the outcome of the trial was a foregone conclusion. What is far more important is the missing children. We do not know why the Erl King wants the children or what he plans to do with them – and they are still being stolen across Britain.'

'But we closed up the tunnel! Have the goblins found another way past the Hedge wards?'

'No, and I have seen far fewer signs of goblin activity here since Midsummer. But I fear he may have some other plan in place. He might even be behind these enchantments,' said the Hedgewitch, tapping the newspaper. 'Farmer Scrump, Mrs Mossley and now Ted Whitby. There certainly seems to be a pattern to the attacks.'

'Aunt Miranda, there's something I have to tell you...' Cassie began. 'Rue, Tabitha and I spent a night in the

'What if she only came this way to lose us? She could have turned back and be halfway to the Hedge by now,' said Cassie, torn between staying to look for Ivy amongst the graves and racing back the way they'd come to stop her before she reached the woods. 'I suppose we'd better at least take a quick look – there aren't too many places for her to hide.'

However, the mist and the darkness made the churchyard seem bigger and stranger than it ever had by daylight and progress was made difficult by the fallen leaves, which obscured the large flat grave markers and fallen tombstones, on which they tripped and stumbled. At one point, a fox darted out from behind a stone cross and Tabitha screeched.

'Don't worry, I'll protect you from any ghosts,' teased Rue. But as she turned to lead them up the path towards the church, they saw something coming out of the yew grove. Tall and slender, it wore a white gown and stretched out long, bare arms. Pale sleeves billowed around it as it rushed forward, seeming to fly over the grass. It let out a low, eerie cry.

'It's a wood wife!' cried Rue. 'Run!'

As one, they turned and scarpered, making for the lychgate, but as they reached it the eerie cry changed into childish laughter.

Turning, they saw that the ghostly figure had been cut in half, or rather, that one half of it was laying in the grass, clutching its side in a fit of giggles. The other half pulled a white sheet from its head and bowed to them. It was Susan and Phyllis Drake, with one of Mrs Briggs' tablecloths.

'Oh, you should have seen your faces!' said Susan, gasping for breath as she recovered from a laughing fit.

'Ivy was right, what a lark! Just wait until we tell the rest of the coven about this,' said Phyllis. 'Call yourselves witches? You ought to know there's no such thing as ghosts!'

'We didn't think you were a ghost, we thought—' began Tabitha.

'Wait, where *is* Ivy?' Cassie asked.

Susan shrugged. 'She said she'd meet us here after. I thought she'd be here to enjoy our little trick.'

'It was *you* we chased down the hill?' asked Cassie. A terrible realisation came over her – the prank had not only been intended to make laughing stocks of them, but to distract them while Ivy got away, making for her dreadful errand within the Hedge.

'We'll have to track her,' said Cassie as they reached the tree line, the point where the village ended and the Hedge began. It was almost pitch black in the woods, the carpet of fallen leaves obscured by the low-lying mist and the trees above reaching out bony branches towards them. None of the girls were keen to dash in without any notion of which direction Ivy had taken.

'Tabitha, have you still got the Followfoot powder?' asked Cassie.

'Yes, only, we need to find at least one of her footprints for it to work – there isn't enough in this jar to cover the whole forest looking for her.'

'She must have come this way from the village, but we'd better hurry, she's gained a considerable lead on us by using Susan and Phyllis as decoys.'

'I can't believe we let them get away with that!' said Rue. 'We ought to have chased them into the duck pond! Now we'll never hear the end of it.'

'This is more important,' said Cassie. 'We have to get to Ivy before she uses the flute!'

'You go right and I'll go left,' said Rue, pointing. 'It'll be hard to see footprints under all these leaves, and she might be on her broom – look out for signs above ground too.'

Cassie and Tabitha walked along the edge of the woods, Tabitha crouching down to inspect the grass while Cassie checked each holly and hawthorn they passed for signs that Ivy had come that way. It felt like such a slow way to go about it – every minute they spent trying to pick up the trail was taking Ivy closer to the Elder Mother.

They could hear Rue crunching through the leaves in the opposite direction, stopping every now and then to inspect the forest floor.

'Over here!' she cried. 'I've found something.'

Tabitha and Cassie backtracked to join her. Rue held out her hand. In it was a small circular fabric badge embroidered with a witch's hat, a clothes-brush and an iron.

'It's an award badge,' said Tabitha. 'For perfect uniform – that's got to be Ivy!'

'It was caught on this thorn bush – she must have come this way,' said Rue.

Together they searched the ground below, brushing away piles of copper leaves.

‘Here!’ called Cassie. Rue and Tabitha rushed over to where she was pointing to a small semi-circular imprint in the mud, no doubt left by the heel of someone’s boot.

‘We’d better be sure,’ said Tabitha. ‘We’ll only get one chance at this and if it’s someone else’s print…’

‘Oh, go on,’ said Rue. ‘I want to see this stuff in action.’

‘All right, have you got your sparkstone?’

Tabitha pulled a small jar of green powder from her pocket. It had holes in the top like a salt shaker, and she carefully dusted the footprint and the area around it, making sure to completely fill the heel-print.

‘Step back,’ said Tabitha. ‘I don’t want you to disturb anything while I recite the incantation.’ She raised her hands over the print and spoke in a clear, calm voice:

‘Follow foot, follow foot, wherever you roam,
Wherever you wander, through leaf or loam.
To me, this traveller’s route betray
And light a path to lead the way.’

Finishing her spell, Tabitha bent down and struck a single spark from Rue’s stone. They each held their breath as it touched the powder. At first, nothing happened, then, slowly, the edges of the print began to glimmer, like a piece of paper set to light. The glow burned through the powder, lighting up the whole print and then fizzled out, but as it did, the other half of the footprint appeared, marked out in glowing sparks on the compacted earth. As this too faded, a second print appeared, just ahead of them, pointing into the woods.

'Quickly,' said Tabitha. 'If we don't keep up, we'll lose them.'

They followed the glowing footprints into the forest as each lit up and vanished, regardless of what lay beneath.

They had to jog to keep up – Ivy had clearly been moving at quite a pace. As they went, Cassie wondered how she'd ever managed to find her way back to the Elder Mother, in the darkness, with no path to follow. It was then she heard the voices, rustling through the leaves above them, just as she had the day she and Ivy had been foraging in the wood.

'Did you hear that?' she asked, grabbing Rue's shoulder.

'What? The wind?'

'No, it was a voice... I'm sure of it, it said... *daughter*.'

'I didn't hear anything, Cassie,' said Tabitha. 'Maybe it was a bird. Come on, we're losing the trail.'

They ran to catch up with the glowing footprints, which led them ever deeper into the woods, through thickets of hazel and wild cherry, under tangled arches of briar rose and past pools of still water filling the root-holes of fallen trees.

They passed a hollow willow tree and reached a narrow stream which cut deep into the earth, making a channel-like drain beneath them.

'Where is it?' asked Rue. 'I can't see the next footprint.'

Tabitha was panting. 'We've lost it, we've lost the trail.'

'No, I don't think so,' said Cassie. 'Look at this last print – both feet are together. She's stopped for something. She had her broom, didn't she? She must have flown from here.'

'But why here?' asked Rue, looking around.

'There!' said Cassie, pointing to the dead willow. Carved into the greying wood was the faery rune, Faru, its feathery arrow shape pointing the way. 'She's left herself markers, just like we did when we were looking for Ambrose.'

'Only, we ran into the wood wyrm,' said Tabitha, rubbing her arms and peering into the gloomy shadows. 'You don't suppose she's about tonight...?'

'Hullo! Here's another rune,' called Rue. 'She must have gone this way, come on. We can fly too, now we've got the path again.'

They mounted their brooms and flew after Rue, who led the way, weaving between tree trunks and ducking beneath low-hanging branches. It was challenging flying in the dark, and Cassie was glad that Rue was leading as it took all her concentration just to stay on Tantivy and avoid the thrashing twigs.

Suddenly, Rue pulled to a stop, forcing Tabitha and Cassie to yank on their brooms to avoid a collision and roll into a thicket of bilberry bushes beside her.

'Shhh!' said Rue, dropping to the ground with her broom and using the witch sign to signal that they do the same.

'What is it?' whispered Tabitha.

But Rue only shook her head and pointed directly in front of them.

Slowly, careful not to make a sound, Cassie rose up on her knees and peered out over the bushes. At first she could not see anything that might have alarmed Rue, just the spindly trunks of young ash trees, still with their clusters of keys clinging to their otherwise bare branches and the mist creeping around their roots. But then she saw a shadow between the trees, just where Rue had pointed. It was hard to make out, for it had no solid edges and appeared only as a deeper patch of darkness in the gloaming. Cassie thought it was merely a shadow cast by some stone or tree, but then it began to move, drifting towards them. It was at least seven feet tall and had a vague, almost human shape, but no face or eyes.

Cassie ducked down, pulling Tabitha with her and pressing her face into the dry leaves, desperately hoping that it had not sensed their presence.

The shadow rolled over them, blocking out the light so that they were temporarily blinded. Cassie hid her face in the crook of her elbow and held her breath. A horrible sensation washed over her, deeply disquieting. It made her think of her mother, of her smile, her soft laughter and she felt the familiar ache of a wound torn open. She remembered the day she had been left at Fowell House, only six years old, abandoned and alone. All the years spent waiting came back to her, suffocating in their weary loneliness. She felt weighed down by hopelessness, exhausted, unable to do so much as lift her head. Then the shadowy shape passed over them and drifted away, taking with it the darkness and the oppressive weight of its presence.

At last, they all three sat up and looked at each other.

'What was that thing? I could hardly breathe...' Tabitha began.

'Oliver,' said Rue. 'It made me think of when Oliver was taken by the goblins, when I thought it was my fault. The fear that he was gone for good...'

Cassie nodded. She couldn't even express her own sense of loss, of utter despair that she would never find a way to save her mother. All she knew was that whatever that thing was, she did not want to encounter it again.

'Come on,' said Rue, helping Tabitha up. 'We need to catch up with Ivy and I want to put as much distance between us and *that* as possible.'

Fortunately, they had not gone far from the last rune, and Cassie soon found the next, leading them on through the darkening wood. Soon, the trees changed again, growing shorter and more twisted. They had left behind the tall and solid oaks, beeches and ash and now found themselves in a grove of twisting grey-green trees, the ground beneath covered in a carpet of ivy and dying nettles.

They halted their brooms in a clearing, landing one by one on the damp earth.

'I can't see any more runes,' said Rue.

They spent a few minutes searching the trees but found nothing. The ground was damp and the trees themselves were covered in pelts of green moss and lichen. Even the mist seemed green with it.

'We must be close,' said Cassie. 'These are all elder trees!'

Above them twisted the branches of a hundred elder trees, each contorted into different shapes, some bushy with twigs, other sinuous and snakelike in their winding trunks, and a few split in half by weight or lightning, their grey trunks strewn across the path.

'There must be a thousand of them!' said Tabitha. 'How are we supposed to find the Elder Mother's tree?'

Cassie turned around in a circle, peering at each tree in turn. They all looked different, but none were particularly big or old, and she could make out no faces or signs in their bark.

Cassie felt a prickly sensation on her hand and looked down to see a small golden spider crawling over her wrist. She brushed it off, and when she looked up again she saw it: a little hut, grey-green like the trees, with a roof of black thatch and a single door. How had they not seen it as soon as they reached the clearing?

'I suppose we should go inside,' said Cassie, bracing herself to approach the hut.

'Inside what?' asked Rue.

Cassie frowned and pointed. 'Inside the house. Ivy must have gone in there. I don't really fancy the look of it, but we have to stop her before—'

'Cassie,' said Tabitha. 'There *is* no house. There's nothing there but an old tree.'

'Turn around, like I did – no, not that way, counter-clockwise!' said Cassie.

Rue and Tabitha spun around, over and over.

'I can see three of the same tree now,' said Rue, wobbling a little. 'But no house.'

Cassie rubbed her own eyes, wondering if she'd fallen under some sort of enchantment.

'Must be a glamour,' said Rue, stepping forward to inspect the tree. She rapped on it with her knuckles; it was solid to the touch. 'Faery magic. Someone doesn't want us to see the house, but for whatever reason, Cass, you can.'

Cassie frowned. She didn't like this sort of magic, it reminded her of the feast in the Riddlewood, the delicious food that had turned to decay and maggots when the spell was broken. She had no way of knowing which was real – the house or the tree.

'I suppose I'll have to go in alone then.'

'We'll be right here,' said Tabitha. 'If you need us, just call.'

Cassie took a deep breath and opened the door.

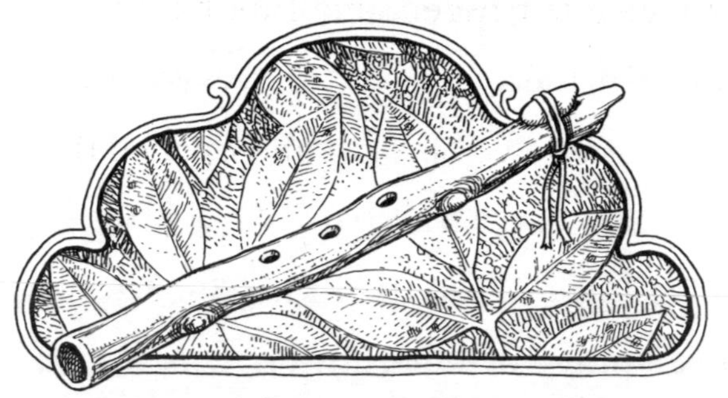

Chapter Twenty-Three

Hyldamor

It was surprisingly bright inside the little house, although Cassie couldn't tell where the light was coming from. She found herself standing in a simple room, with walls and floor of the same pale wood. There were no windows, but there was a second door at the back of the room, a green door, with swirling designs on it, and in the centre of the room, a table. Seated at the table, the flute in her hands, was Ivy.

'You!' she said, leaping to her feet and clutching the flute to her chest. 'You followed me!'

'We had to, Ivy,' said Cassie. 'You can't trust the Elder Mother. Lailoken said she always—'

'Go away! You shouldn't be here, you'll ruin everything!' Ivy snapped.

'Now then, there's plenty for everyone,' said a gentle voice.

Cassie and Ivy turned to see a little old woman standing at the back of the room. She had wispy white hair, like sprays of elderflower, which curled about her ancient, lined face. On her head she wore a black bonnet and her dress was green, with a purple apron. She was carrying a pot of something, but what struck Cassie about her appearance were her eyes, which were small and dark, with no whites to them, and glossy, like elderberries. Cassie had expected the tree hag to be terrifying, all sharp teeth and clawed hands, and was caught off-guard by the glistening eyes and soft smile of this tiny grandmother.

'Here we are now. You poor dears must be so hungry. Why don't you have a seat?'

Cassie and Ivy found themselves seated at the table. There were wooden bowls before them. Cassie was sure the bowls had not been there when she had entered the house.

Into each bowl the old woman ladled a deep purple liquid, somewhat lumpy, like a rich beetroot soup but also, Cassie thought with a shudder, like clotted blood.

A spoon appeared in Cassie's hand, made of the same grey wood.

'Ah, my poor motherless girls,' said the woman, stroking Ivy's short dark hair. 'Left all alone in the world to fend for yourselves. No one to love you, no one to care for you, no one to *feed* you... do eat up, dears.'

Cassie was in no way tempted by the dark mess in the wooden bowl.

'Don't eat it, Ivy. She's a faery – you know we shouldn't touch—'

The old woman shot her a dark look. 'There now, that's no way to accept hospitality. But then, you've not had a mother to teach you manners, have you? Poor love.'

But Ivy was no more interested in the soup than Cassie was. She turned to the old woman, clutching the flute. 'Is it time now? You said if I come on All Hallows' Eve, during the witching hour—'

'Yes, yes, patience, my sweet. It is nearly time, can't you feel it?' She turned to Cassie. 'And you, dear, you've come all this way; you too must have someone you wish to see?'

'Someone?' asked Cassie.

'Someone lost, gone to the other side, someone you long to speak with again...'

Cassie's heart was beating fast. What if it was true? What if the Elder Mother really had the power to bring someone back from Faerie? If Cassie blew on the flute, would her mother hear it? Would she come?

'But I'm the one who brought the flute!' said Ivy. 'It's my wish you're supposed to grant.'

'Of course, my precious girl,' said the old woman, laying her hands on Ivy's shoulders. 'You shall go first. Come now, it is time, the old roads stand open. We must try my little door.'

They were standing once more; the table, the bowls, the spoons had all vanished and the light, which had been bright as day, now dimmed to a late evening glow.

The Elder Mother took Ivy by the hand and led her to the green door, which had doubled in size. Opening it wide, the Elder Mother stood back and Cassie and Ivy peered through. There was nothing on the other side but darkness.

'Now then,' said the old woman, 'three notes, clear and true – just as I showed you.'

Ivy raised the flute to her lips and blew. A single high note pierced the air and, as Cassie watched, the darkness behind the door faded to a pale purple light with pinpricks in it, like stars. Beneath the stars a wood came into view, and beyond the wood, through a break in the trees, they could see rolling hills, winding rivers and, in the distance, mountains, impossibly high. The colours were vivid, brighter than anything in the real world. The grass was greener, the waters bluer and the sky lit by some bright light that came from neither moon nor sun.

'Is that really...' Cassie asked, unable to contain herself. 'The land of Faerie?'

'Yes, my dear,' said the Elder Mother softly. 'The sunless lands, the timeless realm, where it is always summer and never winter, where none are born and none may die. Is that your wish, my darling? To go through that door? To join someone you love?'

Cassie took a step towards the doorway, so as to better see the view. A breeze drifted towards them, and on it they could taste flowers and silver and some spice that Cassie could not name. There was music coming from the trees. Was it birdsong or people singing? She could not tell, but it lifted her spirits and made her heart ache with longing all at once. Wisp lights danced between the shadowy trunks and the leaf of a fern waved at her, just inside the door. She had only to reach out her hand and she might touch it.

Ivy raised the flute again and blew another note, lower this time. The breeze grew colder, and a shadow stepped through the woods towards them. It was a tall figure, made taller by the crown of antlers rising from its head, and as it walked, black tattered robes flowed about it.

'Ivy, stop! That's not your mother,' said Cassie, who had seen the figure once before, when the phooka had taken his master's shape to frighten her.

But Ivy's eyes were closed. She moved her fingers along the bone-like flute and raised it to her lips once more to play the final note.

Cassie leapt forward and snatched the flute from her hands.

'Wait!' cried Ivy. 'Give that back.'

Someone laughed. It was a young man's laugh, warm and light, and it echoed inside the small wooden room.

The Erl King was standing on the other side of the doorway. His tall form threw a long shadow over them, the strange light of Faerie outlining the tines of his stag-skull mask. Cassie took a step back, dragging Ivy with her.

'Who are you?' asked Ivy. 'Are you the faery who cursed my mother?'

They could not see his face, or his hands – he was completely obscured by mask and robes.

'Ah, now this is a familiar scene,' said the Erl King, his voice softer and younger than Cassie had expected. 'Curious, isn't it? The way events reprise themselves in your world. Years fold in on each other like pages in a book, and once again I find two friends, one fair, one dark, come to seek the Elder Mother's blessing, to gain entrance to a world forbidden to mortal kind.'

'We are not friends,' hissed Ivy.

'Ah, but your mothers were. They came to Hyldamor's grove, oh, more than seven years ago it must be, by your time.'

'They did? But why?' asked Cassie, still clutching the flute. In the back of her head a voice that sounded a lot like Montague's was warning her against this, against speaking with the Erl King, against believing a word he said, but she ignored it. Cassie needed to know what had happened that night and until now, no one had ever been able to tell her.

'They came, just as you have, to summon one who was lost to them, only that is not quite how the magic works. Your mother, Cassandra Morgan, saw what she had lost – but could not reach it, not unless she stepped through the door. The temptation was, I fear, too great; she was always an impulsive creature. She saw him where I stand now, her true love, after all those years, still alive and waiting...'

Cassie took a step towards the door. Was he telling the truth? Was that really why her mother had crossed into Faerie, to rescue the man she loved? And could he be...

'My father?' asked Cassie.

The Erl King ignored her question. 'You have the flute, you have only to blow a single note and you may find them yourself. You may step across the threshold, as she did, recover what you have lost – love, family, the truth of who you are.'

Cassie looked down at the flute in her hands. The door was open before her, the way she'd longed to find; she did not need her aunt's permission or Lailoken's help. She could just step through, as easy as breathing. It was all she had wanted since she'd first come to Hedgely, since she'd learned where her mother had gone – to follow her, to find her and bring her back. And yet, she was not the same girl; the summer had changed her and she had grown more in these six past months, she felt, than in all the seven long years before. She had Tabitha and Rue, waiting for her in the grove, and Miranda, Mrs Briggs, Brogan and Montague. She had a home and a coven, and by opening the way, by letting the Erl King through she put all of them at risk. She could have all she desired, yes, but at what cost? Lailoken's words came back to her: *as with most things in this world, those who take the easy way pay the steeper price.*

Cassie raised the flute in both hands and snapped it in two.

'No!' cried Ivy, grabbing at the splintered halves. 'What have you done?'

'A poor choice,' said the Erl King, and Cassie could detect a change in his voice. Gone was the light humour, the teasing lilt. Now there was ice in his words. 'The great magics always require a sacrifice. Your mother was stronger, she freely gave up her own child, abandoning her to this world, to never know who she was, believing always that her mother would someday return, waiting, hoping—'

'Stop it!' said Cassie, covering her ears.

'And my mother? What happened to my mother?' asked Ivy.

'Your mother is not in Faerie, child, she is here, in this very grove. In every leaf and root. Do not fear, soon you will join her, both of you.'

'But I don't understand, how...?'

'Come on, Ivy,' said Cassie, reaching for her again. 'He can't come through. Let's go, before...' But as she turned back to the first door, the one they had come through, she found only a rough knot of wood.

The Erl King laughed again. 'I had hoped to make use of this door, it is true. And I paid the doorkeeper handsomely for the service – two young motherless girls. Her favourite meal. She will have quite the Hallowtide feast tonight.'

Cassie looked about, but the little old woman had vanished; there was only the tree and the door and Ivy, looking small and frightened.

'This is but one of the old roads,' said the Erl King. 'Soon I shall have control of another, once its watchdog is put down. My servant has nearly found the tool I need – in fact, they've just found the perfect assistant.'

The spear, Cassie realised. He was talking about the spear.

'Goodbye, Cassandra, I'll give your regards to Rose.'

The Erl King stepped back into the shadows of the wood, and as he did, their view of Faerie was darkening, fading, receding until it dissolved entirely and the green hills, the purple skies and the white mask of the Erl King himself vanished.

Ivy ran towards the doorway, reaching after him, but the green door slammed shut in her face and was already shrinking, vanishing into the wood grain.

'What have you done?' she said, turning to Cassie, fury in her eyes. 'That was my last chance to bring her back, to see my mother again. You of all people ought to have understood!'

'I do understand,' said Cassie. 'I made the same mistake. I trusted one of them, a faery – I risked everything to bring my mother back, but Ivy, it's never that easy, there's always a price.'

'Easy? You think all of this was easy? I found the Elder Mother's tree, I stole the flute – do you think that was simple? Unlike you, I don't go about breaking the rules just for the fun of it!'

'Ivy, it was all a trick, can't you see that? And now we're stuck inside this house and...'

But as she looked around she saw it was no longer a house, but the hollow inside of a tree. The floor beneath them was leaf mould and the ceiling had vanished, to be replaced by a dark and narrow cavity reaching high above them. Both doors were gone; there was no way in or out.

Cassie ran to the nearest side and beat upon the wood. 'Rue, Tabitha!' she cried. 'We can't get out!' She pressed her ear to the wood but no sound returned, only the groaning of the tree itself, as the wind moved through the branches far above.

Ivy sat down on the leafy ground and wrapped her arms around her knees.

'We have to find a way out,' said Cassie. 'Have you got your knife?'

But Ivy ignored her. 'It's no use, they're going to take her away... there's nothing left to try.'

Cassie dug her own pen knife out of her pocket and inserted it into a crack in the tree trunk. Something wet trickled out over her hand, and the wood groaned and creaked. Cassie tried again, forcing the knife in to make a deeper cut, desperate to make her own door where the other had vanished. The tree groaned again and her knife stuck fast in the wood, she yanked on it, but it would not come out.

What else could she try? A spell to break the enchantment? But she was pretty sure the house had been the glamour and that this hollow tree they found themselves trapped in was all too real.

'Rue!' she called again. 'Tabitha! We're in here!' But whether or not her friends could hear her, there was little they could do from the outside. Perhaps they had already left? Gone to fetch the Hedgewitch or an axe to bring down the tree. An axe – that was it!

Cassie felt around in the pockets of her cloak until she found a small wooden shape that fitted in the palm of her hand – the nightingale whistle that Lailoken had given her, its wings flexed as if in mid-flight, its mouth open. She lifted it to her lips and blew through the tip of the tail. It let out a high, sweet trill, altogether unlike the deep eerie notes of the elder flute. She blew again.

She could only hope that somehow the sound might reach the woodwose.

'It doesn't make sense. My mother – why did she come here in the first place?' asked Ivy.

Cassie sat down in the leaves beside her. 'If what the Erl King said was true, then Tamsin must be the friend my mother mentioned in her letter, the one who offered to help her get to Faerie. I'm sure she thought she was doing the right thing. She can't have known about the price...'

'It's all your fault, Cassie Morgan! Your mother was just as selfish as you are and now my mother is... she's...'

'There must still be a way to help her, we'll keep looking,' said Cassie.

'Don't touch me!'

'I didn't,' Cassie replied, but as she said it, she felt a pressure against her back. It was the trunk of the tree. As they'd sat talking in the dark, the wooden walls had been shrinking in on them. Cassie reached out her hands and they met splintery, wet wood. She was pressed up against Ivy. They couldn't see and they couldn't move. The tree groaned, an echoing, sinister sound. Soon, they wouldn't be able to breathe either.

'Rue! Tabitha!' Cassie cried, beating her fists on the wood. But her shrieks were absorbed by the dense sapwood of the tree.

Chapter Twenty-Four

A Stretcher for Sebastian

There was an ear-splitting crack. Both girls jumped up. The sound came again and the whole tree shook and groaned under the impact. A third blow let a thin strip of light into the hollow, which was quickly blocked by half a face, peering in at them.

'They're safe! I can see them!' cried Rue.

'Step back,' said another voice, warm and dry like bark.

Another ear-splitting crack reverberated through the wood and finally they could see the outside world once more as light flooded into the dark chamber. Rue's small brown hand reached in and Cassie took it. She had to squeeze her way out through the slit in the tree, and caught her hair and cloak on the splintered wood as Rue drew her to safety. Next it was Ivy's turn, but she refused all assistance, pulling herself out and going to stand a few feet away from them, arms crossed and glowering.

'All right, Cass?' asked Rue. 'You had us worried there.'

'You were inside that tree for hours!' said Tabitha. 'We had no idea what was happening. We were about to go and find the Hedgewitch when we heard your whistle. Are you hurt?'

'No, I think I'm all right...' She looked at the broken flute she still clutched in one hand.

Lailoken towered over them, the stone axe in his hand and a deep frown on his face. He wasn't looking at the girls he'd just rescued, but at the split tree. It was in a sorry state, its great trunk rent asunder.

'The Elder Mother, is she dead?' asked Cassie.

'One such as she does not fade so easily, nor is she bound to a single tree, look.'

He pointed to the gash where Cassie and Ivy had emerged and she saw something shimmering and golden. Cassie stepped closer and saw that the rim of living gold was made up of thousands of tiny, yellow spiders. One by one they let out a thread of silk and released their grip on the tree, floating off into the air.

'Come,' said the woodwose. 'The danger has not yet passed, for it is still one of the thin nights and humans should not be about in the woods. I will lead you home.'

Cassie, Rue and Tabitha followed the woodwose immediately, while Ivy trailed behind, staring at her boots. A wind had picked up, blowing away the mist like cobwebs and stirring the branches above them, sending down showers of brown and yellow leaves. Lailoken led them up a narrow path, leaving the elder grove behind and winding between the comforting trunks of oak and birch, rowan and ash.

As they walked, Cassie told Tabitha and Rue what they had witnessed within the Elder Mother's tree.

'Do you mean to say you actually met the Erl King, Cass? In the flesh... or the bone or what have you?' asked Rue, eyebrows raised.

'What did he say to you?' asked Tabitha, frowning.

'A lot of things. He's close to finding the spear, he said something about another of the old roads and putting down a watchdog?'

'Galtres,' said Lailoken. 'It is possible that he means to destroy her.'

'Surely not,' said Tabitha. 'She's the last of her kind. If he kills her...'

'Then he might bring through an army of goblins on the next Crossing Night, and thus control the Riddlewood and the border.'

Cassie, Rue and Tabitha walked on in silence, as the possibility of this sank in.

'He said something else,' said Cassie. 'About my mother and Ivy's mother – they came here together, seven years ago, to seek the Elder Mother's help.'

'A woman,' said Lailoken, frowning. 'I found a woman not far from the elder grove, seven winters past, sleeping as if she would never wake. I brought her to the edge of the wood, in sight of your village. She still lives?'

'You found Tamsin?' asked Cassie. 'Did you hear that, Ivy—'

'Hush!' said the woodwose, holding up a dark hand. 'Someone is coming.'

All four girls stared into the woods, listening with all their might for whatever it was Lailoken had sensed. Cassie thought of the shadow they'd encountered earlier and shuddered.

At first they heard nothing, and then there was a soft clacking, and the crack-snap of a broken twig.

Their heads swung in unison in the direction of the sound.

Two figures emerged from the darkness. Leading the way was a tall dark-haired woman in a long black cloak, walking as silently as Lailoken himself. They'd never have heard her but for the other figure, tripping along behind her in a yellow cloak, her bracelets clattering and her long hair blown about by the wind.

'I'm sure they can't have got far,' said Aoife Early.

'They do not need to get very far to encounter trouble, Miss Early, and I hope you have not been *encouraging* their reckless behaviour.'

The Hedgewitch stopped as she saw Lailoken and the girls. Montague was with her, as was her own familiar, the black cat, Malkin.

'Well met, Hedgewitch,' said the woodwose. 'As you see, no harm has come to your young charges, although they have perhaps learned a lesson this night about treating with tree hags.'

'Well met, Lailoken,' said Miranda. 'Tree hags, is it? Stars forbid you three should spend a Crossing Night at home when you could be out here risking life and limb.'

'We were only trying to stop Ivy,' said Rue.

'Ivy? Whatever possessed you to get mixed up in all of this? I'd have thought you at least had the common sense to avoid such mischief. But I will hear the full tale when we are safely back at Hartwood. I see the four of you remain relatively unharmed, but where is Sebastian?'

'Sebastian?' asked Cassie, as Montague joined her, twining between her legs.

'He's been missing for hours, we thought he'd gone into the Hedge with you!' said Aoife.

'I haven't seen him since the feast,' said Cassie. She had just remembered something, a promise she'd made and unwittingly broken – to take Sebastian with them next time they entered the Hedge.

'He went this way,' said Montague, trotting ahead of them, his tail held up like a flag. 'The boy has been wandering around about like a dizzy woodlouse, but my whiskers indicate he was traveling deeper into the woods.'

It was Montague who had found Cassie in London, what seemed like a lifetime ago. He could always find a Morgan, he'd explained, and she supposed that even though Sebastian was technically a Penhallow he still counted as one of the family. If he'd been stumbling about in the Hedge for hours he might have encountered goblin nabbers, the wood wyrm, or worse. If anything had happened to her cousin it would be Cassie's fault, or at least the Hedgewitch was bound to see it that way. And perhaps she would be right to. Cassie had promised to take Sebastian with them on their next excursion into the Hedge, although she'd really meant mushrooming or catching imps, not chasing after Ivy as she attempted to summon her mother from Faerie. Still, Sebastian would not have seen it that way and she should have checked on him first. If only there'd been more time she could have explained and maybe prevented him from following them. There was no way he could have kept up once they mounted their brooms, and now he was lost and alone somewhere in the deep woods.

Lailoken made his farewells and left the girls with Miranda and Aoife, warning them not to stray near the Riddlewood that night of all nights. Cassie, Rue and Tabitha followed Montague, with the Hedgewitch, Aoife and Ivy trailing behind.

The wind whipped their hair and made their cloaks flap about them as they searched. The Hedgewitch would not let them call out Sebastian's name, for fear of attracting unwanted attention, but she held a sprite lamp to warn them of any faery presence. Cassie watched her aunt's face as the blue flame within flickered and flared, and peered into the dark branches above and the thickets around them. It was a Crossing Night, and every faery in the Hedge would be abroad.

Montague paused at a point where the path forked in two, lifting his nose to the air.

'You've not lost him?' Cassie asked, crouching down beside her familiar.

Montague sniffed. 'Really, Cassandra, I am offended by that remark. You ought to have a little more faith in my abilities by now. I was merely confirming my natural instinct with the faculty of reason, one you would do well to cultivate yourself. The boy has only just passed this way. If you were to use your eyes for once you would not need me to tell you which path he chose.'

The leaves were too deep on the ground to carry footprints, and they were all out of Followfoot powder, but when Cassie looked at the young trees lining either path, she saw that those on the left path had been damaged, their twigs bent or broken off and trodden upon, and one young sapling crushed where it stood in the way. Whoever had gone that way had no idea how to move through the woods carefully and had very likely been running from something.

The path led them downhill into a little gully, rimmed with tree roots. Lying at the bottom in the leaf litter was her cousin. His eyes were closed and he wasn't moving.

'Sebastian!' cried Cassie, ignoring the Hedgewitch's warning.

Tabitha pushed past her and ran to his side, feeling for a pulse. 'He's alive,' she called back, and Cassie let out the breath she'd been holding. 'But unconscious – he must have hit his head falling down here.'

Cassie and Rue joined her. There was blood on Sebastian's arm, which was scraped and bruised, and the angle of his ankle looked all wrong, but he was breathing at least.

Aoife crouched down and laid a hand on his arm. 'He's too cold, we must get him back to Hartwood and see to him there.'

'But how?' asked Tabitha. 'Surely we can't move him, he might have broken something, and what if he's concussed?'

'Cassandra, Rue, your brooms – lay them down here beside him.'

Following the Hedgewitch's instructions, they constructed a stretcher, tying Miranda's long cloak between the two brooms to make a sling into which they rolled the unconscious boy, very carefully. They piled their own cloaks on him for warmth and, with one hand each on their brooms, bade them to rise. The stretcher hovered between them, with Tantivy on one side and Blaze on the other, bearing Sebastian's weight.

They made a strange procession on the way back to Hedgely, with the Hedgewitch leading the way, her sprite lamp held high, followed by a dejected-looking Ivy, and with Cassie and Rue guiding the stretcher and Tabitha constantly fussing over Sebastian. Aoife followed behind, looking for all the world as though they were merely taking a nice stroll in the woods.

Back at Hartwood, the feasting hall was silent and empty of guests, the rest of the coven having returned to their homes and beds. The tables were still laden with half-eaten platters of food, used glasses and guttering candles.

'Oh my gooses and ganders!' cried Mrs Briggs, rushing to meet them. 'Here, give him to me. Tabitha, there's hot water on the stove – I was just about to start the washing up. Fetch it for me, there's a dove, and Rue, see if you can't find some clean towels.' She lifted Sebastian bodily from the stretcher, as if he weighed no more than a loaf of bread, and carried him up the stairs towards his room.

Miranda turned to Cassie and Ivy, who stood before her, neither wishing to meet her gaze.

'Now, you will both tell me what has occurred tonight, in *detail*.'

Cassie looked at Ivy's sullen face and sighed. She would have to explain, there was no way around it.

She described everything, from the moment they found Ivy's trail to Hyldamor, the Erl King and their rescue by Lailoken. Cassie tried to be fair, because she understood why Ivy had stolen the flute, but whichever way you put it, Ivy did not come out of the story well.

'Show me your wrists,' said Miranda. 'Both of you.'

They held out their hands and Cassie gasped as she saw they had matching red marks on their skin, although Ivy's had begun to fade.

'The bite of the dreamweaver spider,' said Miranda, fishing in her cloak for a small silver flask. 'Drink this, a good mouthful.'

Cassie took a swig of the potion, which tasted of bitter herbs and charcoal, and handed it to Ivy to do the same.

'That is why only you two could see the Elder Mother's house. She uses the spiders to lure in her victims. The venom is not poisonous, but has a subtle effect on the mind, enhancing one's dreams and one's willingness to chase after them, blurring the line between truth and reality. I suspect you have not been sleeping well, Ivy?'

Ivy shook her head. 'She showed me things, in my dreams, my mother...'

'It is a powerful enchantment, one that feeds on your own emotions and desires, but it does not rob you of your free will. The choices you made have put the safety of everyone in this village – in this country – at risk. A witch must learn to think of others' needs, before her own.'

'But, Hedgewitch...!'

'I am sure you believed you were doing the right thing by your mother, but the fact remains that you have stolen a magical item and used it to attempt to open a way into Faerie. Had you succeeded, who knows what you might have let through? Your behaviour shows an extremely poor sense of judgement and, were you a licensed witch, would be seen by the Witches' Assembly as oath-breaking. You are hereby suspended from coven and will not take part in the Midwinter play.'

Ivy was stunned. She said nothing, simply staring at the Hedgewitch as if she had been struck. Ivy, the perfect witch who never put a foot wrong, who passed every test and trial with flying colours, who was frequently praised and held up as an example by the Hedgewitch, was now forced to accept her punishment.

'Brogan is waiting on the drive, he will take you home,' said the Hedgewitch, and with that, Ivy was dismissed.

'Cassandra, you should have come to me the minute you suspected that Ivy planned to use the flute.'

Cassie hung her head, awaiting her punishment.

'However, despite the unnecessary risks you and your patrol took this night, you did well to resist what the Elder Mother offered you. I am pleased to see that you have at least learned that much from your past encounters with the folk of Faerie.'

Cassie lifted her head, staring at her aunt. Had she heard right? Had her aunt actually been impressed by her actions? It was hard to be sure.

'We will talk more of this in the morning, for now, get some rest.' The Hedgewitch nodded towards the staircase that wound about the Hartwood tree and watched as Cassie climbed, feeling the fatigue wash over her, making every step an effort.

'Oh, and Cassandra,' called the Hedgewitch as she was halfway up. 'It appears there is now a role in the Midwinter performance that must be filled. You will play Morgana.'

Chapter Twenty-Five

The Attic

Sebastian woke at dawn, a few hours after they'd brought him back from the Hedge, but he was weak and plagued by constant chills. Tabitha had made a poultice from fresh herbs; plantain, marigold and woundwort, to help his arm heal. She showed Cassie how to change it for a fresh one each day. Mrs Briggs kept a close eye on Sebastian too, bringing him warming stews and quantities of peppermint tea.

Miranda had sent an imp to Elliot, asking him to come and collect Sebastian and received a message in return, explaining that Elliot could not get away until Saturday week, leaving his son in their care for another ten days.

Cassie wondered what could be keeping her uncle so busy that he couldn't find time to come to Sebastian's bedside. She felt sure that his presence would make all the difference.

'Well, he'll be right as rain soon enough,' said Mrs Briggs. 'All he needs is good food and good company, if you ask me.'

The following evening, the housekeeper sent Cassie up to Sebastian with a bowl of creamy pumpkin soup, sprinkled with parsley. She placed the tray by his bed.

'You really should try to eat something,' she said. 'You want to be well enough to go home with Uncle Elliot.'

But her cousin merely stared at the ceiling with a vacant expression. He'd said barely a word since he'd woken, and wouldn't tell anyone what had happened to him in the woods.

Cassie tried reading to Sebastian, both from his science magazines and her story books, although he did not pay much heed to either. Finally, she pulled out her dog-eared script and began to go over her lines. She had rather a lot of them now that she was playing the lead.

'The wyrm is banished,' she read. 'But you, sir, shall not leave us. I have here a most potent potion, of nettle root and honeywine, sweet melilot and selumbine. Take but one sip and you shall be restored, to the strength and power you had before.'

Cassie looked up from the script, expecting some comment from her cousin about this concoction. He merely lay there, his eyes vacant. She skipped over Rue's lines to her next bit.

'Arise, sir knight and take up your sword and spear once more!'

Sebastian sat up suddenly and turned to her, a look of intense interest replacing his listless expression. 'The treasure? Have you found it?' he asked.

Cassie, taken aback by this sudden change in his demeanour, shook her head. 'No, we haven't had much time to look this past week, what with Ivy and the flute. PC Griffiths came around to apologise for accusing you, by the way. Aunt Miranda explained what happened and he's told everyone in the village, so your name is cleared.'

Sebastian shook his head as if none of this mattered. 'You haven't discovered anything at all, then?'

It was the most animated she'd seen him since Hallowe'en; a healthy flush had returned to his cheeks and his eyes were bright and eager. Perhaps if she'd included Sebastian in their search for the spear, taken him along on their expedition, he might have been happier here in

Hedgely. In trying to protect him from the dangers of the Hedge, she'd also pushed him away, leaving him out of all the excitement he so obviously craved. Maybe this was a chance for them to start over, and although he wasn't a witch, he was clever enough and they could use some fresh ideas just now. So Cassie told him all they knew – about Toby's journal, Sir Egad and Galtres and the deathly fate that awaited any who touched the spear.

'Well, if this witch Nimue was the last one to have it, and she lived hundreds of years ago, then that narrows things down a bit,' said Sebastian, once she'd finished talking. 'There can't be many places in Hedgely that have been around that long, can there?'

'Hartwood Hall has, I think,' said Cassie. 'Mrs Briggs said it's nearly eight hundred years old.'

'Then that's where we ought to begin. Here, fetch me those trousers, will you? My torch is in the pocket.'

'You want to start looking now?' asked Cassie, a little surprised by his sudden recovery.

'No time like the present,' said Sebastian, grinning.

'Watch your step there, ducks, the rung's missing,' said Mrs Briggs, peering down at Cassie through a hole in the ceiling. Cassie had never been in the Hartwood attic before, and it had taken them nearly an hour to find the entrance – behind a tapestry with a unicorn on it, at the end of a hallway on the third floor.

'Used to be you could climb up here by going through a hidden door in the black-and-white bathroom,' Mrs Briggs had explained. 'But I haven't been able to find it for months.'

Cassie ascended the ladder, which creaked ominously beneath her, and soon found herself in a cavernous space with a sloping roof formed of heavy oak beams. Sebastian clambered up behind her.

Every surface was coated in a fine layer of faery dust, which shimmered softly in the dim light. Cassie lifted her candlestick, illuminating forms and shapes shrouded in sheets.

The attic was stuffed with old unwanted things, the detritus of centuries of Hedgewitches and their families. There were boxes of books and crates of old amulets, brittle-dry herbs that turned to dust at a touch, furniture wrapped in greying sheets like mummies, a bald rocking horse, tennis rackets, old brooms, a witch's hat with an enormous silver buckle, dark bottles sealed with wax and stacks of rusty cauldrons.

'Wha– what's that!' shrieked Sebastian, pointing at a hairy canine head, peering at them from the shadows.

'The beast of Tynton Moor,' Mrs Briggs explained. 'Your great-great-great-great grandmother, Constance Morgan, caught it. Everyone thought it was a whisht hound, but turns out the poor thing was only a wolf, escaped from the circus. She kept it as a pet for twenty years, then had it stuffed when it died. Used to give me a fright on occasion too, which is why I had it brought up here.'

'How long have you been working at Hartwood, Mrs Briggs?' asked Cassie, coughing at a cloud of dust. The housekeeper always spoke as if she'd known each of the Hedgewitches personally, but perhaps she'd only heard stories about them.

'Oh, coming up for six hundred and twenty years now, dove. Watch out for loose nails! I asked Brogan to hammer those down last autumn, but he's clearly forgotten.'

Cassie stopped and stared at her. 'But that's impossible! That would make you...'

'A lady never tells her age, but yes, I've worked for a fair few Hedgewitches over the years. I'm still a spring chicken compared to Brogan, though.'

Cassie had always assumed Mrs Briggs and Brogan were human, like her. They were a little eccentric perhaps, but she'd never seen either of them do anything obviously magical.

Mrs Briggs chuckled, 'Now, what was it you were wanting up here? Costumes for the Midwinter play? I'm sure there's a box of old clothes somewhere.'

'Oh, yes,' said Cassie, casting a sidelong glance at Sebastian. They'd been searching the house top-to-bottom all week, and had found nothing to suggest that the spear was hidden at Hartwood. The attic was the last place they could think to look.

Sebastian was inspecting the beams that ran across the floor, poking about in corners with his pocket torch and an old umbrella.

'Ah, here we are!' said Mrs Briggs, opening the lid of a wooden chest and releasing a cloud of dust and cobwebs. Cassie brought her candle over to see what the housekeeper had found. Inside the chest were piles of velvet, silk and lace, hats and old shoes and what looked like a very real sword. There was a dress of iridescent silver silk that would suit Tabitha as the Faery Queen, and a hat with a feather in it that would look rather dashing on Rue. A simple dress of green velvet with long trailing sleeves looked perfect for Morgana. Cassie held it against herself to see if it would fit.

'Now look, here's some of your mother's old things. Your aunt had me bring them up here when Rose went away.'

Cassie nearly tripped over the long dress in her eagerness to see what Mrs Briggs had found. It was a sturdy trunk, the sort people take on steam ships, with the initials R. M. painted on the lid. Reverently, Cassie opened it. Folded neatly inside were old clothes – pretty summer dresses, thick wool jumpers and a faded, slightly moth-eaten witch's cloak. Cassie lifted these out and put them aside.

At the very bottom of the trunk was a rusty biscuit tin. Cassie pried it open. Inside were two pairs of grey gloves and a bunch of papers – old newspaper cuttings, receipts and the torn pages of a notebook, scribbled in a hand that looked remarkably familiar. As Cassie flipped through, a photo slipped out. It was a picture of a young man with glasses and a shock of fair hair that stood up in all directions.

'Mrs Briggs, who is this?' asked Cassie, holding the faded image up to the light.

'Well now, there's a face I've not see in many years. That's young Toby Harper, he was a friend of your mother's, long ago. Got lost in the Hedge when he first came to Hedgely; your mum's patrol rescued him. Fancy you finding that in Rose's things.'

That meant that the pages... She began to read them. There were sketches too. It was the missing part of Toby's notebook!

'Well, that lot ought to do you for the play,' said Mrs Briggs. 'I'll leave you to sort through it, take what you like and put the rest back. I've a pear tart in the oven and I'd best check on it before it's burned to a crisp!'

As Mrs Briggs eased herself back down the ladder, Cassie called Sebastian over and showed him the pages.

'These are in Toby's handwriting, and the dates match too.'

'What does it say?' asked Sebastian, crouching down beside her.

Cassie held the paper up to the candlelight, reading aloud:

'When I began searching for the spear, I had no real knowledge of what it was, what it had done in the past to those who possessed it. Now I understand all too well. The spear is no glittering treasure from the age of knights, not something to show in a museum or impress the Hedgewitch with – it is only death, cold and hard and real. It does not belong to our world, but to the next, and we ought never to have looked for it. To think what might have happened, if not for Rose's familiar, and now we must live with what we have done. Tonight we bury Maeve, and with her every cursed clue to the location of the spear. Tomorrow I will destroy the sign that guided us there. Rose thinks I go too far, but I cannot risk anyone else finding it.'

Cassie traced a finger over the final sentence. 'So they found the spear after all.'

'And then destroyed all the evidence? What rotters!' said Sebastian.

'It sounds as though they had a good reason. Maeve must have been my mother's familiar, and she died, protecting them from the spear...'

Cassie thought of Montague – he was a grump most of the time, but her throat ached at the thought of losing him.

'What's that there, scribbled at the bottom?' asked Sebastian.

Cassie peered at the scratchy lines in pencil running up the side of one page. 'They're faery runes. Toby wasn't a witch – my mother must have written these.'

'What do they say?'

Cassie shook her head. 'They're not letters – they don't spell out a word, it's more complicated than that. These three are Swef, Tungil and Wyrm – the dream, the stars and the serpent, but they can mean all sorts of things depending on how you use them.'

'So it's a spell?' asked Sebastian.

'Or a clue.'

Chapter Twenty-Six

Castle Hill

Sebastian's father arrived on their doorstep the following Saturday, as promised. Cassie let him into the entrance hall where the Hartwood tree's leaves shivered in the gust of cold air that followed him in.

'It's cold enough to freeze a goblin's nose off out there!' said Elliot. 'Please tell me Mrs Briggs has put the kettle on.'

Cassie led him through to the warm kitchen where a merry fire crackled in the inglenook. Mrs Briggs was elsewhere in the house, changing bed linen, so Cassie filled the teapot with bramble tea and cut them each a slice of ginger loaf.

'Aunt Miranda was called away this morning, but she should be home for dinner,' Cassie explained.

'Oh, I won't be staying, I'm just here to collect Sebastian. How is the boy?'

'He's doing much better now,' said Cassie. 'Although I'm sure he'll be happy to see you.'

'He's certainly sent me enough letters this past month, begging to be rescued.' Elliot sighed. 'Myself, I have splendid memories of Hartwood at Hallowe'en, and Christmas. Speaking of which, I hear you've landed yourself the starring role in the Midwinter play? Your mother would be so proud. She played the Queen of Faerie herself, one year.'

The image of her mother in a shimmering dress like the one she had found in the attic made Cassie smile. She glanced at the door. Cassie had never had much chance to speak with her uncle alone before, to ask him about her mother. She had a hundred questions but right now there was one in particular she needed an answer to.

'Uncle Elliot, did you ever meet a boy called Toby Harper? He used to live in Hedgely.'

Elliot put his cup down in the saucer, very carefully, as if he was afraid to break it. 'Toby? Who's been talking about Toby? He used to come to Hartwood now and then, although he was a few years older than me.'

'Was he a close friend of my mother's?' Cassie asked.

'They were thick as thieves, Toby, Tamsin and Rose. Always off on some escapade or another, in the Hedge or up Castle Hill. They didn't let me join them often. I suppose that's understandable – who wants their little brother tagging along?'

So Ivy's mother had been friends with Toby too.

'They went up to Castle Hill?' Cassie asked, trying to sound innocently curious.

'Yes, they used to love digging about up there. That Toby Harper fancied himself a budding archaeologist. Can't see the attraction myself, it's just a pile of old stones.' Elliot glanced at his watch. 'Is that the time? I hope Sebastian is all packed. I want to get back to London before it gets dark, the roads will be awful in this weather. See if you can find Brogan for me, would you, Cassie? I might need his help loading Sebastian's things into the car.'

But when Cassie returned to the house she found Sebastian standing on a step, halfway up the central staircase that wound about the Hartwood tree.

Her uncle was standing below in the entrance hall, his hands shoved in the pockets of his overcoat and a frown on his face.

'Oh, there you are, Cassie. Tell Brogan we won't be needing his help after all, my boy here insists on staying put.'

Cassie couldn't believe what she was hearing. Ever since Sebastian had arrived at Hedgely he'd been desperate to leave, talking non-stop about what he'd do once he got to London with his father, complaining of boredom and the inconvenience of being in such a backwater village. Although looking for the spear had distracted him for the past few days, she'd assumed he was still eager to get home.

'You sure you won't change your mind?' Elliot called up to him. 'Your mother will be missing you, you know. I said I'd get you back to Cornwall by Midwinter.'

Sebastian shook his head. 'I must stay here. There is something I have to do.'

Elliot shrugged. 'Very well, I'm glad you've settled in then. I knew you'd love Hedgely once you got to know the place, and I suppose you want to see Cassie in the play and enjoy Mrs Briggs' Christmas dinner. Can't say I blame you for that and maybe I'll pop back up for the big day.'

Cassie followed her uncle out onto the frosty drive.

'Well, take care of the boy for me, Cassie. He seems a lot better, up and about and determined as ever. I'll probably see you for Christmas.'

'I still don't understand why you wanted us to meet you here?' said Rue, touching down on her broom at the foot of the great mound that lay to the north of Hedgely. Above them, the ruins of Castle Hill loomed dark against the heavy November sky. Tabitha was already there, bundled up in a wool coat, a scarf and a knitted hat with a bow on it.

Cassie was clutching a handful of papers, which the wind kept trying to tear from her grasp. It was bitterly cold.

'I found the rest of Toby's journal, it was with some of my mother's old things.' She went on to explain what had happened when Toby and Rose had found the spear, and why they'd decided to leave it where it was. 'But my mother scribbled some runes on the last page, they must mean something.'

'Can I see?' asked Tabitha. Cassie passed her the papers.

'What's he doing here?' asked Rue, nodding at Sebastian who was standing behind Cassie, his hands shoved deep in his coat pockets and his nose bright pink.

'He helped me find them,' Cassie explained. 'And it was his idea to look for buildings that have been around since Nimue was Hedgewitch.'

'But why Castle Hill in particular?' asked Tabitha.

'Well, the runes are Swef, Tungil and Wyrm – the dream, the stars and the serpent. The first two can mean memories and time. I think that has something to do with the past, somewhere all but forgotten. And this hill has an older name: Wyrmroot.' Cassie had discovered this in the summer, when they'd climbed through the tunnels of the Netherwood. 'And then there's something Uncle Elliot said, that they used to come up here, my mum and Toby. That they were digging around. They must have thought the spear was hidden here somewhere.'

'Can we get started now? It's freezing,' said Sebastian.

'Here, take these,' said Cassie, handing them each a grey leather glove.

'I'm not wearing that,' said Rue, pulling a face.

'Oh, but they're lovely and soft,' said Tabitha, holding hers up to her cheek.

'I found them in the attic, amongst my mother's things,' Cassie explained. 'Mrs Briggs says they're selkie skin. I looked it up and they're supposed to be magic-resistant. If we find the spear they should protect us. I think that's why my mother had them. There were only two pairs though – that's one glove each, so we'll still have to be careful.'

Together they approached a broken archway that had once been an entrance into the castle. Before them the hill flattened out and the remains of walls and windows could be seen, with great flagstones set into the grass and covered in moss and patchy lichen. They found themselves in what was left of an old hall, looking up at the crumbling sandstone walls and the side of a broken tower. Aside from a handful of squawking jackdaws, it was oddly quiet, as if time itself stood still and the rest of the world was far, far away.

'So, what exactly are we looking for?' asked Rue.

'I'm not sure,' said Cassie. 'Perhaps a secret passageway or a trap door?'

Sebastian scoffed. 'You've been reading too many novels. We need to approach this systematically – split up and make sure we cover the ground evenly. You two head that way and we'll take the left.'

Rue bristled. 'I am not taking orders from him!'

'Oh, come on Rue, he's right,' said Tabitha. 'Let's look over here, we can all meet back in this hall after.' She dragged the reluctant Rue through a crumbling doorway and down a set of steps.

'Shout if you find anything!' called Cassie.

'Let's go,' said Sebastian, marching off in the other direction.

They proceeded through a series of rooms, their shoes echoing on the worn stone and the crumbling walls doing little to block the icy wind. The roof had long since collapsed, leaving the ruins open to the sky above.

They scanned the walls and stopped to inspect fallen stones. Sebastian stuck his head up the flue of a chimney, still streaked with soot, and came out cursing.

'Nothing but an old pigeon's nest,' he muttered, and they continued on.

'Sebastian,' Cassie began. 'Why didn't you go back with Uncle Elliot? You've been desperate to go home ever since you got here, and I thought after Hallowe'en...'

'I never said I wanted to go home. I wanted to go to London. Dad has a flat there, near his work. He lets me visit sometimes, for the weekend, but he wants me to stay in Cornwall and I hate it there. It's nearly as bad as this place.' He waved an arm in the direction of Hedgely.

'But don't you want to be with your family? At least for Christmas...' Cassie was thinking of all the miserable, lonely Christmases she'd spent at Fowell House.

Sebastian turned away from her and a shadow fell upon his face. 'It isn't the same any more. It isn't really home with Dad always in London, and when he does come back they're always in a row and it doesn't matter what I do, they don't seem to care. Sometimes I think they forget I even exist. That's why they sent me here, you know, to keep me out of the way.'

Cassie nodded. She knew exactly what it felt like to be abandoned, left behind, safely out of the way, to hope and wait.

'Besides,' said Sebastian, leading her into the next chamber. 'We've still got to find this spear, don't we? It's clear you need my help – you may be witches but this requires rational thinking and planning. Can't leave you to muddle through on your own now, can I?'

'Cass!' called Rue from behind the wall. 'Over here!'

Cassie and Sebastian ran through the next broken doorway to join Rue and Tabitha on the other side. They were in a long roofless hall, with the stumps of pillars running down the middle in two long rows, like a line of wounded soldiers. At one end, the room was open to the hillside, facing west to the Hedge, at the other was a short dais and on it a stone altar, its top cracked and spotted with lichen.

'I think this must have been the chapel,' said Tabitha. 'But look at these carvings!'

Around the four sides of the altar were images worked into the stone. They'd been worn down by the rain over the years, their outlines softened, rounded, but Cassie could still make out the figures. On the first was a knight in armour astride a warhorse, on the next, the same knight stood beneath two trees and a woman in a long gown was offering him something, but the years had worn it to a vague blob. The third side, which faced north, was clearer however. It showed the knight before a great wyrm, its long body dominating the panel. In one outstretched arm the knight held a spear.

'Sir Egad!' said Cassie.

'It must be,' said Sebastian, leaning in for a closer look.

Cassie rushed to the final side and almost cried out in frustration, for it had been attacked – there was no other explanation for it. The picture that was once there had been chiselled out, leaving only a rough stone surface with great gouges in the rock.

'But who would do this?' asked Tabitha. 'And why?'

'Someone who didn't want us to know how the story ended,' said Rue. 'Or where the spear was hidden.'

Cassie sighed. 'It was Toby Harper. He said as much in his notebook – that he had to destroy the sign that had led them to the spear so that no one else could find it.' She ran a finger over the chipped and broken surface. It was hard to believe he'd really done this, the boy who was so fascinated by history. He must have been terribly angry and afraid to destroy something so old and beautiful.

Cassie stood up and looked at the walls of the chapel, hoping for more carvings, some further clue, but they were decorated only with weeds – pellitory and ivy-leaved toadflax.

'So this really was Sir Egad's castle,' said Rue, coming to stand beside her. 'Wonder what happened to it.'

'I suppose it fell into ruin over the years, after he died,' said Tabitha.

But Sebastian was inspecting some black marks on the wall beneath a small stone ledge. 'Look here, this is soot, only there's no chimney – it must have been a fire.

And look up there, at those grooves in the stone, near where the roof would have been.'

They followed his pointing hand to where four deep, evenly spaced scratches scored the grey stone.

'What could have done that?' asked Tabitha. 'It's almost like... claw marks.'

'I don't think Sir Egad's castle fell into ruin,' said Sebastian, frowning. 'I think it was destroyed.'

Chapter Twenty-Seven

The Midwinter Market

As November dragged on, the cold and darkness swallowed up the evenings and began to nibble at the afternoons. The last of the leaves had fallen and the trees of the Hedge waved bare branches against the grey sky. The Hartwood gardens turned brown and grey, the autumn flowers crushed by the first frosts, and only the rose garden still bloomed, a bright sea of colour amidst the dry grasses.

Cassie, Rue and Tabitha found their short afternoons were crammed full of coven meetings and preparations for the midwinter play. It was too cold and dark to use the patrol den, but whenever they found a spare moment, they put their heads together with Sebastian over the pages of Toby's notebook and the carved stones at Castle Hill, from which Tabitha had taken rubbings with rice paper and charcoal. Cassie kept coming back to the three faery runes and going over all their possible meanings. If they really were a clue to the spear's hiding place, then perhaps her mother had not wanted it to remain a secret after all but had left a message that only another witch could decipher. She ought to be able to figure it out if she were a proper witch, if she were really her mother's daughter.

On Friday afternoons, Aoife had them painting canvas sheets and cutting out paper snowflakes to decorate the coven hall. They had rehearsals twice a week and Cassie practised her lines on the walk home from school, in the bath and while brushing her hair before bed. She was determined not to forget them and make a fool of herself in front of the whole village. Montague did his best to help, prompting her whenever she missed her cue. He even taught her some vocal exercises that he had learned from his great-uncle, Marcel, who had been a theatre cat at Covent Garden. These involved rather a lot of yowling, however, and Miranda soon put a stop to them, complaining that she couldn't hear herself think.

By mid-December, Cassie, Rue and Tabitha could recite their lines in their sleep, but they were still no closer to finding the spear.

On the morning of Midwinter's eve, Cassie woke in her bed at Hartwood Hall to a deep and muffled silence. There was no birdsong, no howling wind about her turret and she felt as though the whole house had been wrapped in cotton wool. Pulling on her dressing gown, she passed Montague, who was curled beside the ashes of her fire, and went to the east window. Climbing up into the deep window seat, she opened the shutters that blocked out the cold night air, and gasped.

Before her lay the familiar hills and fields of Hedgely, only the swathes of green had been swept away in the night and replaced with a sheet of white snow. More snow blanketed her windowsill and the roof of the stable below. The fruit trees had been iced with it and a perfect blanket of pristine, sparkling white obscured the paths and the garden beds.

Her heart racing, Cassie dashed along the corridor, nearly fell down the stairs and hurtled through the warm kitchen, pausing only to pull on her boots and cloak.

When she emerged into the garden, the snow had begun to fall again, a shower of soft white flakes that looked black against the grey sky and stuck to her eyelashes, cloak and gloveless hands, revealing for a moment their star-like crystals before melting entirely.

She laughed and spun about, her boots crunching on the thick powdery ground beneath her. It was the first snowfall of the year, the first real, clean snow she'd seen since she was a little girl, and it had transformed everything. Cassie explored the garden once more, as if she had again arrived at Hartwood for the first time, finding every tree, every bush, every wall changed by the snow's touch.

At last, she came to her mother's rose garden where, sure enough, the whiteness of the snow was broken by red and pink and yellow flowers, somehow surviving beneath the frost. She reached out to touch a big red rose, its petals heavy beneath a cap of snow. They were true faery roses, blooming even at Midwinter.

'Cassandra!' said a voice behind her, and she turned to find Montague wading through the soft snow. 'Whatever are you doing out here? Your aunt is looking for you, and there's breakfast quickly going cold and—'

'But Montague, just look at this! Isn't it magical?'

'It's wet and freezing and likely to give one a chill, if that's what you mean.'

Cassie laughed and swooped down upon him, scooping the cat into her arms, much to his chagrin, and breathing in the lovely scent of snow on fur. 'Oh, very well, let's go and find breakfast.'

But Cassie couldn't remain indoors for long, and after wolfing down a plate of scrambled eggs, sausages and bacon, nearly scalding herself on the tea, and promising her aunt that she would come to the coven hall early to help set up for the play, Cassie grabbed her broom and was out of the door once more into the snow-dusted world beyond.

The sunlight reflecting off the snow was a blinding white, as Cassie flew Tantivy downhill towards the village. For once, she gave the broom its head and whooped in delight as she sped across the bridge and over the first rows of houses and shops. She wanted to see what the village looked like from above and, although her stomach did a small somersault at the height, she rose higher until she could look down on Loft Street and the white-capped rooves of The Pickled Imp, Marchpane's and St Aelfwig's.

There were already footprints in the snow and cart tracks along the street, and they all seemed to be leading towards the market square.

Something cold, hard and damp struck Cassie's shoulder. She banked to the right and peered down just in time to see another ball of hard snow flying towards her face, ducking as it soared past her.

Down below was Rue, laughing in delight and forming a fresh snowball in her mittened hands.

Cassie grinned and dived towards her, knocking her back in the soft snow. Cassie rolled off Tantivy into a particularly heavy drift that covered half the village green and was immediately pelted by another of Rue's expertly aimed snowballs. She reached for a handful of the cold white powder with which to retaliate.

'Oh, would you two stop that,' said Tabitha, who was putting the finishing touches to a snow rabbit she was building. 'I want to see the market.'

Cassie, Rue and Tabitha made their way up Loft Street towards the market square. All the shops, aside from Whitby's, were shut for the day, their windows strangely dark and silent. But there was a buzz of chatter and the prancing sound of someone playing the fiddle coming from up ahead of them.

Soon, they reached the first of the wooden market stalls, decorated with boughs of holly, trailing ivy and bright lanterns. The street was crowded but the three girls dived in, ducking beneath arms and weaving between wool jumpers and fur coats to reach the stalls. It seemed everyone in the village was out doing their Christmas shopping.

'Hedgely has the best Midwinter market in the whole county,' said Rue, beaming. 'Everyone says so – some folk even come over from Oswalton to shop here.'

Some of the stalls were familiar – Mrs Bellwether was selling great cheeses and hams, while Farmer Scrump had barrels of sweet apples and casks of cider. Widdershin was sitting on a high stool behind teetering piles of books, reading from a small purple volume and largely ignoring his customers, while Saltash was carefully arranging rows of jars and bottles – cures for winter ills – and Selena Moor was selling tins of her special tea blends. They hurried to Miss Marchpane's stall, where they found half the girls in coven already lined up to buy striped candy poles and sweet vanilla snowflakes. They each bought a gingerbread goblin and a mug of hot spiced cocoa to sip as they browsed the more exciting stalls, set up by travelling traders. You could buy blown-glass witch-balls in a rainbow of hues or pots of winter-blooming hellebore in purple and green. A little old man was selling wind-up birds and insects and Cassie bought a clockwork cricket for Sebastian that whirred and chirped. There was even a stall selling exotic witchcraft supplies and Cassie and Tabitha spent ages looking through bottles of saffron ink, gemstone rune sets, obsidian mirrors, clumps of Icelandic moss and amulets of amber and coral, so that Rue eventually got bored and went to look at another stall selling fishing tackle.

There were carol singers and a piper and someone playing the fiddle and, in a clearing at the centre of the market square, fire jugglers threw flames into the air – bright blue, purple and green, like wisp-lights. They were enjoying the performance when Tabitha glanced at her wristwatch. 'It's a quarter to four! We'd better head to the coven hall...'

'Surely we can stay until the end of the show?' said Rue, watching a woman swallow a sword.

But Tabitha gave her a pleading look and the three of them set off up Nearwood Row, away from the crowds and music. It was then they saw Aoife, heading away from the festivities. At first they thought she was also on her way to the hall, but then she made a sharp turn, back towards Loft Street and the village green. She was walking slowly, her head bent low and each step careful and plodding, far from her usual dancing gait.

Cassie grabbed Rue's sleeve. 'Look at Aoife. There's something off about the way she's walking and what is she muttering about?'

'Maybe she stubbed her toe?'

'You don't think she could be...?'

'Enchanted?' asked Tabitha. 'But she's a witch.'

Rue sniffed. 'Not a very good one.'

'The Erl King said his servant had found the perfect assistant – what if he's enchanted Aoife? She was in the Hedge on Hallowe'en, he could be using her!'

'Can you smell that?' asked Tabitha.

'Smoke!' said Cassie.

'Come on,' said Rue. 'I've still got a handful of rowan berries in my pocket, just in case.'

They hurried after Aoife, turning the corner in time to see her slip into The Pickled Imp.

The Pickled Imp was the last building on Loft Street before the river marked the end of the village proper. It had two storeys and a sloping thatched roof that looked like it might slide off if not for the sprawling ivy that covered the walls and held the old place together. On an ordinary day it tended to be full by lunchtime, but the Midwinter market had drawn most of its regulars away, leaving the benches in the garden empty, their seats pillowed by mounds of snow.

Cassie had never been inside the pub before. It smelled strongly of wood polish, cider and roasting meat. The roof was low and beamed with dark oak, like the kitchen at Hartwood, but the windows were smaller, the atmosphere close and dark. The walls were hung with old hunting trophies: antlers, a boar's head, a trout in a glass case and an imp preserved in a bottle of yellow liquid.

'Don't worry your head, lass!' said a voice from behind her. 'He was a goner when they bottled him. We're not in the habit of hunting the good folk round here. Why, your aunt'd have my guts for garters!'

The voice came from Emley Moor, the proprietor, a broad hulk of a man, so tall he had to stoop slightly under the low ceiling. He was drying a glass with a dish cloth.

'What can I do for you, then?'

'Miss Early... which way?' gasped Cassie.

'She's gone through to the back room.' He pointed with a thumb.

'Thank y—' said Tabitha.

'Now hold it right there! What'll you be havin' to drink?'

'Oh, we were just...' Cassie stuttered.

'You come to The Imp, you have a drink. Them's the rules!' He lowered his voice, 'Don't worry, I've got something suitable for young witches.'

They watched as he pulled out three pewter tankards and filled them from a cask behind the counter.

The liquid inside was ruby red and there were small scarlet berries floating in it. Cassie took a cautious sip. It fizzed on her tongue, sweet and warm at first, but then the spices kicked in and she gasped – her tongue was on fire!

Emley Moor roared with laughter. 'Cinnamon Punch! They're not jokin' about the punch, but you'll get used to it. Here, have a watermint. Might help.'

They thanked him and carried their tankards with them, sloshing, as they hurried towards the doorway through which Aoife had vanished.

The next room was much bigger and heated by a roaring fire in a vast inglenook. There was a scattering of tables, chairs and old church pews, all of dark, polished wood. The ceiling was low enough that Cassie could reach up and touch it. She realised that the building itself must be very old, perhaps even as old as Hartwood Hall.

Aoife was on her knees before the fireplace, running her hands over the rough stones of the hearth.

'Now, where is it? It must be here somewhere, I'm sure of it...' she muttered.

'Stand back,' said Rue, raising her fist. 'Cass, can you remember the incantation?'

'By the bitter berries of Rowan, I release you!' cried Cassie, as Rue threw a handful of dried brown rowan berries at the witch.

'What on the good green earth?' said Aoife, rising to her feet as berries cascaded to the ground around her. 'Girls, whatever is going on here?' She looked surprised and confused, but her eyes were their usual clear hazel and her shadow fell harmlessly against the stone wall.

'I'm sorry, we thought you'd been enchanted,' said Cassie, feeling the colour rise to her cheeks. 'Only, you were walking strangely and muttering, and then we saw you searching for something...'

'My bracelet,' said Aoife. 'I lost it last night when I joined Brogan for a drink. I was checking the path on the way here.' She laughed. 'Wait, the three of you thought I'd been enchanted, like Ted Whitby and the other villagers?'

'We smelled smoke,' said Rue.

'Well, given you've all been standing next to the fire jugglers at the market for the past half hour, that's not terribly surprising, is it? Your cloaks reek of the stuff.'

They each sniffed their woollen cloaks and had to admit that Aoife was right.

'Come now, why don't you help me find my bracelet and then we can sit down and you can finish those drinks. I don't suppose any of you know a good seeking spell?'

Tabitha used a short incantation her gran had taught her, and they soon found the missing bracelet, which had slipped down behind one of the firedogs.

'Now then, I appreciate you all running to my rescue, but as you can see, I'm perfectly well, and not at any great risk of faery enchantment. That's why I wear these, actually.' She held up the bracelet she'd just recovered. It was made of some dense black material, like stone, carved with a pattern of faery runes. '*Abonos* – bog oak, from Ireland. It's made from wood that has been preserved under water for thousands of years. That gives it unique properties, including a certain protective power. Here, take one. In fact, I'll give you one each.'

She handed the girls bracelets from the stack she wore on her arm. The wood was warm to the touch and Cassie slid the bracelet over her hand so that it sat against her wrist. It was a little big but very beautiful, with the light of the fire reflected on its glossy, polished surface.

Aoife tapped her cheek with a finger. 'Now then, you're clearly an observant patrol. What else have you noticed about the villagers who've been enchanted?'

So Cassie, Rue and Tabitha described the signs they'd noticed – the smell of smoke, the odd shadows and the victim's loss of memory once the incident was over.

'It sounds to me like the work of a brollachan,' said Aoife, frowning. 'One of the formless ones – a faery with no physical body or shape to call its own. They seek out human hosts, taking over their minds and bodies for a few hours or days. Pitiful creatures really, all they desire is a home, a name, somewhere to belong...'

'Well, I hope you don't expect me to feel sorry for it,' said Rue. 'It took my dad. He could have been hurt!'

Aoife smiled sadly. 'I understand your anger, but do not worry, it could not have possessed your father for long in any case. The brollachan can only enter a mortal when they are at their lowest point – it seeks out an emptiness in the heart and takes up residence there. We all have our bad days, yes, but those of us who are loved and cared for cannot play host to such darkness for long. That is why the brollachan must wander from body to body; it can only stay if it is invited in, welcomed by one who has given in to despair.'

'I was just thinking...' said Cassie, and she told Aoife of the dark shadow they'd encountered in the Hedge, the way she had felt when it swept over them as they huddled together in the bushes. The three girls shuddered at the memory.

Aoife looked grim. 'It is almost certainly a brollachan, then. It must be hiding in the woods, coming down into the village only when it senses misery and the possibility of a new host.'

'But how do we stop such a thing?' asked Tabitha.

'Well, witches of the past have tried to bind the poor creatures. With the right incantation they can be trapped inside a bottle or a box...'

Cassie felt a sinking feeling in the pit of her stomach. 'Or a teapot?'

'An unusual choice, but yes, I suppose that would work. Oh my, but look at the time! Have you all finished your punch? We'd best get along to the coven hall – the play cannot begin without its leading ladies!'

Chapter Twenty-Eight

The Wyrm, the Witch and the Faery Knight

'Well, that was embarrassing,' said Tabitha, pulling her Faery Queen dress on over her head. 'The look on Aoife's face when you threw those berries at her, Rue, I could have melted into the floor – and she was so nice about it. I told you, she's a good sort, really.'

'I'll admit, she's not *completely* hopeless.' said Rue. 'But why did you ask her about teapots, Cass?'

Cassie bit her lip as she climbed into her green velvet dress. 'I think *I* might have released the brollachan.'

She told them about her visit to Bramble's with the Hedgewitch, and the tea that tasted of tears.

'Well, I wouldn't beat yourself up over it,' said Rue, giving her sword an experimental swish. 'Sounds to me like you were set up; a goblin sells the teapot to Eris Watchet, someone was bound to buy it and, sooner or later, the brollachan would break free. Just bad luck that it happened to be you.'

Tabitha nodded. 'And nobody else has been enchanted, not since Rue's father. Perhaps it has given up?'

Cassie frowned. 'I wish I could believe that, Tabitha, but I don't think the Erl King gives up so easily. When I saw him through the Elder Mother's door, he told me his servant had just found the perfect assistant. If the brollachan is serving him, helping him to find the spear then his assistant must be someone in the village. Someone who has given in to despair, as Aoife said, who the brollachan can control completely.'

While they were dressing, dusk had deepened into night. Lamps were lit about the coven hall and outside along the path, where they made the snow shimmer in blue and gold.

Finally, Miranda deemed the hall in good order, and Aoife gathered them all to run through some warm-ups as the first of the villagers began to arrive. It was only then that Cassie's nerves set in.

'This skirt is so long, what if I trip?' she whispered. 'And I'm never going to remember that long speech, the bit about the girdle.'

'Oh, don't overthink it, you know the part, you'll be splendid,' whispered Tabitha. 'It's Rue I'm worried about, the way she's swinging that sword about she's likely to behead anyone sitting in the front row.'

Tabitha's own costume, a glittering silver gown, made her look like a creature of the snow herself, delicate and enchanting. Meanwhile, Rue strutted about in her knightly get-up without any sign of stage fright.

Aoife had gathered Alice, Heather, Eliza and Harriet to begin a Midwinter chant, accompanied by Nancy on the tin whistle, while the rest of the coven waited behind a makeshift curtain.

'When the winds cease blowing, and the night draws in,
Snow coats field and meadow, keeping all within.
Witches light the hearth fire, burn the yule log bright,
Warding home and village against the fading light.'

Anika – who was to be the tail of the wyrm – had misplaced her tights and Phyllis and Susan were frantically helping her search for them.

'Holly bright of berry, hang on lintel high,
A candle in each window as the dusk draws nigh.
Ivy over threshold, keeps the dark at bay
Wakefully we watch now, 'til the break of day.'

Cassie chewed her thumbnail as she waited behind the canvas sheet they had painted with tall, dark trees. More and more people kept coming in, rugged up against the cold. There was old Mrs Blight, Tabitha's grandmother, insisting that a boy in the front row give up his seat so she might claim it. There were Rue's parents, standing at the back and chatting to Eris Watchet and Selena Moor, holding earthenware mugs of hot spiced cider in their hands. She could see her schoolteacher, Miss Featherstone, and Mrs Briggs and Brogan, and finally, standing in the doorway as if he hadn't decided whether to join them, was Sebastian.

'Hear the silver sleigh-bells of the faery steeds,
Listen for their laughter, all who hear, take heed.

Keep within your household, iron near at hand,
For this night the fair folk roam across the land.'

The Hedgewitch rang a brass bell and the hall fell silent, until all you could hear was the crackle of the fire and the breathing of the audience and, Cassie thought, the soft *shush-shush* of snow falling outside. The play was about to begin.

'We welcome you tonight, on Midwinter's Eve, to the Hedgely Coven hall,' Miranda began. 'As you all are aware, tonight is one of the four Crossing Nights on which the wards that guard the Hedge are weakened and folk may cross between our world and that of Faerie. It has always been considered the most dangerous of the Crossing Nights, for it is also the longest night of the year. And so, I thank you all for making the journey here, and ask, when you leave, that you go with great care and never alone. For, while you are safe within these walls, we cannot know what danger may lurk without.'

Cassie peered at the waiting faces. Some of the children looked frightened at these words, but most of the villagers listened with merry smiles and calm eyes. They had lived all their lives beside the Hedge and knew well its dangers, accepting them without fear or panic.

'As is tradition, we gather tonight to keep safe around the hearth fire, where the yule log will burn through the night. The 1st Hedgely Coven will perform a traditional Midwinter play – *The Wyrm, the Witch and the Faery Knight* – and while the story is fictional, it may serve as a reminder of the very real threats faced and overcome by the witches of old.'

At this, Eliza and Harriet, the leaders of Thorn and Ash patrols, walked onto the area designated as the stage. All eyes were on them.

'Once upon a time, when the folk of Faerie walked this land...' Eliza began.

'... and the way between the worlds stood open,' said Harriet. 'There came upon the village of Hedgely a great and monstrous peril.'

At this, Nancy banged upon a small drum and the great wyrm rushed into the light, writhing and roaring. It was made up of Susan and Phyllis Drake, with Anika trying to keep up as the tail. They tramped about the room, hissing at the small children in the audience, one or two of whom began to cry, and making the older folk laugh with their antics.

'The villagers were terrified as, one by one, the great wyrm devoured their sheep!' said Harriet.

Heather Shuttle, with a sheepskin on her back and a pair of papier-mâché horns, shuffled in front of the canvas sheet. The head of the wyrm turned, sniffed the air and then pounced after her, chasing the genuinely frightened Heather about the hall to much laughter and applause.

'They called upon a brave knight to save them from their plight!' said Eliza, as Rue jumped out to place herself between the wyrm and poor Heather, brandishing her sword.

'Begone, foul beast! I am the bravest of all knights and surely I shall defeat you!'

The audience cheered.

Susan, who held the wyrm's head aloft above her own, gave an almighty roar and tried to bite the eager knight, but was driven back by the sword. They fought for a moment, but then the wyrm lashed out with its tail and dashed the sword from Rue's hand. The wyrm fell upon her, driving her to the ground in a heap of scales and feathers.

'But the knight was not strong enough to defeat the wyrm, and was gravely wounded,' said Harriet.

'Aaaargh! My foot! I mean, my head! I am poisoned, ugh!' cried Rue, as the wyrm retreated behind the canvas.

'And there the knight lay, and might have died, but a witch was passing on her broom and heard his cry,' said Eliza.

That was Cassie's cue. She took a deep breath and swept onto the stage, her dark cloak wrapped around her and Tantivy clutched in her hand. Cassie crouched over the fallen Rue, both of them trying not to laugh.

Nancy played a mournful tune on her whistle.

'Sir Knight! What has befallen you?' asked Cassie. 'I see by the coldness of your skin that a terrible poison is at work in your blood.'

'The wyrm, the wyrm!' cried Rue, rolling about as if in agony.

'Alas, I have no medicine to counter that poisonous bite, but see here, I have the sap of the Hartwood tree, and if you would drink but a few drops you will not die. I shall seek out this wyrm and see what might be done to save you and this village!'

The audience cheered again and Cassie felt a wave of relief at having delivered her first scene. If only she could remember the rest.

'And so the witch, finding a helpful sheep nearby, asked it the way to the wyrm's lair and there she encountered the beast itself,' said Harriet.

Heather took Cassie's hand and led her back around the canvas, emerging again to face the waiting wyrm.

Cassie took a deep breath and addressed the beast before her. 'Wyrm, you have done great harm to the people of this village, stealing their sheep and frightening their children, and now I find that you have injured this good knight, even unto his death!'

Susan, Phyllis and Anika squirmed in their costume.

'But I know that in truth you mean no evil and are only lost, here in this strange land. If you will come with me I shall lead you back through the woods to Faerie, where you shall trouble these people no longer,' said Cassie.

'And so the witch bound the great wyrm with her girdle,' said Eliza, as Cassie tied her belt around the wyrm's snout. 'She led the creature, meek as a lamb, into the depths of the Hedge, but once there, they quickly became lost.'

Cassie, who had plenty of experience getting lost in the Hedge, found this the easiest part of the play to imagine. Leading Susan by the belt, she wandered about the hall, peering into the darkness as if the audience were a thicket of trees.

'But behold! They came upon a woman, bright as the dawn,' said Harriet, as Tabitha emerged from behind the canvas to a gasp from the audience. Her dark curls shone in the candlelight and she wore a mysterious and radiant smile. In her hand she carried a branch, painted white and wrapped with silver tinsel.

'I am the Queen of Faerie!' cried Tabitha, and even Cassie was taken aback by the clarity of her voice. 'And I will take that beast from you and grant you medicine to heal your knight, if you can but answer me a riddle!'

Cassie drew near Tabitha, leading the wyrm behind her. With a sweep of her arm she threw back her hood and stood before the audience in her green gown.

'I am the Hedgewitch, and I will accept your challenge!'

'Hear me and answer well, for if you fail I shall take you away with me to Faerie to be my servant and you shall never see these lands again,' said Tabitha.

'Speak and I shall answer,' said Cassie.

'Here is my riddle: I am soft as bread, dark as the night, made by living hands for no living man. Who sleeps in me shall never wake but their name will be remembered. What am I?'

Cassie knew the answer, of course – they'd practised it a dozen times, but as Tabitha spoke she began to think of her mother. Rose Morgan had played the Faerie Queen herself, had spoken those very words, all those years ago. The play might be fictional, as Miranda had said, but there was once a real faery knight living at Castle Hill, who had fought a great wyrm and died from his wounds. What if the play held a germ of truth, a secret wrapped inside the story? An answer to another riddle; the three runes her mother had scrawled in the notebook: swef, tungil, wyrm – memories, time, death. Cassie gasped. She knew where the spear was hidden.

'Cassie!' hissed Tabitha, under her breath. Someone in the audience stifled a cough.

'The grave!' Cassie cried. 'It's in his grave!'

Tabitha frowned at her, Morgana's line was simply 'a grave' – she'd messed it up in her excitement.

'Indeed, you have answered my riddle correctly, or close enough, anyway. Hand to me that girdle and I shall relieve you of this beastly burden. Here is the potion you seek that shall save your fair knight.'

The rest of the play passed in something of a blur as Cassie revived Rue, helping her up off the cold floor, and the sheep and the villager, played by Heather and

Alice, cheered and begged Morgana to stay in the village always and protect them.

Afterwards there were bows and applause, and Aoife conducted them all in another Midwinter chant while Nancy played a piping reel.

'What was that all about?' asked Tabitha, once the audience had finished clapping and everyone was queuing for hot cocoa, mulled wine and Mrs Brigg's homemade fruit mince pies. 'I thought you knew your lines?'

Cassie drew Rue and Tabitha aside, looking about to be sure that none of the nearby adults were listening. The Hedgewitch was talking to Miss Featherstone, and Sebastian was standing beside her. 'It's the spear, I know where it is! The answer is in the riddle.'

'A grave?' asked Rue.

Cassie nodded. 'Think about it: Sir Egad may have lived in the castle, but when he died he would have been buried at the nearest church – St Aelfwig's. It must be at least as old, maybe older, and it fits with the runes my mother left us too – the dream, the stars and the serpent; a place where we go to sleep under the stars for all time.'

'And you think the spear might have been buried with Sir Egad?' asked Tabitha.

Cassie nodded. 'We have to go now, while everyone is here.'

'Tonight?' asked Rue. 'You want us to go into the churchyard on Midwinter's Eve and dig up a grave?'

'She's right, it can wait until morning, surely? We'll hardly be able to see anything under the snow and in the darkness,' said Tabitha.

'But we're not the only ones looking for it – the brollachan is seeking the spear and it could be hiding inside anyone in this room – what if they get there first? What if they succeed, and the Erl King slays Galtres? He could bring an army of goblins through the Hedge!'

Rue and Tabitha threw their cloaks over their costumes, and went to collect the selkie-skin gloves from Oak Patrol corner.

'One of the gloves is missing,' whispered Rue. 'There should be four, I stored them here after we went up to Castle Hill.'

'Never mind that, we still have one each,' said Cassie.

With a backwards glance to ensure that neither the Hedgewitch nor Aoife were looking, they snuck out the door, stooping to take a lantern each from the path.

The snow had begun to fall again, and with the darkness a deep chill had set in, turning their breath into clouds of white mist and biting at their fingers and noses. The three girls trudged single file through the eerily quiet village. Even The Pickled Imp was silent, its windows dark and its sign swinging in the wind. Everyone was at the coven hall, safe and warm and enjoying themselves – or, almost everyone.

'What's that?' asked Cassie. 'I heard a sound behind us.'

They spun about, looking for some shape or figure in the darkness, but could see nothing, only the three rows of deep footprints they themselves had left in the snow.

'Come on,' said Rue. 'The sooner we find the spear, the sooner we can get back to warm fires and mince pies.'

They trudged on, past the village green where the pond had begun to freeze over, rimmed by a border of transparent ice, and up to the ivy-covered stone wall that ran around the churchyard. They paused for a moment under the lychgate to brush off the snow that had gathered on their cloaks and to relight Rue's lantern, which had blown out.

Before them lay the churchyard, glowing white under its shroud of snow. The pristine sheet was

broken here and there by ancient headstones, with the dark spires of the yews and the tower of the church itself rising into the night. Cassie thought of Phyllis and Susan's trick and hoped that there was nothing worse than a tablecloth-ghost abroad that night.

'I suppose we had better spread out and look at the dates on the headstones,' said Cassie. 'See if we can find the oldest part of the churchyard.'

The three girls each took one of the narrow paths that wound between the graves. Through the flurries of falling snow they were visible to each other only by their lanterns, dipping and bobbing as they stopped to brush snow from a gravestone or stooped to read an inscription by lamplight.

1918 – Jonathan Saltash, Cassie read. *1746 – Mary Bellwether*.

Many of the surnames were familiar, belonging to members of old Hedgely families who'd been there for hundreds of years, while others, like 'Harold Morpeth – a visitor to this town, laid to rest 1825' were stranger, leading Cassie to wonder about their stories. None of the graves she saw were old enough, however, to belong to a medieval knight.

After a gruelling hour of searching, they met in the doorway of the church itself, shivering and exhausted.

'I don't think I can go on much longer,' said Tabitha.

'She's right, Cass, we've had a good look. Maybe he wasn't buried here after all, or perhaps something happened to the gravestone. We can come back tomorrow and look again by daylight.'

Cassie looked up at the tower, its stones dusted with white. 'What about *inside* the church?'

Chapter Twenty-Nine

Here Lies Sir Egad

The door to the church was unlocked, but it creaked ominously as they let themselves into the gloomy interior.

Cassie had been inside the church once or twice before with Rue, but always in the light of day, when the stained-glass windows glowed with bright colours and the stones seemed warmed from within. It was a very different place by night, almost as cold as it had been outdoors, although at least they were out of the wind and falling snow. The air was still and deathly silent.

The girls spread out once more, Rue taking one wall, Cassie another, and Tabitha the aisle between the pews.

Their footsteps sounded overly loud on the stone and their lanterns cast only small circles of light, leaving much of the church in shadow.

Cassie inspected the north wall, which was set with the coats of arms of ancient families – stars and arrows, the head of a deer and a moon-gazing hare. There were names, too – the dedications to various individuals who had paid for windows or a new organ, or to fix the roof.

Cassie lifted her lantern high to inspect the stone figure of Saint Aelfwig himself, a kindly looking man with a long beard, holding a cup in one hand and a book in the other. Then she heard something fall to the floor with a thud and nearly jumped out of her skin.

'Rue, was that you?' she hissed, but Rue's lantern was down the other end of the nave and Tabitha was by the font. Slowly, Cassie crept towards the source of the sound and found a hymn book lying open on the flagstones. She picked it up and examined it, but there was nothing remarkable about the book. The shadows were deep and dark beyond her lantern. If there was someone else in the church, it would be easy enough to hide.

Cassie glanced down again, and then she saw it, the name they had all been searching for. It was right beneath her feet.

'Rue! Tabitha!' Cassie called, her voice echoing off the cold stone.

They hurried over and she showed them what she'd found: a great flagstone some four feet long, and on it carved words, worn nearly smooth by years of footfall.

'*HIC IACET EGADUS MILES*,' read Tabitha, 'What does it mean?'

'It's Latin,' said Cassie. 'We had to learn some at Fowell House. It means "Here lies Sir Egad".'

'Do you think he's buried in the floor? I don't think we can lift this stone, it's mortared in,' said Tabitha.

'He must be in the crypt,' said Rue.

'The crypt?' asked Cassie and Tabitha together.

Rue nodded. 'Beneath the church, there's a vault. I only know about it because Angus dared Bran to sneak in there one summer. He told us there are big stone coffins down there. Sir Egad must be in one of them.'

'How do we get in?' Cassie asked.

Rue led them back outside, into the frozen churchyard, and then around the building to a set of steps that ran down beneath the wall. They were all grown-over with ivy and thorny brambles. In the darkness at the foot of the stairs they could just make out a door.

'It'll be locked, though,' said Rue. 'Mr Kirkwall, the caretaker, shut it up after Bran came out screaming and woke him from his afternoon nap.'

But they found the wooden door ajar, and what's more, there was a line of snow on the dark stone floor and two wet footprints.

'Someone else has been down here tonight,' said Cassie. 'Do you think it's Mr Kirkwall?'

'I don't think so,' said Tabitha. 'I saw him at the coven hall before we left, talking with Mrs Mossley.'

It was deathly cold beneath the church, and the darkness there seemed thicker, pooling around the wide stone columns that held up the floor of the church above them. They went forward together, elbows touching, lanterns held aloft, barely breathing in the still, dry air.

Bran's description held true – between the columns were great stone boxes, some carved with ornate patterns, others very plain. One lid had cracked, and a gaping darkness showed within. Cassie tried not to look at it or imagine what lay inside.

'Here!' said Rue, rushing forward. 'It's him!'

Before them on a stone box lay a body – no, it was merely a statue; a knight in full armour, laid out upon the sarcophagus with his head resting on a pillow and his eyes staring up at the stones above. Clasped in one hand he held a long spear shaft, but the head of the spear was broken off.

Sure enough, as they brought their lanterns close, they found the same words running around the side of the coffin: HIC IACET EGADUS MILES.

'We've found him,' said Cassie, relieved that they would not need to explore the depths of the crypt any further. 'But the spear, it's broken.'

'It's just a statue, though, what if...' Tabitha took a deep breath. 'What if the spear is inside, with his—'

'Don't say it,' said Rue, 'whatever you do, don't say it.'

Cassie sighed. 'I don't like the idea of it any more than you do, but we have to at least look. Have you got your gloves?'

They each put on one of the selkie-skin gloves and took up position along the edge of the coffin.

'Ready?' Cassie asked. She counted, and on three, they pushed, but the heavy stone would not budge. The figure of Sir Egad lay staring into the darkness.

'We need a lever... something to wedge it open,' said Tabitha.

'Will this do?' asked Rue, holding up a wooden pole. 'I found it, there against that pillar.'

Cassie frowned. How had it got there? It was a little too convenient, unless someone else had been there before them.

They heaved again, and were able to shift the stone knight just enough to insert the pole. With all three of them pulling down on the sturdy wood, they inched it open – just a crack, but enough to see inside.

'I'll hold it,' said Rue. 'You look.'

Tabitha and Cassie exchanged a worried glance, neither of them really wanted to see what was left inside the coffin.

'Come on,' said Cassie. 'It can't be that bad after all these years.'

'Oh, do hurry up!' said Rue, grimacing under the weight.

Together, they lifted their lanterns and peered through the crack.

Tabitha gasped. 'It's empty! There's nothing there!'

Rue groaned and released the wooden pole, letting the stone fall back into place with a heavy thud. 'What do you mean?'

Cassie frowned. 'She's right, it's just dust. There was no sign of the spear. I must have been wrong about the runes...'

A laugh rang through the crypt.

'Who's there?' said Rue, holding up her sword and stepping in front of Cassie and Tabitha.

A shadow broke away from one of the pillars and came towards them.

'Sebastian!' said Cassie. 'You frightened us, we thought for a moment...'

'That I was the ghost of Sir Egad?' He laughed again.

'What are you doing down here? Did you follow us from the hall?'

'Ha! As if I needed your help, cousin. It was obvious, really – the only place in the village where something might lie undisturbed for hundreds of years, while the knight who carried it crumbled to dust.'

'But the coffin's empty!' said Tabitha.

'It is now,' said Sebastian. He held up his left hand, which was protected by a silvery selkie-skin glove. It clasped a shard of black stone as long as a knife and fiercely pointed. Its chipped edges glittering darkly in the light of their lanterns.

'Be careful!' said Cassie, stepping towards him to take the spear, but Sebastian stepped back.

'No, you can't have it. I found it, it's mine.'

Cassie frowned, there was something strange about her cousin – he stood taller, straighter than usual and the smile that played about the corners of his mouth was unfamiliar. His eyes had a peculiar, misty cast and—

'Cassie, look! His shadow!' cried Tabitha.

The light of the three lanterns cast their own shadows against the walls of the crypt in long, thin columns, but Sebastian's shadow, where the light fell upon him, curled and twisted like a column of smoke. It was moving, reaching out spectral arms to grasp his shoulders.

'Sebastian, put the spear down,' said Cassie, slowly. She didn't want to startle him, but she couldn't go near him while he held it.

'Why? So you can take it to Aunt Miranda? You may be desperate to impress her, but I don't care one jot what she thinks.'

'What are you talking about? What's come over you, Sebastian?' She shook her head. 'Just give me the spear and we'll go home together.'

'Home?' he asked. As he said it his voice began to change, growing deeper and stranger, echoing in the stone chamber. 'Home? I have no home. Long years have I wandered, without shape, without form, searching, seeking, until the Erl King found me. He promised me a home, a body to be mine, to live and breathe as mortals do, to walk the earth and feel the wind, a body in exchange for this.' He held up the spear once more.

'Sebastian!' cried Cassie, stepping towards him, but Rue and Tabitha pulled her back.

'That's not Sebastian, Cass,' said Rue.

'Or, not only him,' said Tabitha. 'It's the brollachan, inside him.'

'I can't go back,' said the boy, his voice changing again to Sebastian's familiar tone. 'There's nothing to go back to. My family, my home, it's gone. I broke it and now I have nowhere to go.' Tears were creeping down his cheeks and the shadow behind him grew, a dense, dark smoke, rising up and swirling about his face and body.

'That's not true. Uncle Elliot, your father—'

'My father left! He left my mother, left our home, and then he left me *here*, in the middle of nowhere. He doesn't care what happens to me, he doesn't want me around.'

Cassie didn't believe for a moment that her uncle felt this way, but she did not really know what things were like at home for Sebastian. She could not truly promise him that it would all be fine.

'He will give me a home,' said Sebastian, his voice deepening once more. 'He will change the world so that it is ours again, and none can drive us from it, he will free all who have been bound and wake the sleepers. The very land will sing his name.'

'Fine, you can have the spear,' said Cassie. 'But leave my cousin alone! Get out of him and leave!'

'I need him to carry out this task, to return while the old roads stand open this night, to join my lord and offer this gift, to claim my reward.'

'You cannot have him!' she cried. 'Let him go!'

'But he has already welcomed me in! I can only take those who have lost something, a memory, a precious belonging, a dream for the future. The loss creates a hollow that lets me enter. Most only allow me to fill a small part of themselves but this boy, he has a far greater void within him, an emptiness he longs to fill. It was so easy, so very easy to claim him; he did not resist.'

They had no juniper water, no rowan berries this time, nothing with which to cast out the shadowy creature that held her cousin captive. Even if they had, Cassie doubted the strength of those methods. Sebastian was not in a daze, like Rue's dad had been, he seemed to be there, awake and aware, and working with the creature, almost welcoming it. If she wanted to drive it out, she'd need to get through to him.

'Sebastian,' she began, softly this time. 'I don't know what you've been through, but I'm sure that none of it is your fault. And I do know what it's like to feel as if you have no one, to be alone, and to be willing to do anything to change that. But he's wrong – you're not empty, you're full of ideas and hopes and dreams. You told me yourself, you're going to be a pilot and a scientist and... and... fly to the moon!'

The boy stared at her, his eyes vacant and wide. The shadow had grown again, a dark cloud wrapping about him like a shroud. It wasn't working. It wasn't enough.

'And you have another home!' she cried. For a moment, Sebastian looked up, as if he had heard her, really heard her for the first time.

'You have a home here, with us, with Aunt Miranda and Mrs Briggs, with Brogan and me. We are your family too, we want you around, and you are always, always welcome at Hartwood!'

Sebastian lifted his chin and shook his head. The shadow retreated, drawing back from him.

'Cassie?' he asked, as if seeing her for the first time. 'Where am I?'

He stumbled and fell, the spear falling from his hand, clinking as it hit the stone floor.

Tabitha and Cassie rushed to his side, while Rue stooped to claim the spear, holding it carefully in her one gloved hand.

'He'll be all right,' said Tabitha, checking Sebastian's pulse and forehead. 'He's just passed out, but we need to get him away from here, take him somewhere warm.'

They hefted the unconscious boy between them, dragging him back towards the door, but before they reached it, they heard a whoosh of wind and the door slammed shut, leaving them in darkness.

Chapter Thirty

The Brollachan

The crypt was silent but for Cassie, Rue and Tabitha's heavy breathing. Sebastian lay unconscious, supported by Tabitha, as Cassie tried the door again.

'It's jammed shut.'

Rue hammered at the rotting wood with her fists and the hilt of her sword.

'Shhh,' said Cassie. 'What was that?'

They all heard it this time, the grinding of stone moving against stone.

Cassie and Rue took a step towards the sound, wielding their lanterns. It was coming from Sir Egad's tomb. The stone knight lifted its head, jerked stiffly into a sitting position and swung its legs down from the sarcophagus. They stared as first one foot, then another, touched the cold stone floor. The knight rose up to his full height, lifting the broken spear shaft. Around him the shadows thickened, curling wisps of smoke twined about his arms and legs. His face remained expressionless, framed by a mail hood, and when he moved it was with the slow, jerking motions of a puppet or a sleepwalker.

Rue stepped forward. She raised her costume sword, her mouth set in a grim line. 'Stay back!'

As it drew closer, the knight seemed to awaken more fully. Its staggering pace grew swifter, more natural, as if it remembered what it was like to be flesh and blood and not cold stone. Rue held her ground while Cassie and Tabitha dragged Sebastian against the wall and pulled on the door handle with all their might.

Turning, they saw the knight bearing down on Rue. With a sweep of one stone gauntlet he struck the flimsy sword from her hand.

The knight raised its broken shaft, a rod of stone, and swept it low, knocking Rue to the ground. She cried out in pain and Tabitha ran to her side. The spear, a shard of black in the darkness, fell from Rue's hand and skittered across the floor towards Cassie. She stooped to pick it up in her gloved hand. She could feel the coldness of it through the leather, and the sharpness of its edge. If she were not careful it would slice through the selkie-skin gloves like paper.

The knight loomed over Rue and Tabitha, raising its weapon once more.

'Wait! I have what you want!' called Cassie, holding the spear above her head and lifting her lantern so it might see what she held.

The knight stopped in its motion and came towards Cassie.

She swallowed the fear that was rising in her. Her stomach churned, she was chilled all over and she felt she might be sick as the horrible, heavy figure of the knight marched towards her.

'You can have it, I'll give it to you,' she said, as calmly as she could. 'Only, I don't believe this is what you really want.'

The knight paused, its fist still raised. It was not Sir Egad, come back to haunt them, but the brollachan, the shapeless faery creature Aoife had described, and if it was a faery, then it could be bargained with.

'You don't want the spear, not really, you want a body – that's what the Erl King promised you.'

The knight loomed over her now and Cassie looked up into the stone mask of its face. The brollachan could animate the stone but not, it seemed, make it speak.

'What if... what if I gave you a body, a home?' she offered.

'Cassie, what are you doing?' called Tabitha. 'You saw what it did to the villagers, to Sebastian.'

But Cassie had no intention of letting the creature take her, or any of them. Another idea was forming in her mind. What if Aoife was right and a witch's duty was not only to protect her community, but to help faery folk as well – to work with them, not against them? What if she could protect her friends, her cousin, not by fighting this thing, but by saving it?

'I have a home, a place called Hartwood Hall, and it is missing something. It doesn't have a brownie – a protector. There's a place for you there. That's what you need, isn't it? Come with me and you can make it your own.'

The knight raised its weapon over Cassie, taking another step towards her. She flinched and shut her eyes, turning away from the oncoming blow.

'Cassie, look!' said Tabitha.

The knight had frozen in place. The stone rod fell from its hand and shattered on the floor. Shadows began to pour out of it, from every crevice in its armour, from the mail hood, gauntlets and breastplate. The wisps of darkness rejoined to form a mass, a shapeless, shifting shadow. It was the thing they had seen in the Hedge on Hallowe'en, a creature with no form, no body, no face, only emptiness – the absence of everything, even light. Cassie felt that same dreadful sense of loss wash over her as it came nearer. The bog-oak bracelet Aoife had given her grew warm against her wrist. She felt that warmth pour through her and the emptiness fill with a soft, gentle hope, with fond memories and the sure knowledge that she belonged, here in Hedgely. The brollachan may once have been able to take her, before she had come to this place, when she had been as lonely, as desperate as Sebastian was, but no longer. It was not only the bracelet protecting her now, but her own memories, fresh and new, of coven and village and home, of family and friends.

The brollachan hovered behind her and whispered in her ear, 'Show me, show me this place you call home.'

When they tried the door again, it swung open easily, but the journey back to Hartwood was exhaustingly slow.

Rue could walk but was clearly in pain; she had sprained her ankle as she fell. Sebastian was still unconscious and Cassie and Tabitha had to manage him between them, carrying him over the deepening snow while Cassie held the spear carefully in one gloved hand, constantly afraid that she might drop it. All the while the shadow clung to her, trailing them through the snow and Cassie could feel the constant, painful emptiness at her back.

The road over the river and up the hill between the beeches had never seemed longer, but at last they found themselves standing before the open gates of Hartwood. With a groan, Sebastian opened his eyes and staggered to his feet. Although he was weak and disorientated, he was able to walk through the gates with Tabitha supporting him. Rue limped behind them.

Cassie turned to face the shadow, a dark hollow between the beech trees. It stretched long tendrils of smoke towards the lights of Hartwood.

'I cannot enter,' it whispered. 'Not without his body. The witch's wards are too strong. You must invite me in.'

Cassie took a deep breath. She could walk through those gates and the creature would not be able follow them. She could run into the house, find her aunt and have the Hedgewitch deal with it, banish it back into the

Hedge where it belonged. But she had made a promise, had offered it a home, as she had Sebastian, and what sort of witch was she if she broke her word?

'I don't even know your name,' she said to the formless shadow.

'I have never been given a name. I am always alone with none to call it.'

'In that case, I'll give you one.' Cassie raked her memory for something appropriate. She settled on one of the names she'd read on the gravestones – its owner no longer needed it, after all. 'Morpeth, I'll call you Morpeth.'

'Mor-peth...' said the shadow, savouring the syllables. 'I am Morpeth.'

Cassie took a deep breath. She would no doubt have a lot of explaining to do when her aunt found out, but she knew what it was like to need a home, a real home where you could be safe and happy. Now that she had such a place, she found she must learn how to share it.

'Morpeth, I invite you into Hartwood Hall.'

The creature sighed, a soft, hissing sound, and seemed to expand as it drew nearer. As it grew in size it faded from a dark, heavy shadow to a fine mist and then, as it reached the walls of Hartwood, disappeared altogether.

It had been a long night for the three members of Oak Patrol. Sebastian was put to bed with a hot water bottle, being far too weak to tell his side of the story, but the Hedgewitch kept Cassie, Rue and Tabitha in the kitchen until they'd told her everything about Sir Egad, the tomb and the brollachan. The spear lay on a gossamer cloth in the middle of the table, catching the light from the fire in dark flickers. When Cassie explained the deal she'd made with the shadowy creature to let them escape the crypt, her aunt sat bolt upright in her seat, nearly knocking over her cup of nettle tea.

'Do you mean to tell me, Cassandra, that you welcomed this creature into Hartwood? The one place in all Hedgely it could not enter? The one place you might be safe?'

'But it's already been here, hiding inside Sebastian – ever since we found him in the Hedge on Hallowe'en. We had no other way to stop it and I thought...'

'You thought this monstrous creature, which has been taking over the minds and bodies of innocent villagers would make a good house sprite? It is no helpful brownie, Cassandra. Tell me again, the name you gave it.'

Cassie told her and the Hedgewitch went into the pantry and returned with a small jar of some dry herbs. She tossed a pinch of it on the kitchen fire. The flames turned blue and silver sparks flew out.

'I adjure you, Morpeth! As the chatelaine of this house, appear before me now!'

At first, there was no response, but then they heard a scratching, rasping sound at the kitchen door. Miranda quickly crossed the flagstones and threw it open, letting in a flurry of snow.

Before her, a short, bulky creature squatted, outlined in black against the whiteness of the garden. It had horns, wings and grasping claws.

Miranda stepped aside, letting it into the house and Cassie recognised it as one of the gargoyles that usually perched on the roof.

As it entered the kitchen, bringing a gust of cold wind with it, they could hear its stone claws clacking on the flagstones. Melting snow dripped from its beak.

'Well, as my niece has inadvisably invited you to into Hartwood, we might at least see what assistance you can provide. You can begin by telling me why the Erl King was seeking this.' The Hedgewitch pointed to the black spear.

The gargoyle turned his stone head to look at Cassie. She nodded. 'It's all right, he can't reach you here.'

'The Lord of Rags and Tatters seeks the slaying spear,' said the gargoyle in its raspy voice. 'He would kill that which cannot be killed. The third watcher, the one who guards the way.'

Miranda took a sharp breath. 'He seeks to slay the wood wyrm. Are you sure?'

'Morpeth was tasked to find it, to bring it to him. He is waiting, he is almost ready, many have joined his cause.'

'So he *is* building an army,' said Rue.

The Hedgewitch frowned. 'While a handful of goblin smugglers might sneak through each Crossing Night, he could not bring an army, not with the weirstones and the Watchers guarding the way. That is why he has been destroying the stones. Galtres is our final line of defence against such an incursion from Faerie.'

'But the wood wyrm tried to kill us!' said Tabitha.

'The Watchers do not discriminate,' the Hedgewitch explained. 'They are the ancient guardians of the wood, they keep the balance and do not care whether one is mortal or faery. To pass them one must pay their price, and when it comes to Galtres, that price is one's life. No, while the wyrm is a danger to all who enter the depths of the Hedge, she is a threat that in turn grants us protection. So this is why he sought to win Hyldamor to his side – he hopes to gain control over the border. If the Erl King were to slay Galtres he could bring through his people at the next Crossing Night and make himself lord of the Hedge. It would give him a foothold in our world.'

They turned as one to look at the spear.

'I will send a message to Elliot in the morning. Wayland Yard must be informed of this, and we will need to find a safer place to keep the spear,' said the Hedgewitch. 'But for now, Morpeth, I am grateful for this information, but I cannot accept you as brownie of Hartwood. You have done much harm to the people of this village and allied yourself with the Erl King. If not for the interference of these young witches, I do not doubt you would have handed him the spear and brought about a great evil.'

'But Aunt Miranda,' said Cassie. 'I promised him!'

'And you would do well to think about the consequences of such a promise before you make it, Cassandra. By rights, he ought to be banished to Faerie, but I have yet to reach a decision.' She turned back to the gargoyle. 'In the meantime, I must bind you in some vessel.' The Hedgewitch looked over the contents of the kitchen. 'Tabitha, pass me that mustard pot. Is it empty? Good.'

'Long weeks I spent in confinement, constantly flooded with boiling water and foul-smelling herbs. Mistress, you would not make me suffer so again!'

'You'll be perfectly safe and comfortable in here,' said the Hedgewitch, removing the lid from the small ceramic pot. 'If you do as I say, it will count in your favour.'

The gargoyle gave one last stony glance at Cassie and then it went rigid. Wisps of shadow leaked from the stone, re-joining and forming a dark mass that flowed into the mustard pot, pooling inside. The Hedgewitch put the lid on once more and whispered a quick spell over it.

'And now, I think that is quite enough excitement for one Midwinter's Eve—'

But Miranda was cut off by a hammering sound that reverberated through the house.

Cassie, Rue and Tabitha followed the Hedgewitch to the entry hall, where she drew open the door, letting in a gust of snow and icy air. Standing on the doorstep was Mrs Mossley, Emley Moor and Rue's dad, Ted Whitby. They held flaming torches and their wide eyes glittered in the light from the fire.

'Thank goodness you're here, Hedgewitch,' said Mrs Mossley. 'You must follow us, quickly. There's a great wyrm, come to destroy the village!'

Chapter Thirty-One

Galtres

'It came out of the woods at midnight, as we were going upstairs to bed,' said Ted Whitby. 'We heard a loud bellow, and the sound of splintering wood.'

'The size of it!' exclaimed Emley Moor. 'Never seen anythin' like it, not in my father's time neither – and it's heading for the market square.'

The Hedgewitch turned to face Cassie, Rue and Tabitha. 'Stay here, all three of you. Do not set a foot beyond this door, do you understand?'

'But—' said Cassie, as Rue tried to push past Miranda to reach her father.

'Listen to the Hedgewitch,' said Ted Whitby. 'This isn't the time for young witches to get involved, that thing's enormous. I'll come back for you when it's safe, Rue.'

They watched as the Hedgewitch grabbed her cloak and bag and called her familiar, Malkin, away from the kitchen fire. Seconds later, she was flying downhill to the village with Emley Moor, Ted Whitby and Mrs Mossley running after her.

Rue, Cassie and Tabitha remained in the hall beneath the spreading boughs of the Hartwood tree. A single leaf fell at Cassie's feet, green-gold and shaped like a heart. She stooped to pick it up. 'Galtres,' she said. 'The weirstones are weaker because it's Midwinter's Night she's found a way through.'

'But why attack the village?' asked Tabitha. 'It's so far from her territory, and we've done nothing to provoke her.'

'It's just like the play,' said Cassie. She thought of the claw marks on the stones of Castle Hill. Perhaps this wasn't the first time a great wyrm had come out of the woods.

Rue's fists were clenched tightly as she stared at the door. 'It's the Erl King, he knows we've found the spear. He's driven the wyrm towards us, made her angry... it's revenge.'

Cassie frowned. There was more to it than that. The Erl King had nothing to gain from destroying the village, it would not get him the spear.

'We can't just wait here, doing nothing,' said Rue, pacing back and forth in front of the great oak doors. 'I don't care what the Hedgewitch said, I'm going down.'

Tabitha placed a hand on her arm. 'But what can we possibly do? We barely escaped with our lives last time we met Galtres.'

Her aunt was already furious at them for going after the spear alone, but they couldn't just stay here, safe and warm while a great wyrm terrorised the village.

'She's right,' said Cassie, leading them back towards the warmth of the Hartwood kitchen. 'You're both right. We can't just sit here, but if we want to help we need a plan.'

On the table before them the spear glimmered darkly.

'We have to use the spear,' said Rue. 'It's the only thing that can put an end to this.'

'No!' said Tabitha. 'We can't just kill her.'

'Now's not the time to be soft, Tabitha. Aoife's being-nice-to-faeries stuff is all very well when it comes to goblins and brownies, but this is a *great wyrm*. You can't reason with it. You heard Emley; that creature is heading for the market square – it's heading for the shop and my family!'

Cassie shook her head. 'No, don't you see? If the Erl King *is* behind this, then that's exactly what he wants. He's forcing us to do his dirty work. We cannot kill the wood wyrm, to do so would put Hedgely in even more danger. But there is another way.'

She reached for the mustard pot.

It was not hard to find the wood wyrm, they simply had to follow the trail of destruction through Hedgely. There were great brown gashes on the village green beside uprooted trees. The picnic benches outside The Pickled Imp lay flattened and the roof had lost a good chunk of thatch. Loft Street itself was battered, with signs ripped from the shops, broken windows and a hole in the wall of Marchpane's.

Cassie urged Tantivy onwards, flying high over the rooftops, the mustard pot clutched tight in one hand, Rue and Tabitha close behind. They could see a column of smoke and the bright glow of fire up ahead, and flew towards it.

They passed villagers running the other way, up the hill to Hartwood or east to the safety of the farms and fields. Some were carrying small children, others clutched precious belongings. Widdershin was piling books into a small cart hitched to a rather flighty pony.

'Oh, and the Archimelius! Cannot forget the Archimelius... hold still, you cowardly creature! And Ficino's *Catalogue of Planetary Influences*, that's a first edition!' Cassie heard him say as he rushed back into the shop for more books.

As she flew over the broken shop fronts and running, frightened village folk, a new fear grew in Cassie's stomach – what if something happened to her aunt? What if Miranda herself was hurt, or worse?

'Over there!' cried Rue, pointing, her face and arm illuminated by the glow of fire.

The great wyrm had wound itself around the fountain in the market square, crushing the wooden stalls of the Midwinter market beneath its coils like matchsticks. One clawed foot had gone through the window of Whitby's shop and its mossy tail lay in the ruins of the schoolyard wall.

A trail of broken masonry led to Darnwright's. The wyrm had smashed through one wall and the forge had set fire to the rest of the building. Down below they saw Aoife Early organising a small crowd of villagers, including Rue's dad and Eris Watchet, who had gathered to try and put out the fire before it spread to the rest of the village. They were holding buckets, but could not reach the fountain to draw water.

This is what the Erl King wants, thought Cassie, *fire and destruction, chaos and fear. He knows we'd do anything to put an end to this, to protect these people, that we'd kill to save those we love. He's counting on it.*

Then she saw Miranda. She was standing upright on her broom, which hovered before the wyrm, her arms out on either side and her long cloak flapping around her.

The Hedgewitch was facing Galtres. In her right hand she clasped a knife which flashed in the firelight. In her left she held something small and round. It looked like a ball of green twine, and it stretched in a line away from her and around the branching antlers of the wood wyrm. She held the string taut, like a fisherman with a particularly big catch on the line, and she was chanting, her voice raised over the crackling fire and the villager's shouts and screams from below. Cassie strained to hear the words but soon realised they were in a strange language, entirely unfamiliar to her.

Cassie, Rue and Tabitha hovered at a safe distance, watching. Cassie had seen her aunt at work before, offering remedies for urchen bites and finding jewellery stolen by imps, but that had been the minor day-to-day business of witchcraft. Only now did she see what it truly meant to be the Hedgewitch, to be the first line of defence against the dangers of Faerie.

'She's binding it,' said Tabitha breathlessly, hovering at Cassie's side. 'That twine, it's a witch's ladder – see the knots? It won't get away now.'

And truthfully, it did not look as though Miranda needed their help. She was intent upon her work, focused on the chant that rang through the night air in her cool, clear voice.

But then there came another noise from behind them, a blast of heat and the rumble of crumbling stone. Cassie, Rue and Tabitha saw that the chimney of Darnwright's forge had collapsed and the sound had drawn Miranda's attention, making her pause for just one breath in her chanting.

The wood wyrm roared, rising up on its hind legs until it towered above the shops and houses and wrenched its great antlered head away from Miranda, pulling the ball of twine from her hand and unbalancing her.

Cassie gasped, but the Hedgewitch regained her balance and crouched upon the broom.

But now the wood wyrm was free. It came crashing down again on all fours and raised its tail from the ruins of the wall. The great length of it swung towards Miranda, forcing the Hedgewitch to clutch her broom and dive before it hit her.

The control Miranda had over the creature was lost. Cassie grasped the mustard pot. She could not wait to see what her aunt would try next, could not wait at a safe distance while the wyrm destroyed her village, her home and the one person in her family who had always tried to protect her. But she couldn't do this alone either – the wood wyrm would see her coming, she wasn't a good enough flyer to evade its jaws and complete the task she had in mind. She needed her patrol.

'Rue, Tabitha, I hate to ask this, but could you distract it for me?'

Rue nodded, already turning her broom. 'We need to draw it away from the village. I've got half a dozen goblin bombs in my bag. I've improved the witch salt recipe so they should have more oomf. They won't do much damage, but they'll annoy it a bit. I'll get its attention, then Tabitha, I need you to fly as fast as you can towards the Hedge, get it to follow you if you can.'

Tabitha nodded once and gave her the witch's salute.

'Cassie, will you be all right with that?' She nodded at the mustard pot.

'I just need to get close enough and hope Morpeth can do the rest.'

'Right, well, here goes nothing!' said Rue, flashing them her best grin. She dived off on Blaze, a goblin bomb ready in one hand. Tabitha was close behind her.

Cassie gave them a head start, and then flew towards the school, until she was hovering beside the clock tower. Carefully, holding tight to the broomstick with her legs, she used one hand to remove the lid from the mustard pot and explained her plan to the brollachan lurking inside.

Then it was time. Rue dived at the wyrm, pummelling its head with the small bundles of dried herbs and salt. That certainly got its attention, as the creature turned away from Miranda and snapped at Rue, who dived out of harm's way just in time.

Tabitha whizzed past the wyrm's open maw. She paused just long enough to let it see her and then dived towards the Hedge.

Enraged by Rue's witch salt, it scrambled after her, up the hill towards Nearwood Row and Tabitha's own cottage.

Clutching Tantivy with one hand and holding the mustard pot tight with the other, Cassie flew as fast as she could after them. This was the sort of flying Tantivy lived for, and she was soon gaining on Tabitha and the wyrm as the wind whistled past her ears.

'Cassandra!' she heard her aunt cry and glanced down to see the Hedgewitch flying beneath her, but her aunt would not catch up with her before she reached the wyrm.

The great beast tore through a cottage as it dived after Tabitha, who was still flying up to the Hedge. She saw Tabitha dip down between the trees, using them for cover and disappearing from the wyrm's line of sight. Cassie was right behind it now. She could see the mossy scales of the wyrm's back, like wooden shingles, could see the small trees that still clung to its hide, and the great branching antlers that crowned its serpentine head. She flew in, as close as she dared, took a deep breath and threw the mustard pot at it.

The pot shattered as it hit the wyrm's wooden hide, falling in a shower of terracotta shards. Cassie turned and sped away from the wyrm, until she was out of reach of its claws. From there she thought she saw the shadow that was the brollachan rise, free from the confines of the pot and drift towards to the wyrm's head, but it was hard to make out in the darkness. The wyrm paused, one claw raised, and snorted, as if it had breathed in some undesirable scent. Its great, golden eyes slowly closed and then opened once more, looking glazed and unfocused.

'Cassandra!' said Miranda, finally catching up with her. 'I told you to stay at Hartwood. What in stars' name do you think you're doing?'

But Cassie simply pointed at the wyrm. 'Look!'

And they watched together as the beast gathered itself up, lifting each limb from the earth in a slow, staggering walk. It made its way sedately back into the Hedge, leaving a trail of broken branches and muddy snow in its wake.

'How...?' asked the Hedgewitch.

'It was Morpeth. He can take over humans, control us, force us to do things against our will, so I thought maybe he might be able to control the wood wyrm too.'

'And what made you think that could possibly work?'

'The brollachan can only take over the body of one

who has suffered a great loss,' Cassie explained. 'And Galtres is the last of her kind.'

The three witches of Oak Patrol landed beside the Hedgewitch in the square. The ruins of the Midwinter market were all around them, and beyond that were broken walls and windows, hanging gutters and signs. Rue saw the gaping front of Whitby's and ran towards it.

'Mum!' she cried.

'It's all right,' said the Hedgewitch. 'She got away before the wyrm reached the square, and your brothers are safe too.'

Aoife was picking her way across the rubble towards them, her bright-yellow cloak vivid in the darkness. 'Hedgewitch!' she called. When she got closer, panting and out of breath, they saw she was smeared with soot, her hands nearly black with it. 'We've put out the fire, it spread to the house next door but didn't get any further. Thank goodness for the snow. Is everyone all right?'

'All of the villagers were evacuated safely – thank you for overseeing that – and miraculously these three young witches are unharmed, despite their extremely reckless behaviour tonight.'

Aoife smiled at them, but then a look of horror crossed her face and she pointed behind them.

'Hedgewitch – that shadow!'

They turned to see a shape over the fountain. It was darker than the surrounding night and seemed to absorb the light of the stars, moon and the flickering lantern Aoife held.

'Well, brollachan, I see you are willing to earn your keep after all,' said the Hedgewitch, addressing it. 'I trust you have taken the wyrm deep enough into the Hedge that it will not disturb us again any time soon?'

Cassie heard the voice again, coming from everywhere and nowhere, as if some invisible presence were whispering in her ear.

'The wyrm sleeps once more, it will not be so easily woken this time.'

'Please, Aunt Miranda,' said Cassie. 'Does this mean Morpeth can stay? He's protected the whole village – surely he can help protect Hartwood?'

The Hedgewitch pursed her lips for a moment. 'He may stay, but as for the rest of you, I've had just about enough of your foolish risk-taking for one night. Back to Hartwood, all of you! I want you safe in bed by the time I return.'

Chapter Thirty-Two

The Lost Library

Tabitha and Rue slept over in Cassie's room that night. The three young witches sat around the warm glow of her small fireplace, discussing the events of the evening – which had seemed exhaustively drawn out, even for the longest night of the year. They eventually fell asleep in a pile of cushions and familiars and did not wake until nearly midday, when the sun peered in through Cassie's window.

Descending to the kitchen in their borrowed pyjamas, their stomachs growling, Cassie, Rue and Tabitha found the Hedgewitch waiting for them. From the shadows under her eyes it was clear she had been up all night, no doubt dealing with the aftermath of the wood wyrm's visit to Hedgely.

'Sit down,' said Miranda, folding her hands on the table. 'I don't imagine any of you recall my forbidding you to leave the house last night?'

They perched in a row and did their best to look remorseful while shooting surreptitious glances at Mrs Briggs, who was frying up something that smelled delicious over the open fire.

'I do not make these rules and prohibitions to restrict your freedoms, I do so because my role as your Coven Mistress and Cassie's guardian means I have a duty to protect you from the dangers you are not yet ready to face.'

The three girls looked down at their hands, bracing themselves for a scolding.

'However,' the Hedgewitch continued, 'I cannot deny that your quick-thinking last night very probably saved the good people of Hedgely from waking amid ruins this morning. You listened to each other and demonstrated admirable teamwork as a patrol. This time, it has worked out for the best, but you may not always be so lucky. Please do not take such risks so lightly in future.'

'Yes, Aunt Miranda,' said Cassie. Rue and Tabitha nodded.

'Now, I suspect from the grumblings I hear echoing from your side of the table, the three of you are ready for Mrs Briggs' pancakes?'

Over the weekend between Midwinter and Christmas, and the whole of 1st Hedgely Coven were mobilised to help repair the damage caused by the wood wyrm. Ash Patrol helped those who were temporarily homeless find spare beds and a place to stay with their neighbours, retrieving their possessions and distributing supplies. Thorn Patrol assisted Ted Whitby and Emley Moor on repairs to The Pickled Imp, Whitby's and the other shops that had been wrecked by the attack, cleaning, painting and fetching wood and nails. Meanwhile, Oak Patrol followed Miranda into the Hedge to check the remaining weirstones, counting those that still stood, for a report to the Witches' Assembly. They worked from dawn to dusk, and went home exhausted each night, too tired to think of the upcoming festivities.

On Christmas Eve, Mrs Briggs handed Cassie a basket full of freshly baked shortbread and asked her to deliver it to the displaced families. She was crossing the bridge onto Loft Street, when she saw Ivy, sitting alone on a bench by the duck pond. Cassie summoned up her most convincing smile and made her way across the green.

'Happy Christmas Eve.'

Ivy looked up at her through reddened eyes, her face stained by tears. She drew her lips together and glared back. 'That's all very well for you to say, Cassandra Morgan, I'm sure you'll have a wonderful Christmas, but it isn't a happy day for all of us!'

Cassie hesitated, unsure quite how to respond. With a small sigh, she brushed the snow from the wooden bench and sat down next to Ivy.

'What's happened?' she asked.

'My mother. She's gone. The menders from Convall Abbey came to get her last night, to take her away to the witches' hospital in Devon, and this is... this is the first Christmas I've had without her.'

'Ivy, I'm so sorry...' Cassie began.

'This is your fault, Cassandra. If you hadn't stopped me, I would have made the Erl King break the curse – she would be well again. I wish you'd never come to Hedgely, you ruin everything. Just leave me alone!' And with that, Ivy ran from the green, leaving a trail of footprints in the snow.

Cassie didn't see Morpeth again until Christmas morning, when she woke early to a tapping on her windowpane. It was freezing in her room, the fire having burned out overnight, and Montague was curled up in a ball by her feet. At first she thought she'd imagined the sound, but then it came again, on the west window, the one that faced the Hedge. It was still dark outside and she did not find it easy to leave the warm comfort of her bed and stand on the cold wooden floor while she searched for her slippers. Only the driving force of curiosity could have made her get up. The tapping came again, insistent this time.

'Hold on, I'm coming!' she said.

Montague stirred and lifted his head to watch her as she crossed the moss-green rug to open the casement window.

Two stone claws gripped the snowy windowsill as Morpeth heaved himself into the room.

'Good morning,' said Cassie. 'Where have you been?'

'Morpeth has been everywhere,' said the gargoyle. 'High and low, within and without, Morpeth has been door and window, lamp and beam, chimney and roof tile and winding stair! Never has Morpeth had a home such as this, alive it is, and yet not alive. Awake and sleeping, open and hidden. There is much to be, much to hear and see and show.'

'Show?' asked Cassie.

'Yes, Morpeth has come to show Cassandra, to thank her.'

Cassie started looking for her dressing gown; it really was freezing. 'Well, just mind you listen to the Hedgewitch. Don't give her any excuse to send you away.'

But Morpeth wasn't listening, it had scuttled away to the door of Cassie's bedroom. 'Come, come now, Cassandra.'

'Montague?' called Cassie.

'The sun isn't even up yet,' the cat grumbled. 'And you want me to follow that ludicrous garden ornament who knows where?' But he came with her all the same.

Morpeth led Cassie down the dark corridor and, to her great surprise, as he went before her the lights came on. This would not be altogether remarkable in an ordinary house, but although Hartwood had light fixtures on all the walls it had no electricity to supply them. Mrs Briggs had explained to Cassie when she'd first arrived that they'd tried to install wiring but the old brownie hadn't liked it. She'd got used to carrying a lamp or a candlestick with her at night, but with Morpeth ahead of her there was no need. Her only concern was that the light might wake her aunt, Mrs Briggs or Brogan, but as she looked back down the corridor behind her she saw the hallway was dark once more. Morpeth was lighting only those fittings directly above them.

That was the first change Cassie noticed in the house, the second was that they did not get lost, even once. Usually the house was at its most restless at night, and if you got up to use the lavatory you inevitably found yourself in a spare bedroom, or the music room or wandering through the great hall as doors refused to open onto the same rooms twice. Now, however, the house felt settled, content, and they soon found their way down the back stairs to a part of Hartwood Cassie rarely entered.

At the end of a short hallway was a door Cassie had never seen before. It was painted blue and had a little brass plaque affixed to it, just above Cassie's head. The plaque bore one magic word.

'Library,' Cassie read. 'Surely, it can't be... is this really it? The lost library?'

'Morpeth will show,' said the gargoyle and, without either of them touching the knob, the door swung open.

The first thing Cassie noticed was the dust. A thick layer of it, pale and sparkling on every surface. Montague padded ahead of her across the parquet floor, which had some design hidden beneath the powder, leaving a trail of pawprints behind him.

In the centre of the hexagonal room she turned to look about her and as she did, the chandelier that hung above her came to life, illuminating the whole space. The walls rose up to twice the height of an ordinary room, with the second floor accessed by a tight spiral staircase. It must be in one of Hartwood Hall's two turrets, Cassie realised, directly beneath her aunt's study. All these years, Miranda had been unable to access the library, even though it was right beneath her feet.

There was a desk and a sofa and a deep armchair by the empty fireplace. A great globe showed the stars and constellations and two bronze hares guarded the mantlepiece. The walls themselves were lined with bookshelves right to the ceiling and each was stuffed with leather-bound tomes. Far tidier and more orderly than Widdershin's shop, the books also seemed older, some with faded titles on their spines and others without any indication of what may lie within their pages. She crossed to the nearest shelf and brushed a fine layer of dust from a fat black spine. It was Grieve's *Herbaria Magica* – a reference book on magical plants she'd only glimpsed in Saltash's apothecary, and here was their very own copy that she could read whenever she wanted. Cassie rushed across the room to the opposite wall and pulled out another book, a slim blue volume titled *The Trials of Nimue*, about the legendary Hedgewitch.

Clutching the book to her chest, Cassie turned slowly about, looking up at the shelves. These books had belonged to every Hedgewitch who had lived at Hartwood, for hundreds of years. Everything she could possibly want to know about the history of Hedgely, about Faerie, about witchcraft, was right here!

'Cassandra,' called Montague. 'Over here.' He had jumped up on the heavy oak desk which sat like an island in the middle of the room, with several chairs tucked neatly under it on either side. One chair was pulled out, as if its occupant had just risen and forgotten to push it in behind them. In front of this seat was a pile of papers, a book and an old fountain pen.

Montague nudged the book with his nose. 'It is rather faint now, but this smells like your mother's things.'

Cassie picked up the book, sneezing as a cloud of dust rose from its cover. It was called *The Wanderers*, and seemed to be a book of poetry. A slip of pale-pink writing paper fell out. Cassie picked it up and as she saw the handwriting, her heart skipped a beat. It was her mother's.

Monday, 21st December

My love,

Please forgive me for all I said last night, for I see now that you have been right all along. I should never have trusted him, but now he has shown his true nature and I see that behind his promises, behind the hope he held out, is only great bitterness and deceit. He has used me, and if it were not for you I should have betrayed my family, and all I have been taught to hold dear.

But I know better now, and there is still time to make amends for my mistakes. I shall return the key, *she does not yet miss it, I think, and then we must flee this place, for he will seek to punish us.*

Come to the copper beech at midnight tonight. I have one last thing to tell you that I dare not put into words, but it changes everything.

Yours always,
Rose

'Cassandra? Is that you?' called a voice from the doorway. Miranda stepped through, dressed in a black nightgown and robe, her own slippers leaving a track across the dust.

'The library – however did you find it?' The Hedgewitch's gaze ranged over the shelves with a hunger Cassie could well understand.

'It was Morpeth, he showed me.' She turned to thank the gargoyle and found only an open window, a breeze ruffling the papers on the desk. 'Aunt Miranda, I found another letter from my mother, look.'

Miranda took the paper from Cassie and scanned it quickly. Her hand flew to her mouth as she read. 'She was putting it back, that night we argued... She wasn't stealing the key, she was returning it.'

'But who was she writing to?' Cassie asked.

'The letter is not addressed, but the library has been lost for nearly ten years now, the paper is old, Rose must have written it before she left Hedgely. And the date – December 21st – Midwinter's Eve.'

'Toby Harper,' said Cassie. 'Mrs Whitby said he went missing, fourteen years ago, at Midwinter, and that my mother blamed herself. She and Toby were friends.'

'Possibly more than friends if this was truly meant for him.' The Hedgewitch read the letter again, pausing on the final line. 'If it was from the year Toby Harper disappeared, that places this letter six and a half months before you were born, Cassandra.'

'She would have known about me by then,' said Cassie, softly. 'Could it... could that be what she wanted to tell Toby about?'

But before Miranda could respond, Cassie dashed from the room, leaving the library door open behind her.

The sun was just beginning to rise and the snow beneath Cassie's floating feet was pristine, almost blue in the low light.

She landed her broom at the foot of the copper beech in which they had their den. It was too cold to huddle up there now amidst the bare grey branches, so Oak Patrol had abandoned it until spring returned.

Crunching through the snow, huffing great breaths, Cassie approached the tree. It was here they were supposed to meet – Toby and her mother, on Midwinter's Eve, all those years ago.

Cassie walked about the tree, making a ring in the snow, looking up at its bare branches and willing it to tell her what it had witnessed.

Then she saw it, above a knot in the wood, rough scratched markings. She brushed away a patch of dry snow and ran her finger over the shapes, almost indiscernible now as the tree healed itself over the years, but she could just make them out. They were letters: RM + TH – Rose Morgan and Toby Harper. Her parents.

Chapter Thirty-Three

The Holly and The Ivy

When Cassie arrived back at Hartwood, the sun had risen and turned the snow gold and pink. She found everyone in the kitchen waiting for her – Miranda, Mrs Briggs, Brogan and even Sebastian, who looked much better and was tucking into a healthy serving of eggs, bacon and toast.

'Took your time about it,' said Sebastian. 'You realise we've had to wait for you to open presents?'

Cassie reached for a slab of toast and spread it with butter and marmalade while Mrs Briggs poured her a cup of hot spiced cocoa. Hungry from her early flight, she wolfed it down as Sebastian wiped his own plate clean and Miranda sipped her nettle tea. As soon as she was finished, she followed Sebastian into the great hall where the Hartwood tree was dressed in its festive finery, hung with coloured glass witch-balls and fragile silver snowflakes. When it moved, as it did occasionally of its own accord, little gold bells strung on its branches tinkled. At its roots were a pile of packages, wrapped in brown paper with tartan and velvet ribbons. Had they been there when Cassie dashed out of the door at sunrise to visit the copper beech? She'd barely spared a glance.

Brogan carried chairs in from the parlour so that he, Miranda and Mrs Briggs might sit in some dignity during the present-opening ceremony, but Sebastian sprawled happily on the floor and Cassie soon joined him, nursing the last of her cocoa as her cousin picked up a package and shook it.

In a flurry of torn paper and flying ribbons, cries of delight and surprise, the presents were unwrapped. Cassie's own gifts to the household – a new shoehorn for Brogan, a wooden spoon for Mrs Briggs, its handle inscribed with runes, and a bottle of blackberry ink for her aunt – were all well received. She'd made each using the skills they'd learned in coven and while working on her Woodwitch badge. Sebastian was delighted with the mechanics kit his father had sent, and there was a package from Elliot for Cassie too: a silver charm bracelet with a tiny silver cat on it that looked just like Montague, and a tiny silver broom and witch's hat. From Brogan she received a pair of slippers in blue velvet, lined with soft lambswool. Mrs Briggs gave her a hand-knitted scarf and hat, beaming as Cassie tried them on. 'You'll be needing those, now the snow's arrived!'

Finally, Miranda handed Cassie a flat, rectangular parcel which she knew immediately to be a book, but was surprised on tearing away the paper to find its pages empty.

'It's high time you had your own grimoire,' explained her aunt. 'To record the spells and potions you learn as you work towards your Sapling Test.'

The notebook was bound in warm chestnut leather and had a red ribbon bookmark, and there was a green fountain pen with a gold nib like the beak of a goose.

Mrs Briggs went back to the kitchen to fetch a plate of gingerbread goblins, and as she left there was a rapping on the great oak door.

'I'll get it,' said Cassie, as Sebastian was far too engrossed in his mechanics set, constructing some sort of aircraft with a tiny screwdriver.

'Hello, Cassie. Happy Christmas!' said Elliot, standing in the doorway and stomping snow off his nice leather shoes.

'Uncle Elliot!' she said, and thanked him for the bracelet.

'Dad?' said Sebastian, slowly rising from the floor.

'Now, what sort of trouble have you been getting yourself into, my boy?' asked Elliot.

Without a word, Sebastian leapt over his presents and ran to embrace his father.

Elliot was to stay for Christmas lunch, and as Cassie was helping Mrs Briggs set the table in the feasting hall, she heard the great oak door creak open again and rushed to see who it was.

'Oh, hello, Cassie,' said Aoife Early. She wore a fuzzy knitted hat with a purple pom-pom. In her arms she carried trailing vines of green ivy. 'I've been out on my morning walk and thought I'd harvest some last-minute garlands. Is there somewhere I can put these?'

'Of course!' said Cassie, and hurried to help her with the branches.

'The Hartwood tree,' said Aoife, stepping forward to admire its decorations. She smiled at Cassie. 'Do you know, the old legends say this tree was planted by

Morgana herself, and that the house was built around it? The seed came from Faerie, of course. There isn't another like it in all of Britain or Ireland.'

'Aoife,' Cassie began, plucking at a dead ivy leaf. 'I wanted to say thank you, for everything you taught us this year, about the summoning spells and the brollachan and, well, I'm sorry if we weren't exactly welcoming when you joined the coven, but we couldn't have done any of it – found the spear or stopped the wyrm – without you.'

Aoife smiled. 'Do you ever wonder, Cassie, why people are afraid of Faerie?'

'Well, there was the war... and they harm humans all the time, enchant them and trap them and steal their children...'

'But why do you think they do that? Why does a snake or a spider bite? Not because it hates you, but because it is afraid. I've tried to show you a different way to deal with faery folk, beyond iron and fire and salt. All I ask is that you keep your mind open. Listen to both sides and try to understand what you fear, rather than attacking it without thought.'

'But does that mean... Are you leaving us?' Cassie asked. Although their work with Aoife had been unusual and even unwelcome by some of the coven, it was hard now to imagine Fridays without Aoife's cheerful face and jangling bracelets.

'Yes, I am heading back to Ireland tomorrow, the mistress of my own coven is retiring and I am to take her place. I will miss you girls, though. Oh! Before I forget,' said Aoife, putting down the rest of the ivy. 'I have something for your patrol.' She fished around in her pockets until she found three small round fabric patches and handed them to Cassie. They were embroidered with a pair of crossed brooms and each broom was sprouting leaves.

'But these are…!'

'Woodwitch badges, yes. It appears you have earned them.'

'But Aunt Miranda said they removed the badge from the handbook, that she wouldn't be able to get them for us anymore.'

Aoife tapped the side of her nose. 'Not in Britain, no. I had to send home to Ireland for these. I shouldn't wonder if you're the only young witches in the country to have it. You'll be the envy of the coven, no doubt!'

Cassie thanked her profusely.

'There you are, dove!' said Mrs Briggs, coming through the hall with an enormous roast goose. 'Be a dear and fetch the potatoes, oh, and check on Sebastian, I sent him to get the sprouts but the poor boy doesn't know a carrot from a cucumber! Hello, Aoife dear, right this way, there's a place already laid for you.'

When they were all sat down for Christmas lunch, Cassie was glad she'd had only a slice of toast for breakfast as it meant she had plenty of room to tackle the heaping piles of food about her. Aside from the goose and the golden roast potatoes, there was glazed ham and honeyed carrots, pigs in blankets and sprouts, which Cassie didn't like, with chestnuts, which she did. For dessert they had a blazing Christmas pudding with toffee custard, and more gingerbread and mince pies and cocoa and mulled cider until nobody could move. But Cassie had promised to meet Rue and Tabitha, and so she pushed her chair back, asked to be excused and fetched Tantivy from the kitchen.

Cassie swooped across the river on her broom, past The Pickled Imp, where Emley Moor waved to her from the doorstep, looking as jovial as Father Christmas himself. She arrived on the village green to find Rue and Tabitha already waiting for her.

‘Happy Christmas!’ they chorused,

‘Happy Christmas! Is that it?’ Cassie asked, pointing to the basket Tabitha was carrying, which was covered over with a tea towel.

Tabitha nodded. ‘I baked them this morning, do you think he’ll like them?’

‘You should probably let me taste them first,’ said Rue, reaching for the basket.

Tabitha yanked it away from her grasp.

‘Here,’ said Cassie, handing them each one of the small, round badges that Aoife had given her.

‘But I thought...?’ said Tabitha.

‘It was Aoife, she had them sent from Ireland, and Aunt Miranda says it’s all right, although she wants us to stick to officially approved badges from now on.’

‘You know what this means, Cass?’ said Rue, grinning. ‘You can start working towards your Sapling Test!’

They walked in single file, back through the village and up the hilly slope towards the Hedge, with Rue leading and carving a path for them through the snow. They did not stop at the edge of the woods, but found a way in past the thickets of elder and blackthorn.

The snow had obscured all the paths, but the leafless branches made the going easier, revealing more of the way ahead than was visible in the summer. They came to a clearing, a rough circle of pristine white bordered by holly trees, the only green in the black-and-white wood.

'Surely this is far enough?' asked Tabitha.

'I suppose it will do,' said Rue. 'Got your whistle, Cass?'

Cassie fished the bird-shaped whistle from her pocket. She hesitated. 'He said to use it only in great need.'

'Well, surely he can make an exception for Christmas?' said Tabitha.

Cassie put the whistle to her lips and blew a long, high note. It was the only sound in the silent forest. They waited for a good ten minutes but Cassie's call went unanswered. She tried again.

'Can't we light a fire, or something?' asked Rue. 'Tabitha's shivering.'

'He doesn't like fire, remember? I don't think he'll come if we do.'

They huddled together in the centre of the clearing, waiting, ears pricked for the lightest sound of breath or footfall, each peering out in a different direction, wanting to be the first to spot him, if he came.

They were all shivering, and even Cassie was on the verge of suggesting they return home when a voice startled them.

'It is a cold day to be out walking in the woods.'

'Lailoken!' cried Cassie, and the three girls hurried to where he stood by a holly bush. He had arrived without a sound and somehow, despite the clear winter's day, without them sensing his approach. He wore his cloak of leaves, and over it a great fur mantle, dusted with snow.

'Hush now,' he said. 'You do not appear to be in mortal danger, but even though the trees are sleeping, the forest still has eyes and ears. Why have you summoned me on this day?'

'Because it's Christmas!' said Rue.

'And we wanted to thank you, for helping us. I've made you some cheese and herb scones.'

'It was my idea!' said Rue. 'And we all picked the herbs.'

Cassie frowned. 'I hope it was all right to call you, only we did want to thank you, and I have something to ask.'

'Very well,' said Lailoken. 'Although I know not of this human holiday of which you speak, we will be safe enough here while the sun is high.' He spread his fur mantle on the snow and they all piled onto it. Tabitha unwrapped the scones and handed them around, with a little knife and a knob of butter. There was a Thermos too, filled with hot spiced tea. Although the walk through the wintry forest had given Cassie some of her appetite back, she was still too full to manage more than one scone, and as soon as Lailoken himself had finished eating, she turned to him.

'I think I know why my mother went to Faerie, why she sought out Hyldamor and blew the elder flute.' Cassie took a deep breath. 'I think she went after my father. He disappeared, fourteen years ago, on Midwinter's Eve. His name was Toby Harper.'

Tabitha and Rue stopped eating to listen.

'And I was wondering,' Cassie continued. 'If you saw anything? I just want to know what happened that night, why he left and why my mother ran away from Hedgely; why she kept all of this from me.'

'They did not come to me for aid,' said the woodwose, shaking his head.

Cassie sighed.

'But if they came through the Hedge, the trees will remember. Most are sleeping now, but you could ask the holly and the ivy.'

'Ask the *trees*?' said Rue.

'Come with me, witchling,' said Lailoken, gesturing for Cassie to follow. They approached the largest of the holly trees that ringed the clearing. 'Put your hand on the trunk.'

Cassie reached through the spiny leaves, which scratched her skin and caught in her sleeve. She pushed through the dense boughs until her fingers brushed the firm trunk beneath.

The woodwose placed a hand on her shoulder. 'Now ask your question, loud and clear.'

Cassie took a deep breath. 'I want to know what happened to my parents, fourteen years ago at Midwinter, when they came to the Hedge.'

At first, there was no sound but the dripping of snow-melt off branches. Then Cassie heard a soft rustling above her, as though a breeze was passing through, though she felt no wind on her cheek. The sharp holly leaves pricked her face and caught in her hair as they moved, but she did not flinch or pull away.

'I want to know!' she said again, louder.

Then the whispering began, the same soft susurrus she had heard when she and Ivy had found the silver seernuts, all those months ago. The voices of the trees murmured in their own strange language, and this time

Cassie could make out no words she knew. She shut her eyes tight and then she saw it. An image flashed before her eyes, quick as lightning, dreamlike but clear as day – the Hedge under a carpet of snow; her mother, with her halo of red curls; and before her, a young man, fair-haired and unconscious at the foot of a tall, dark figure, a figure with a face hidden by the pale mask of a stag's skull.

Cassie gasped as the vision vanished, and pulled herself away from the tree, the image still burned into her mind.

'Cassie, are you all right?' asked Tabitha, as she and Rue ran forward to support her.

'The Erl King...' said Cassie, breathless. 'The Erl King was there; the night Toby went missing.'

And she told them what she had seen, what the trees had shown her. She still had so many questions.

'It is growing dark,' said the woodwose. 'You three ought to return to the safety of your village before nightfall.'

They scattered the crumbs for the birds and gathered up the picnic things.

'Will you find your way back?' asked Lailoken, standing at the edge of the clearing.

'I think we'll be all right,' said Rue, grinning. 'We're Woodwitches now!'

Arm in arm, Cassie, Rue and Tabitha headed back towards the warm yellow lights of the village, leaving the Hedge and its secrets behind them.

Acknowledgements

They say second books can be difficult, but this one was made infinitely easier by Felicity Alexander; the kind, patient and clear-sighted editor all authors dream of. She knows how to ask the right questions and often understands my characters better than I do. This book would not have been possible without her. My thanks also go out to Emma Roberts and Lois Ware for their thorough and thoughtful copyediting and proofreading.

I'm deeply grateful to Margaret Hope and illustrators Saara Katariina Söderlund and Tomislav Tomic, who have once again made this book a thing of beauty, inside and out. Their attention to detail and love of the natural world comes through in every image, and truly brings Hedgely to life.

The brilliant team at Welbeck Kids including Jane Harris, Susan Barry, Lorraine Keating and Jess Brisley have done so much to help my books find their way into beautiful bookshops and magical libraries. I also offer my heartfelt thanks to the Welbeck ANZ team who have helped Cassie fly all the way to readers in the Southern Hemisphere.

I am indebted to my legendary agent, Philippa Milnes-Smith, and the incredible team at The Soho Agency and ILA who have championed Hedgewitch since the beginning and continue to celebrate every milestone and guide this fledgling author with their invaluable advice.

Over the past year, I have been fortunate to meet many wonderful authors, both new and experienced, who have shared their wisdom and inspired me with their courage and perseverance. Special thanks to the 2022 debut group, Leah Mohammed, Jessica Scott-Whyte, Alex Mullarky and Natasha Hastings.

My family and my partner, Neil, have been my unfailing supporters through the highs and the lows and deserve special badges for their understanding and encouragement.

Finally, my unreserved gratitude goes to the booksellers, teachers, librarians, authors, bloggers, reviewers and organisations who do such amazing work encouraging young readers, and who have helped so many discover the world of Hedgely. Meeting and talking books with you has been the highlight of my year.

Skye McKenna

Scotland

Midwinter 2022